The First Thrust

The First Thrust
The Chichester Festival Theatre

Ronald Hayman

DAVIS-POYNTER
LONDON

First published in 1975 by
Davis-Poynter Limited
20 Garrick Street London WC2E 9BJ

Copyright © 1975 by Ronald Hayman

ISBN 0 7067 0152 6

Printed in Great Britain by
Bristol Typesetting Co. Ltd,
Barton Manor St Philips Bristol

To Monica and Imogen

Contents

Acknowledgements

I am grateful to Leslie Evershed-Martin for telling me so much about the theatre's prehistory, and to the playwrights, directors and actors who described their experience of the theatre : Michael Aldridge, Sarah Badel, John Clements, Peter Coe, Peter Dews, John Dexter, John Gielgud, Margaret Leighton, Keith Michell, Peter Shaffer, Maggie Smith, Robert Stephens, Carl Toms and Michael Warre. I would also like to thank David Fairweather and Anne Hillier, the Press Officers at Chichester, whose helpfulness went beyond reasonable limits.

1
The Paradox of Chichester

Not everyone would agree that Chichester is the most exciting theatre in England, but until the Crucible was built in Sheffield it was our only major theatre with an open stage, and it is still the only one within easy reach of London. Now that Sir Laurence Olivier's four-year régime has been followed by Sir John Clements's eight-year régime, we have forgotten how difficult it was first of all to bring the theatre into existence, and then to keep it alive. At the beginning there was a tremendous amount of local hostility, and long-range critical missiles were aimed at it from all over the country. Why build a theatre that was suited to some plays and not others? How could audiences be content to watch actors' backs? How could they create intimacy when they had either to shout or be inaudible to half the audience?

People enjoyed complaining, but soon it was obvious that they also enjoyed going there. It is very pleasant to arrive, to park in a spacious car-park, to breathe in country air, looking at a vista of superb elms and green fields, to walk into a bright, glass-fronted foyer, to stroll out on the lawn during the interval, and afterwards to be served with smorgasbord by friendly, unwaitressy girls in a well-managed restaurant. In thirteen years the theatre has given an incalculable amount of pleasure to hundreds of thousands of people, and it has an unrivalled place in the affections of nearly all those who have worked there. Peter Shaffer is not alone in describing his time there (working on *The Royal Hunt of the Sun*) as the happiest in his life. Though a great deal of very intensive work is done, the predominant feeling is of being on holiday, and happiness shows in the resultant performances. Actors seem to enjoy Chichester more than Stratford-on-Avon, a beautiful country town which has fallen irretrievably into the hands of the tourist industry. At Chichester they are also nearer the sea, and actors as dissimilar as Albert Finney and Margaret Rutherford have enjoyed a daily swim. There is boating on the Solent, and in the parkland that surrounds the theatre there is cricket to the north and archery to the east and tennis within easy reach.

Chichester is one of the few theatres where there is no straight line to divide the front-of-house from the backstage area. Everything is planned on the circle, and until the new extension was built in the winter of 1966-7, all the dressing-rooms were on the circumference. Even now, with the star dressing-rooms in a separate wing, everybody tends to see far more of everybody else in the company than would happen in London.

But for anyone who cares about the development of theatre as an art form, it is impossible not to have very serious misgivings about the way the theatre has been used. Because it is unique, the wasted opportunities matter all the more. A bright new airy building in which the audience horseshoes around a hexagonal thrust stage could be a stronghold for experiment, a playground where new techniques could be evolved to meet the challenge of the architecture, and new ways found of combining the visual and the verbal elements that constitute the theatrical experience. If performance consists of filling a space, a new theatre shape should elicit a new theatrical style.

The Chichester theatre was created against overwhelming odds. There had been no theatre in the city since 1847, and all the evidence indicated that the townspeople did not want one, that they mostly found horses, boats and fish more interesting than the arts. If any theatre ever owes its existence to a single enthusiast, the father of the Chichester Festival Theatre is a local ophthalmic optician, Leslie Evershed-Martin. He was watching television one Sunday evening in 1959, with his wife knitting by the fireside and with their two sons, when Tyrone Guthrie appeared on the screen, being interviewed about the open-stage theatre in

Stratford, Ontario. It struck Evershed-Martin that the population of Chichester was roughly equal to that of Stratford, where it had been the initiative and persistence of one indomitable private citizen, Tom Paterson, that had brought the theatre into existence. He had succeeded in interesting Guthrie in the project, and then they had constructed a tent-covered amphitheatre in a park outside the city, not investing in a permanent structure until they were sure of having sufficient public support.

To a man with a professional interest in the way three-dimensional scenes are transformed into images on a retina, the idea of an open stage was particularly appealing. A proscenium can appear to flatten the actors, whereas a thrust stage pushes them forward into three-dimensional solidity. And to a man of Leslie Evershed-Martin's temperament, the notion of a theatre in a park was almost equally attractive. He did not find it difficult to enlist the support of Guthrie, who always behaved like a compulsive midwife whenever an opportunity arose of assisting at the birth of a new theatre, but he was quick to explain to Evershed-Martin that even if he succeeded in raising enough money to build a theatre at Chichester, it might turn out to be a disastrous failure. There was so little live theatre in Canada that *aficionados* thought nothing of travelling a hundred miles to see a show. But at Chichester, Brighton was only thirty-one miles away and London only sixty-three. In fact if Laurence Olivier had not surprised everybody by agreeing to be the theatre's first Artistic Director, it might never have attracted either such a good company or such good publicity, and if it had not got off to such a good start it might not have survived.

Olivier's appointment to the directorship of the National Theatre was announced two months after the opening of the first Chichester season, so the second was inevitably something of a public preview before the Grand National First Night, and the third and fourth seasons consisted of visits from the newly-formed National Theatre company, which in turn consisted largely of actors, directors, stage management and administrative staff who had worked for Olivier at Chichester. So for four successive seasons, audiences were treated to the finest theatrical experiences that Olivier could contrive for them.

This is not to say that he took no risks. On the contrary, he opened with two little known and rather inferior Jacobean plays, Fletcher's *The Chances*, in the Duke of Buckingham's adaptation, and Ford's *The Broken Heart*. The final production of his first season, *Uncle Vanya*, was a safer choice in that the play is popular, but there was no knowing whether such a claustrophobic proscenium play could be effective on an open stage. In fact it was so successful that he repeated it in his second season, together with *St Joan,* which was safe, and a new play, which was anything but safe – *The Workhouse Donkey* by John Arden. His third season contained another new play, *The Royal Hunt of the Sun* by Peter Shaffer, an epic about the Incas and the conquest of Peru, a subject which might easily have intimidated potential ticket-buyers. His final season contained two more new plays by the same writers – *Armstrong's Last Goodnight* by Arden, and Shaffer's *Black Comedy.* So there were four new plays during the first four seasons (an average not subsequently to be matched) though, oddly, *Black Comedy*, the only play to be written specially for the occasion, benefited less than the other three from the open stage.

If John Clements, who was to control the next eight seasons of the theatre's history, appears to have been a good deal less interested in new writing, and experiment generally, two points must be made immediately in extenuation. One is that Olivier, with the top job in the English theatre waiting for him, did not have to worry about his future, as Clements did. The other point is that John Clements had to attract a larger audience, needing to fill the theatre over a longer season. Knowing it would be difficult to persuade good actors to commit themselves to Chichester salaries for a long engagement, Olivier had advised him to resist the pressure the Board would put on him to lengthen it. Clements's solution was to do four productions each year instead of three, lengthening the nine-week season at first to fifteen and later to nineteen weeks, but splitting it down the middle, so that no play stayed in the repertoire for more than ten weeks. Leading actors, then, could sign on for either half of the season. This helped Clements to collect a new constellation of famous names each year, but it also increased the feeling of discontinuity in the company's work. As soon as the supporting actors are acclimatized to one cluster of stars, they have to get used to supporting another.

While Olivier, himself a star, had imported famous actors like Michael Redgrave and Sybil Thorndike into his Chichester company, he had not built it around them but – from his second season onwards – had given a more central place to actors and directors who had been working under George Devine at the Royal Court, where the orientation was more democratic and less commercial than in the West End. In choosing his actors Olivier was influenced by John Dexter and William Gaskill, who were to become his Associate Directors at the National and who had both grown to artistic maturity under Devine, a great teacher and a strong influence on their developing attitudes and taste in actors. It was they who were responsible for bringing in Royal Court actors like Colin Blakely, Robert Stephens and Frank Finlay. Joan Plowright, Olivier's wife, had also been influenced by Devine and her experience at the Court. Altogether the tension between the component caucuses in the new company contributed enormously to its vitality.

Clements did not surround himself with younger men who had been trained in the new methods. He has given several productions to Peter Coe (1967-70), several to Peter Dews (1969-73), and several to Robin Phillips (1971-2) who was still in his twenties when he started working at Chichester but none of them was ever appointed as Associate Director. Like Clements, Olivier had been an actor-manager in the West End, but whereas he changed his methods on his appointment to Chichester and the National, Clements continued the line he had developed in the West End during the fifties. He has kept going back to the same playwrights – his favourites, apart from Shakespeare and Chekhov, apparently being Shaw, Anouilh, Pinero and Ustinov. And he has consistently given primacy to the stars, never putting a play into the programme until he was sure of casting it impressively, and sometimes giving stars the choice of which play they would most like to appear in. Brecht's *Caucasian Chalk Circle*, for instance, was produced at the instigation of Topol.

This unapologetic survival of the star system has provoked critics into stigmatizing the theatre and the festival with phrases like 'the temple of the Establishment' (Frank Marcus), 'that Henley regatta of the theatre season' (John Mortimer), and 'that Glyndebourne for the unmusical' (Ronald Bryden). Unlike Olivier's classical revivals, many of Clements's have been open to the charge that Mervyn Jones brought in *Tribune* against Lindsay Anderson's production of *The Cherry Orchard* when he called it a Haymarket production :

> By that we understand – or hitherto understood – a production of a modern classic (Shaw, Wilde or Chekhov usually) in which famous actors and actresses give competing performances of the main parts along lines chosen by themselves, and which dispenses with any overall design or interpretation of the play. The Haymarket tradition is what's wrong with the English theatre, or so we've been told for years by directors like Lindsay Anderson. Celia Johnson plays Madam Ranevsky as in *Chin-Chin*, with echoes of *Brief Encounter*. Meanwhile Hugh Williams plays Gaev like an Earl in one of his own plays.

Although two of the main entrances to the Chichester stage are through the auditorium, with actors debouching through a 'vomitory' into the aisle, their relationships with the audience have become very much what they used to be in the West End theatre during the decade after the war, before the Royal Court had become an influence. At Chichester there are often rounds of applause when the lights go up on a pleasing set and when a favourite actor makes his first entrance or makes an exit following an effective speech. Olivier had been so intent on eliminating applause except at the end of an act that he put a note into the programmes, requesting the audience to refrain. But gradually and invisibly the whole theatre seems to have been swung back to a system in which almost the only objective is to bring gratification and reassurance to a fairly sedate audience.

Theatre can be at its best only when it challenges, provokes, stimulates at the same time as it entertains. If there is no sense of danger, no possibility of embarrassment, the experience is too lulling. Outstanding productions like the Berliner Ensemble's *Mutter Courage*, Brook's *Marat-Sade*, Ingmar Bergman's *Hedda Gabler* with the Royal Dramatic Theatre, Stockholm, the Open Theatre's *America Hurrah!* directed by Joseph Chaikin and Jacques Levy, or Andrzej Wajda's *The Possessed* with the Cracow Stary Theatre, have been at once entertaining and disturbing, satisfying and unsettling. The only productions I have seen at Chichester which made anything of this kind of impact were during the Olivier régime : John Dexter's production of *The Royal Hunt of the Sun*, which he co-directed with Desmond O'Donovan, and *Armstrong's Last Goodnight*, which he co-directed with William Gaskill. This is not a level which can be achieved very often, and while it might seem unreasonable to disparage the Clements régime for falling short of greatness and for succeeding better with light comedies like *The Magistrate* and *An Italian Straw Hat* than with more ambitious plays like *Peer Gynt* and *Antony and Cleopatra*, there is reason to think that it has been a matter of policy – partly conscious, partly unconscious – to avoid giving offence, even at the cost of making a piece like *The Beggar's Opera* look less subversive, or making *The Taming of the Shrew* less upsetting to people who feel strongly about Women's Lib. The intention seems to have been to lull the audience into comfortable confidence that the management would not expect it to watch anything disagreeable.

Not that it would have been easy for anyone in Clements's position to compromise satisfactorily between aiming for success on the highest artistic level and aiming for success with a large public. The theatre seats 1,360 people and it has never received more than a small subsidy or guarantee against loss from the Arts Council. Now that the season has been extended to nineteen weeks, each of the four plays receives about thirty-seven performances, and to fill the theatre, over 50,000 tickets would have to be sold for each production. Since Chichester, with its population of about

20,000, would not be large enough to keep the theatre half full, even if every single inhabitant came to every single play, people from miles away have to be given an incentive to make the journey, and it would be unrealistic to argue that good productions of good plays could attract sufficient crowds without the glamour of star names. What is questionable, though, is whether the stars could not be integrated better into a programme, a policy and a style, without paying for their services by giving them so much power to determine all three.

It is also questionable whether a more heterogeneous audience could not have been built up, depending less exclusively on the upper-middle class and the upper middle-aged. Sussex University is not far away but very little has been done to attract students, young married couples, people with less money to spend on theatre tickets, and people with less conventional theatrical tastes. It would surely have been feasible, for instance, to include at least one or two Sunday night productions of new plays in each season. During the day in the first half of each season many of the actors are rehearsing the two plays which will constitute the second half, but once these are launched, the actors have time on their hands and would be only too glad to work on an exciting experimental project, which could give bigger opportunities to some of the small part players at the same time as testing out new plays, new writers and new ways of using the stage. Many people who never normally come to the theatre might be enticed inside it, and some of them might then buy tickets for other plays. At the moment the management seems to be far too complacent about the rather complacent audience it has built up. Of course it is important to have the theatre full, and Clements has succeeded most impressively in enlarging its public. In his first year at Chichester 136,000 tickets were sold; during 1972, about 247,000, the average capacity being ninety-four per cent. And of course it would be impossible to put on good productions of good plays in a half-empty theatre, especially when the actors have a well-lit view of the empty seats. But have the directors, designers and actors been encouraged to follow too meekly where the audience seemed to lead? How much has been lost in fitting a square public into a hexagonal theatre ?

The Chichester Festival might have developed on quite different lines if the reins had been put into the hands of directors, rather than actors. Leslie Evershed-Martin's idea had been that Tyrone Guthrie should be the first artistic director, and if the building could have been completed a year earlier, Guthrie might have launched the new theatre himself and then handed over to another director like John Dexter or Michael Elliot or Michael Langham, who all have a driving interest in the techniques of directing for the open stage, and the theatre itself might have come much more into its own. When the company from Stratford, Ontario, performed there in 1964, critics and audiences were very excited by the vigour and variety of the productions, the quick changes of mood and atmosphere, and the surges of crowd movement that resolved into carefully worked out choreography. Directorial expertise was the fruit of experience, but though Stuart Burge, after directing *The Workhouse Donkey* at Chichester, was invited to work with the company at Ontario, none of the directors who have worked continuously there or at Guthrie's other open stage theatre in Minneapolis have ever come to direct at the Chichester Festival. The importance of technical skill in directing for the open stage has been consistently underestimated, and the Board of Management, having accepted Olivier's recommendation of John Clements as his successor, then went on to appoint another actor to succeed him, Keith Michell. Unlike Olivier and Clements he has no experience of directing or management, but what should be an advantage is the visual flair he has developed as a painter. Much will depend on whether he is good at surrounding himself with good directors, but there is hope that he will not allow the theatre to be used as if it had an invisible proscenium.

While it is possible that Clements was not given such a free hand as Olivier had, it is difficult to gauge how much pressure the Board has applied. Sometimes the most important pressures are the invisible pressures of expectation, and these affect not only the Artistic Director but everyone who works under him. As the designer Michael Annals has put it: 'As far as decor is concerned, you have to bear in mind that it is the spectator's standard of taste which counts. Far from imposing his own ideas on a reluctant public, and moulding their taste to his preconceived pattern, the artist who is most successful follows where they lead.' Presumably Clements's personal taste largely coincides with that of the Chichester audience, or he could hardly have succeeded in building up box office business as impressively as he did.

Directors without experience in using the space and exploiting the possibilities of an open stage need encouragement and technical advice from the Artistic Director, who influences their work both through discussion and invisibly – through expectation. So a great deal depends on how free he has himself broken from thinking in proscenium terms, how much use he likes to make of scenery, and whether he regards the seats at the side and the seats in the middle as equally important. When Evershed-Martin paid his first visit to Stratford, Ontario, in 1961, he noticed how the production of *Love's Labour's Lost* 'showed what really can be done to use all the stage so that those on the sides felt the production was giving them equal presentation to that seen by people in the central seats.' At Chichester there had been no price differentiation under Olivier, but Clements made the side seats cheaper. At Stratford, Ontario, it was the principle of Michael Langham, who succeeded Guthrie as Artistic Director that there should be no scenery; Clements has been concerned to give his audience as much scenic variety as possible, and many of the plays he has put into the repertoire have been written for the proscenium theatre and could not have been produced on an open stage except by approximating to proscenium conditions. In 1967, when Peter Coe did his first Chichester production, *An Italian Straw Hat*, he was exposing the back wall of the theatre as it had been exposed in *The Chances* (1962). He had it painted white and the railings painted red, so what he was using was not actually a set, though it was praised as if it were. But in his three subsequent Chichester productions, *The Skin of Our Teeth* (1968), *The Caucasian Chalk Circle* (1969) and *Peer Gynt* (1970) he found that instead of profiting from the experience he was gaining of what could be done with the theatre's space, he was exploring and exploiting it less. Had he and the other directors who have worked there during the Clements régime been under less pressure to play safe and more pressure to experiment in different ways of using the shape and the space, a reservoir of experience and technical expertise could have been accumulated which would have helped directors, designers and actors to make the best use of the new open-stage theatres which will soon exist at the National and the Barbican. As it is they will be starting virtually from scratch.

2

The Man and the Money

If anyone had tried in the fifties to predict where the first English open-stage theatre would be built, one of the last places on any list of possibilities would have been this small, quiet, beautiful West Sussex city. It had to happen somewhere, of course. At the 1948 Edinburgh Festival, when Tyrone Guthrie and his designer, Tanya Moiseiwitsch, devised a platform stage in the old Assembly Hall for Sir David Lindsay's *Satire of the Thrie Estaits*, which had not been performed for nearly 400 years, the production was so successful that it was revived at the next year's Festival and again in 1959. In 1953 Guthrie accepted an appointment as Director of the new Shakespeare Festival at Stratford, Ontario, and with Tanya Moiseiwitsch he had a similar stage built, roughly to the Elizabethan pattern. The four trial years, in which the only covering was a tent, proved that there was a sufficient audience, and the stage was retained when the new theatre was built around it, with a conical roof and an auditorium sweeping in a semi-circle around the acting area. There are now 2,225 seats but originally there were only 1,500, all contained within thirteen rows, so no one was more than seventy feet away from the actors. Ideally, Guthrie said, there should have been only ten or eleven rows.

The reason Chichester became the home of the only equivalent theatre in England is that Leslie Evershed-Martin lived there – an extraordinary man who had so far lived a fairly ordinary life. In his youth he had founded an amateur theatrical society called the Chichester Players, and he had twice been mayor of the town, though he later came to regret the amount of time he had given to civic work during eighteen years on the City Council. A philanthropist who believed in the Toc H maxim that we should pay rent for our place on the earth, he had committed himself to civic work in the conviction that someone ought to fight against the streamlining of Philistine town-planners for the preservation of the city's higgledy-piggledy Georgian streets, but retrospectively he was to feel more gratification from the work he did for charities. To succeed in raising the money for an old people's home is to know that a number of old people – twenty-six in this case – are living in better conditions than they otherwise would be. The experience in fund-raising was also to stand him in good stead when it came to finding the money for the new theatre.

His own highly readable book, *The Impossible Theatre*,* describes how Guthrie's television interview sparked the idea in January 1959. It was illustrated with filmed excerpts of the Stratford Ontario production of *Henry V*, which reminded Evershed-Martin of the moments he had most admired in productions at Stratford-on-Avon, when the scenery had faded to insignificance as the actors advanced onto the apron stage. He had also been to see several productions – some in-the-round, some three-quarters in-the-round – at the Pembroke Theatre, Croydon, and it had struck him that in competing with television and cinema, the theatre was handicapping itself unnecessarily if it presented pictures that looked as flat as a screen instead of thrusting the actors forward to create more stereoscopic images.

Apart from the size of the population, the other common factor between Chichester and Stratford, Ontario was the park just outside the city. The local Council had just bought forty-three acres of parkland to the north of the city walls. A plan to build a stadium there had been abandoned, and though it was only a quarter of a mile from the city centre, the park was used very little except for tennis and football. It was also well placed in relation to main roads, so for Evershed-Martin the question was not 'Why Chichester?' but 'Why not Chichester?'

* Phillimore, 1971.

21

Guthrie was in Israel, but due at Stratford-on-Avon in March to start rehearsals for *All's Well That Ends Well*. On March 12 Evershed-Martin drove with his wife to meet him there. Later Guthrie was to describe him as appearing 'to be a person with more than normal common sense and a very driving energetic fellow. I felt confident that if anybody could get a crackpot scheme going somewhere, he could, and I was all out to help in any way I could.' And when Evershed-Martin asked whether he would accept the directorship of the new theatre, if it ever got started, he answered that while it was impossible to predict what his other commitments would be, he would not be uninterested. Privately it was his intention to accept the position, and later on he approached Sir Laurence Olivier about acting in the first season there. Perhaps a Shakespeare and a Shaw for three or four weeks, if he could find time.

Evershed-Martin's meeting with Guthrie convinced him that he was not setting himself an unattainable objective, and knowing he would be in a better position to fight for it if he were no longer on the City Council, he decided that he would not apply for re-election for what would have been his seventh three-year term. Soon he was testing out his new idea on the Town Clerk and the Director of Education for West Sussex, who were both encouraging. The first negative reaction came from the consultant architect to the cathedral, who had been involved in an abortive project six years previously to create an Arts Centre at the Corn Exchange. He was convinced that Evershed-Martin would never be able to raise the money. But next he approached Lord Bessborough, a director of ATV, who arranged for him to meet Ian Hunter, one of the creators of the Edinburgh Festival. If he thought the project was feasible, Bessborough would try to persuade the television companies to donate money.

Visiting Hunter in his Wigmore Street office, Evershed-Martin explained the three principles he had derived from the Ontario example: the new theatre should have a thrust stage and a capacity of at least 1,400; the best available actors, designers and directors should be employed; the fund-raising campaign and the building should proceed in phases, so that if the project had to be abandoned, a good proportion of the money could be returned to the donors. Hunter's verdict, after listening to an outline of Evershed-Martin's plans, was that Chichester was an ideal place for a festival, and that if he kept resolutely to his three principles he could not fail. Triumphantly Evershed-Martin went on to secure the patronage of the Duke of Norfolk and then to consult a heart specialist about whether he was fit to stand up to the pressure that lay ahead. He came away with another favourable verdict.

Leslie Evershed-Martin is not one of those men who can ask for money without feeling embarrassed. Nor is he a man who can take time off whenever he feels like it. He had lost a lot of money during his two years as mayor, when many of his patients had assumed he would be too busy to see them. His working day is from nine till five and to take an afternoon off he normally needs to make arrangements three or four weeks ahead. But he was accustomed to going out every evening and every weekend while canvassing for municipal elections, and he now earmarked all his spare time for the theatre project.

The first man he approached for money was Lord Woolton, who had retired to a village outside Chichester and worked actively for Cathedral charities. Instead of money, he gave Evershed-Martin only advice. When he was raising funds for Manchester University, he said, he turned down a donation of £15,000, telling the well-known businessman who was offering it that he could have afforded £25,000, and that if other people heard about it they would reduce their own contributions proportionately.

Evershed-Martin was soon able to put the advice to good use when approaching a successful property-developer, who offered a few hundred and agreed to make it a thousand when Evershed-Martin explained how useful it would be if he could mention it to lever other people up to the same level. After securing three other offers of £1,000 and one of £500, Evershed-Martin was confident enough to form a committee which could later become the nucleus of a trust. It included the four people who had given money, the

Bishop and the Dean of Chichester, the Duke of Richmond
and Gordon, the Town Clerk, the Director of Education,
the City Surveyor and the City Treasurer. Then in June,
within six months of the television interview that had trig-
gered it all, Tyrone Guthrie was invited to Chichester to
meet the committee. He enthused about the site and soon
he was visualizing a ceremonial opening of the theatre with
a procession of robed clergy and all the dignitaries of the
county, marching under fluttering banners from the cathedral to the theatre to symbolize the link between religion
and drama.

The next step was to approach the Council: would it
agree to the principle of granting the theatre a ninety-nine-
year lease of three and a half acres of Oaklands Park at a
peppercorn rent? Evershed-Martin did not discover until
afterwards that the reason the councillors consented so
readily was that once the theatre had been built, they would
have nothing to lose and a building to gain if it turned out
there was no audience for it. Meanwhile Evershed-Martin
had persuaded the consultant architect to the cathedral to
draw up a preliminary design for the theatre, but his idea
was that the auditorium should be subterranean, and he
withdrew from the project after it had emerged in a discussion with Guthrie that tunnels would have to be dug to
enable the actors to make entrances through the audience.
Evershed-Martin's next idea was to approach Philip Powell,
whose father was a Canon of the Cathedral and who, with
his partner, Hidalgo Moya, had designed the skylon, the
central symbol for the 1951 Festival of Britain. Their skylon
was a slender, 300-foot tall aluminium pencil, tapered at
both ends, held aloft from a low cradle of steel wires and
illuminated at night from inside.

By 1959 Powell and Moya were extremely successful and
so busy that they had declined an invitation to submit
designs for Churchill College. They were working mainly on
hospitals and had no experience of theatres: few architects
had – theatres were being pulled down all over England,
and not being replaced. Philip Powell's first impression of
Evershed-Martin was that he was a big, serious-looking
man, who became more and more like an excited schoolboy

when he talked about the project. They had no intention of accepting the commission but just as Evershed-Martin was leaving their office, Powell said 'It's the most exciting thing we've ever turned down'. Sensing that there was some hope but not wanting to coax or coerce, Evershed-Martin invited him to discuss it with Moya over the weekend. On Monday they rang up to say 'yes', and when they saw the site they declared it magnificent. Their briefing was to design an amphitheatre that would hold an audience of at least 1,400 on three sides of a thrust stage; and to keep building costs down to a minimum.

Evershed-Martin then had to go ahead with the fund-raising without knowing how much would be needed. On his committee now there was a strong faction, headed by an ex-Governor of the Bank of England, that wanted to bring out an expensive brochure and use it to approach the big banks and insurance companies. Evershed-Martin realized that this would be very dangerous. Big organizations were unlikely to contribute unless their shareholders or employees were going to benefit, and a rejection from the influential City magnates would be extremely damaging, if not fatal, to the whole enterprise. He believed, though, that there was money to be had from the ordinary theatre-going public. Some large amounts would possibly be contributed by trusts and commercial and industrial concerns; the balance, he maintained, could be raised from the people who would use the theatre when it was functioning.

In November 1959 he learned from Powell and Moya that the theatre they had designed would cost £70,000 if it were built in the near future, though rising costs could push the price up to £100,000 within a few years. Instead of digging the amphitheatre out of the ground, they proposed to put it on stilts, with dressing-rooms under it and corridors to give the actors access to the front-of-house. The hexagonal shape was determined by the need to economize – it would be cheaper than building rounded sections. There would be no space for storing scenery because the intention was that little should be used, and tents could be erected, if necessary, to provide extra space backstage for actors and costumes, until there was enough money to build an extension. The architects believed the roof would be the first in the world to be completely suspended, slung on cables stretching between the points of the hexagon and keeping the cables taut by its own weight. Later, to economize, rods were substituted for the cables. Originally the stage was to be pentagonal, with a point at the centre of the downstage area, but when Evershed-Martin showed the model to Alec Guinness, who had worked at Toronto, he pointed out that it would be difficult for an actor in this downstage position to face towards either side because the character he was talking to would have to be upstage of him. So the flexible hexagonal stage, with its blunter point, was evolved.

Eight contributions of £1,000 had been promised when the first press conference was called in London, on 2 February, 1960, to display the model and explain the project. The conference was timed to coincide with the meeting of the City Council at which the decision would be taken about whether to confirm the provisional arrangement about leasing the land to the theatre. When the news arrived from Chichester that the Council's decision had been favourable, Evershed-Martin held up the peppercorn he would pay as rent.

It was agreed that the building work was not to start until substantial funds were in hand, and everyone who contributed was promised that his money would be returned (minus seven and a half per cent for promotion expenses) if the theatre did not materialize. Outgoings, therefore, had to be kept minimal. Salaries were paid to the Development Fund Secretary and a typist, but Evershed-Martin never reclaimed the money (about £1,000) that he spent during the first year of the campaign on travelling, entertaining, stationery, postage stamps and telephone calls.

He resisted the idea of employing a professional fund-raiser or one of the firms that charge about £1,000 for sending out appeal literature to rich people they have listed as contributors to charities. As he says in his book: 'The person who can best get the money is the one who is not only working voluntarily, but also obviously shows sincere conviction in the project. Paid collectors are always suspect, since the donor feels that part of his donation is going to pay that salary.' He knew that in opting for the personal approach he was taking the main burden onto himself. He is not a shy man but it was a new effort for him each time to put the question 'How much are you going to give?' But he seldom asked it in vain, and he took enormous pleasure in the new friendships that he made and in the growing certainty that his efforts were not going to be abortive. His method was to write to the people who had been recommended as possible donors, asking whether he could call on them to talk about the theatre. He would follow up each letter with a telephone call, and this was the moment he hated most, though in fact he was hardly ever rebuffed.

When he had collected enough money to employ a Development Fund Secretary, a retired naval commander was appointed to share both the round of personal visits and the lecturing. Taking a model of the theatre with them, they addressed Rotary Clubs, Townswomen's Guilds, Women's Institutes, religious organizations and amateur theatrical groups, but much of this activity turned out to have been more valuable in laying the foundations of the future audience than in accumulating capital. It was their policy to avoid the word *appeal* and never to suggest it was anyone's *duty* to support the project. The emphasis was on entertainment and pleasure: this was what a new theatre would provide, and people had the right to join in if they wanted to. One of the most effective of the fund-raising ideas was Founder Membership. Anyone who donated £100 or covenanted seven annual payments of £10 would have his name inscribed in the foyer.

A. T. Smith, the Chairman of Bryanston Finances, who was later to take over from Evershed-Martin as Chairman of the theatre's Executive Board, was introduced to him in 1960 by the Managing Director of a motor accessories company who was on the fund-raising committee. Once Smith was convinced that Evershed-Martin's commitment to the project had no ulterior motive, he threw himself energetically into the fund-raising activity, importuning business associates for covenants and forming a London Committee which met at his flat in Bryanston Court and raised several thousand pounds by arranging charity previews of West

End shows, a tombola at Arundel Castle and a night on a liner in Southampton docks. Alan Draycott, one of the first donors of £1,000, was a director of a building company, which offered a bungalow near Littlehampton as prize in a competition. Over 20,000 tickets were sold, yielding £2,000 for the fund, and another good source was the competition which became an annual event at Fontwell Racecourse with a horse as prize. A great variety of fund-raising events was organized, including jumble sales, coffee mornings, cocktail parties and concerts, but it was the direct personal approach that yielded most of the money. According to Evershed-Martin's calculations, A. T. Smith, Alan Draycott and he himself were each responsible for about £30,000.

Mrs Henny Gestetner, another donor of £1,000 who was later to be on the Executive Board, raised £8,000 in a single evening by throwing a champagne party in her house at Bosham. Alan Draycott and his wife organized a 'Star Night' at the Ham Manor Golf House with stalls manned by showbiz personalities who lived locally, and this produced £1,300. The Gulbenkian Fund was approached in vain, but the Pilgrim Trust contributed £2,500; the Portsmouth Evening News group £1,000; Southern Television an annual £1,000; and Brickwoods, the brewers, made a gift of the foyer bar and later built the bar extension. The Arts Council's initial grant of an annual £2,500 was used to pay instalments on the cost of electrical equipment. A Theatre Society was formed on the same lines as the one at the Mermaid, and from subscriptions of £1, donations and the sale of souvenirs, and by organizing competitions and events, it was eventually able to contribute over £10,000 to the fund, while building up its own membership to over 8,000.

Only £15,000 of this money had been collected when the Theatre Trust held its first meeting on 21 June, 1960 in a committee room of the House of Lords, and it was decided that no date should be fixed for the building work to start until £35,000 was in the kitty, although A. T. Smith was against waiting so long, arguing that money would pour in much faster once building was under way and offering a personal loan of £10,000. By the middle of July £22,000 had been raised, and there was an exciting possibility that McAlpine would accept the building assignment for a first payment of £30,000, the balance to be spread over eight years with only nominal interest. If the trustees had then accepted Smith's offer of a loan to bridge the gap, building could have started almost immediately, the theatre could have opened in 1961, and Tyrone Guthrie, who was waiting for his theatre to be built in Minneapolis, might have been Chichester's first Artistic Director. Unfortunately the trustees became too concerned about their liabilities and reputations, alarmed by a millionaire's story of his bad experiences in raising funds for a nursing home. But by the end of November they had £34,000, partly in cash, partly in grossed-up covenants, and it was agreed that contracts should be exchanged with McAlpine for building to start on 1 May 1961.

It was before that, in January, when Evershed-Martin and his wife went to visit Guthrie in Ireland to discuss possible directors, that Olivier's name came up. They were going through the Arts Council's unofficial list of suggestions categorizing directors as past and faded, up and coming, new but strident, good, down and out, possible or impossible. Evershed-Martin was making detailed notes of Guthrie's comments on each one. Olivier's name was not on the list, but after a couple of hours' discussion, when they were pausing for a coffee, Guthrie sat back and suggested him. 'Leslie, you keep on and on about only having the best of everything at Chichester, so why don't you go for the best? Ask him.' Olivier was then in New York, playing in Anouilh's *Becket*, first as Becket and later as Henry II. Guthrie knew that he was not enjoying New York. He was about to get married (on 19 March) to Joan Plowright, and possibly he would feel like committing himself to something totally new. Guthrie's advice was to offer him a salary of £5,000 a year.

On 11 January 1961, exactly two years and one week after seeing the Guthrie interview on television, Evershed-Martin wrote to Olivier at length, describing how the project had developed and enclosing plans of the building. There was no reply for a month, for Olivier had taken the play on tour, but the two pages of questions in Olivier's letter were encouraging. Would he have full artistic control? Would he have a say in the construction of the stage? In March, Lord Bessborough, who was now one of the trustees, happened to be in New York, and called on him to tell him more about the theatre. A few days later Evershed-Martin went to see Olivier's agent, Cecil Tennant, at the MCA building in Piccadilly and made the offer of £5,000 a year. After withdrawing from the discussion to telephone Olivier from another room, Tennant came back to say that he would accept £3,000 a year. When Ian Hunter heard the news, he said 'If you've got him, you're made', and when Olivier's letter of confirmation arrived, Evershed-Martin sent him a telegram : 'The Sussex Downs will shout with joy to welcome you.'

A press conference was rapidly arranged and, predictably, the newspapers, television and radio all reported it at length. If the theatre had been a public company, share prices would have rocketed. Olivier came back to England in June and gave an interview on television to Lord Harewood. First of all he was filmed walking over the half-finished building and saying how exciting it was to be in a theatre that was going up, after 'having had two London theatres pulled down round about my ears'. This was a reference to the St James's, which he had run for eight years, and the Stoll, whose life had ended with his *Titus Andronicus*. When he was asked what he felt about acting with the audience all round the stage, he answered 'I did it once. I did it by accident. I was playing Hamlet in Elsinore many years ago, and the rain was falling down so hard in the courtyard of the castle where we had to act that it was abandoned and we suddenly had to put it on at no warning at all in the ballroom, and there we found ourselves in just such circumstances. It was very exciting. Here it will be planned, and the star will be the theatre, apart from what goes on inside it . . .' That phrase, 'The star will be the theatre', was to lodge itself in Evershed-Martin's brain and become a yardstick for what subsequently happened.

3
The Actor and the Chichester Stage

Whether you're an actor or not, stand in the middle of the Chichester stage and you'll immediately be struck by the extent of the area between you and the encircling seats. Audiences equally get an impression of expansiveness, and reviewers have peppered their notices with phrases like 'Chichester's wide open spaces' and 'the desert expanses of the Chichester open stage'. In fact different geometric shapes produce different optical illusions and the hexagon is smaller than it looks. At the Shaftesbury – to take a West End theatre of roughly the same seating capacity – the width of the proscenium opening is 10.1 metres, and at Chichester the width of the stage is 11 metres. The depth of the acting area in any theatre varies according to how far the set comes away from the back wall. The total depth (ignoring the set) is 9.7 metres at the Shaftesbury, and 12.8 at Chichester. Nevertheless, the hexagonal stage creates formidable problems in the actor's relationships both with his fellow-actors and with the audience, and there's no denying that the problems might have been less formidable if the architects had been *au fait* with the technical problems involved in creating and maintaining the kind of contact an actor needs with both.

His two main weapons are his voice and his eyes, and he expects to be able to bring them simultaneously into play. At Chichester, unless he is near the back of the unusually deep stage, it is dangerous for him to turn his head in the middle of a sentence, because his eyes suddenly become invisible to one sector of the audience and visible to another, while the quality of the sound he is making deteriorates for the one sector and improves for the other. It might seem to follow from this that the strongest position is upstage. This is the only area from which he can take the whole audience in with his eyes without turning his head, but it is not a commanding position because of the apparent size of the intervening stage and the abnormal difficulties of lighting the upstage area so that actors in it are clearly illuminated not just from the front but from every angle. And sometimes there is a structure at the back designed to provide a small acting area on a higher level, corresponding to the stage gallery of the Elizabethan playhouse. This is useful and often necessary but the actor on it is too high to be in a good position for contact with the audience, and the actor immediately below is liable to be overshadowed.

Further downstage actors cannot avoid turning their sides and backs to large sections of the audience for a large proportion of the time. Ideally, every part of an actor's body should be expressive and interesting to look at, but the tradition of English acting has tended to cultivate the voice and the head at the expense of the rest of the body. A reaction against this rarefication was well under way before the Chichester theatre was built, and drama schools are now devoting much more of their curriculum to training the body; the existence of Chichester and other theatres more or less modelled on it will provide both an incentive to this development and a playground in which the new physical skills will be cultivated and deployed to greater advantage than they could be in the old proscenium theatres. In the meantime, critics and audiences become discontented if they are required to look at backs and heads which are not moving, while the actors themselves have mostly had so little experience of working on open stages that it is hard for them to hide their feeling of being handicapped, and directors vary in the extent to which they can help them to overcome the feeling that they owe an apology to the people who are not seeing their eyes.

But Evershed-Martin's initial instinct about pushing the actor forward to create a more stereoscopic image than he

can in the picture-frame stage has largely been validated by
the Chichester experience. In a conventional theatre the
actor cannot but be aware of the fact that to the audience
he is little more than part of a two-dimensional picture. His
performance needs to look good from the front, but it can
look very different to another actor watching from the
wings. At Chichester the performance must stand up to
scrutiny from any angle. As Margaret Leighton has said, 'I
think you can't cheat as much'. Or as Clive Swift* put it:
'Total Exposure. No "safety area" as with proscenium
arches where you can turn upstage and clear your throat
without being spied on. At Chich (as "in the round") you
get away with nothing. If you "corpse" or "send up" a
fellow actor or comment (even silently) on the audience's
unquick wit you are seen doing so.'

But this need for a greater honesty constitutes only one
of the reasons that actors feel more exposed and defenceless
when they are almost completely encircled by the audience.
In a picture-frame set the centre of the audience's field of
vision is well above the actors' heads, and most of the space
inside the frame is filled by the set; on an open stage the
attention of the public is concentrated much more on the
actor, his movements and his costume, but his costume
should act almost like a magnifying glass to emphasise what
he is doing inside it. His responsibility therefore is greater
than in the proscenium theatre, and his contact with the
public more exhilarating at the same time as being more
frightening. Most actors are victims of two contradictory
forces, one of which makes them want to appear in public
while the other pulls them sharply towards privacy and
withdrawal. In a proscenium theatre their desire for privacy
is gratified and their insecurity appeased by the sense of
containment within a five-sided box formed by the set, the
stage and the grid. If they forget their lines, the prompter
in the prompt corner will help them; if anything goes
disastrously wrong, the box can be closed by bringing down
the sixth side, which is the curtain. At Chichester there are
no sheltering wings to the stage, the prompter is in a remote

* *Theatre Quarterly*, July–September 1973.

box at the back of the auditorium and there is no possibility of retreat. One is caught in a huge pincer of onlookers.

Whether secretly or unashamedly, many actors regret the disappearance of the footlights which used to illuminate their make-up flatteringly from below and to form a rigid barrier, like an electric moat, between stage and auditorium. The whole tendency of the modern movement in the theatre is to destroy frontiers between acting area and auditorium, to merge performance and public, requiring the actor to overcome his natural shyness. The proscenium frame still survives in most West End theatres, but the National Theatre at the Old Vic and the Royal Shakespeare Company at the Aldwych have built out apron stages to bring the actor closer to the audience, and the Chichester stage brings him closer still. England does not yet have a full-scale, purpose-built theatre-in-the-round, and on the Chichester stage the actor feels less exposed than he would if he were completely encircled by the public: at least there is one angle from which no one can look at him. But the further downstage he goes, the narrower it becomes, and the more he feels that his body is a centre from which the perform-ance has to radiate in every direction. Albert Finney (who played at Chichester during Olivier's final season in *Arm-strong's Last Goodnight*, *Miss Julie* and *Black Comedy*) put it rather well in an interview he gave the *Western Mail*: 'The question of focus is very difficult. It's very difficult to time things and project things through such a wide angle of reference. You keep wondering whether people alongside or behind you have caught something you want to put over. In *Black Comedy* there were two lines where I knew I could do it. Apart from that every role has this recurring problem.' Downstage you can easily be misled by the feeling of closeness to the front rows: you also have to make con-tact with the remoter parts of the house you cannot even see.

In the proscenium theatre one of the functions of the set is to act like a lamp shade around the electric light bulb which is the performance, concentrating both the sound and the energy and reflecting them forward. At Chichester the size and shape of both stage and auditorium make is necessary for the actor to manage without this kind of reflector, to generate more vocal and physical energy, moving about more often and traversing greater distances. When the audience is watching through a proscenium, an intimate scene between two people might very well be played down-stage on a sofa with a distance of only a foot or two between them and without either of them changing position. At Chichester this would be impossible. Situate the sofa upstage and they are visible but remote : there is too much empty stage between them and the audience for their dialogue to hold the attention. Situate it downstage centre, and the favoured few in the middle would have a good view of both actors while the majority would be watching the sides and backs of their heads, and for many people one of them would be almost invisible – hidden by the other. If the sofa is parallel to the back wall, this happens wherever it is situated, except in the upstage area. If it is angled along one of the diagonals that point to the vomitories, the masking problem is reduced because the spectators sitting above them are high enough above stage level to have a reasonably good view, but both actors have their backs to a large section of the public. When only two actors are on stage, the people unable to see the face of one are going to find the experience almost intolerable unless they see the face of the other – which means that the two actors cannot be facing in the same direction for more than a moment or two. Nor can spectators be expected to go on looking at one face and missing the other for very long at a stretch – which means that they must be kept on the move. By now we are thoroughly acclimatized to listening to a duologue in the cinema or on television without seeing both faces at the same time. The camera makes our choices for us, cutting from one to the other, showing whichever expression or reaction or face the director thinks more significant or more interesting or more photogenic. The director in the open-stage theatre has the whole of the actors' bodies to use, no possibility of close-up, and no possibility of presenting the whole audience with the same picture. A point which one side of the house is going to understand from the expression on the face of the speaker may have to be picked up by the other side three seconds later from the reaction of the listener.

Partly to obviate problems of masking and partly to open out the action and generate enough vocal energy to fill the space of both stage and auditorium, the director at Chichester needs to avoid situations in which two actors stay close together for more than a very short time. In *St Joan* John Dexter managed the protracted conversation between Warwick and Cauchon by seating them at opposite ends of a long table. Sometimes directors – over-anxious about sharing out the actors' faces between different sectors of the audience – make them move restlessly about, introducing irrelevant stage business to justify movement which corresponds to nothing in the dialogue or the situation. What the actor finds then is that besides the physical energy he needs to cope with the hectic hither-and-thithering, he must expend additional mental energy on the concentration needed to counterbalance the movement, and extra vocal energy on controlling passages of dialogue which were written to be spoken quietly.

It is impossible to calculate energy quantitatively and some actors insist that (except on the long walk from the dressing-rooms to the stage) they use up no more energy at Chichester than in any other theatre. But Michael Aldridge, who has had more experience of the Chichester stage than any other actor, having played important parts there during seven successive seasons from 1966 to 1972, estimates that actors need to generate about four times as much energy there as in an average London theatre. When there are cast changes in productions that transfer from Chichester to the West End, the actors new to the company always find during the pre-London rehearsals that the others seem to be working much harder than is necessary, and they are right. The original actors always find they now need to cut down on what they were doing in Chichester.

It is also significant that Michael Aldridge, who is a large man, finds that at Chichester his size is a great advantage. The more cubic space that one's movements fill, the better, whether it is a matter of levering oneself up out of an armchair, pacing up and down, or gesturing frenziedly to someone behind someone else's back. Conversely a small actor or actress is somewhat at a disadvantage, and, similarly nuances of behaviour, subtle changes of tone and slight changes of facial expression are hard to project. These require the audience's whole attention, aural and visual, to be focused on the same point at the same instant, and at Chichester this is not always possible.

It is hard to listen intently to an actor when you cannot see his eyes, and it is generally more difficult at Chichester for the actor to catch the spectators' attention at the moment he most needs it, when their whole field of vision is so much wider and deeper than usual. In theory it is the director's responsibility to devise a production which always focuses the audience's attention where it is most needed, but in practice it is often the actor's personality that keeps attracting attention. Actors like Olivier, with his animal magnetism, or Edith Evans, with her extraordinary presence, or Alastair Sim and Margaret Rutherford, with their amiable eccentricity, have been at a great advantage in Chichester, cashing in automatically on every audience's love of the unpredictable, its natural curiosity about what is going to happen next with intriguing personalities of this size. But a great many actors whose technique is highly efficient and highly tuned to the requirements of a normal proscenium theatre have felt uncomfortable as soon as they walked on to the Chichester stage and never subsequently come to feel at home with it. One well known actor walked straight off again for a stiff drink. It is not the ideal launching pad for Irene Handl's comedy, and it is a difficult stage for actors like Nigel Patrick whose technique depends largely on establishing short range contact with other actors.

One of the hardest tasks that the Chichester theatre imposes on the actor is to retain a feeling of great closeness when he is at a considerable distance from his partner in a scene. Sarah Badel, who played with Alastair Sim in *The Clandestine Marriage* in 1966, found she could achieve this in her scenes with him but not to her own satisfaction with any other actor in any of her seven subsequent roles there. It is not difficult to arrive at a momentary rapport with another actor under these conditions, but it cannot be sustained without enormous concentration and enormous flexibility. Nor is it merely a matter of the distance between two partners in a scene. Many lines have to be angled not inwards towards him but outwards towards the audience, and this can produce artificiality, simplification and exaggeration, as well as rigidity and insensitivity to the detail of one's partner's work. Responsiveness is rare anyway, but for instance when Paul Scofield and Anna Calder-Marshall were playing Vanya and Sonya in *Uncle Vanya* at the Royal Court, their scenes together would be slightly different from night to night, for each of them was alert to variations in the other's inflections and secure enough within the overall shape of the scene to react accordingly. At Chichester the extra force that has to go into projecting performances centrifugally makes it all the more difficult for actors to watch each other closely enough, or listen to each other intently enough, to interact with as much subtlety and spontaneity as this.

The difficulties are exacerbated by the acoustic problems of the theatre, which are so awkward that Olivier was at one point seriously considering whether to install microphones. Since then the acoustics have been substantially improved, and there are boards at either side of the stage which help to reflect the sound, but noises from outside can still interfere, and rain would sometimes sabotage the one surefire laugh Tom Courtenay had in *The Cherry Orchard* in 1966, when he was playing Trofimov. 'I delivered my line and just got one small reaction from the people in front of me. Because of the rain, people upstairs couldn't hear.'

In general, men are at an advantage over women in the Chichester acoustic, which, unlike that of most theatres, favours the bass at the expense of the treble. Of the men, actors with a light tenor voice are worse off than actors like Clements, whose voice is deep and distinct. Gielgud found the theatre 'terrifying'. 'You have to be careful directing your voice on the diagonal, not the square.' You often need to address lines – as you hardly ever do in the proscenium theatre – to an actor upstage of you at a sharp angle, and you need to be especially careful about falling inflections at the ends of sentences.

But if the Chichester stage reduces the actor's freedom in some ways, it increases it in others. While a scene requiring quiet intimacy between the characters is difficult, it is possible to achieve intimacy with the audience, to give it the impression of being drawn inside the area where the action is taking place. And this is only one of the factors that make the actor-audience relationship unusually direct and exciting. Theatres vary in the speed at which the public's reaction becomes apparent, and at Chichester the laughs seem to come very quickly. They also sound very loud, and they gather momentum in a very gratifying way, spreading from one sector to another, even if different sectors are laughing at different facets of the same piece of comedy.

The actor's freedom is also increased in effect by the extension of the area of his responsibility. In the Shakespearian theatre there was virtually no scenery and it was therefore left to the actor to create the necessary sense of place, to evoke the necessary atmosphere. At Chichester he is helped by changes of lighting which were unavailable in the sixteenth century, but in most of the plays written in the last 200 years he is not helped by speeches whose main function is to evoke atmosphere. Even Chekhov expected this to be done through scenery, lighting and sound effects rather than words. But the less scenery there is, the more the audience's attention is concentrated on the actor's movements and the more willing the audience is to apply its own visual imagination to supplement what it sees. In Peter Shaffer's play *The Royal Hunt of the Sun* there is a laconic stage direction which reads 'They climb the Andes'. The challenge to the director's ingenuity was deliberate, but it would have been difficult to solve the problem satisfactorily in a proscenium theatre through mime and stylized movement. At Chichester this was one of the most highly praised sequences in the whole production.

Even without stylization, the possibility of making the audience look closely at what a three-dimensional actor is doing with his body suggests – as Olivier was quick to realize – a possibility of using that body to make a statement about place. In *Uncle Vanya* the first act is set in the garden outside the house and the other three acts are indoors, but Olivier, with his designer, Sean Kenny, decided not to change either the set or the furniture. The lighting changed, but 'It was the actors, by their *behaviour*, Sean and I maintained, from whom the audience should tell whether they were outside the house or inside it, and what sort of a room they were in – a drawing-room or an estate office.' The movements of our bodies do, of course, vary perceptibly according to whether we are indoors or out of doors, in our own homes or someone else's and whether we are in the presence of strangers we want to impress or of intimates, but it is all too seldom that either actors or audiences are required to register variations of this sort. One of the functions of an open-stage theatre should be to play a part in training both to observe physical movement more carefully.

The entrances and exits at Chichester produce problems of their own. In a box set a door creates at least a clear punctuation between being off-stage and on. At Chichester, especially when the set is minimal, the actor feels exposed almost before he has made his entrance. He is in view before he is in a good position to speak, and the problem of getting himself into a good position is as formidable as in theatres like the Palladium, with very large stages. You feel you should walk quite a long way before you open your mouth. The problem of making an entrance through one of the vomitories is different, but not easier. Because the audience cannot see the door, there is again no clear punctuation between being off-stage and on, and again you are in view before you are in a good position to speak. So you sometimes have to choose between the risk of letting your opening words be semi-audible and introducing an artificial pause between appearing and speaking.

The vomitory doors have been cut fairly low in order to avoid sacrificing too many seats above them, and this makes it extremely difficult for processions of soldiers to go out with any brio, especially if they are carrying flags, pikes or spears, as they often are. It is even difficult for actors in bulky costumes, and costumes at Chichester do tend to be bulky. The bigger they are, the more help they are to the actor in filling the space, and a clever costume can make a small actor look big. Carl Toms, who has designed seven productions there during the Clements régime, says that one of the reasons modern-dress productions are so difficult is that sweaters and jeans do not help the actor towards the size of performance and projection that the theatre demands.

The sight-lines are also difficult, and ideally the actor needs a detailed knowledge of the problem areas. During the rehearsals of *Heartbreak House* for the 1967 season, Irene Worth, who was playing Hesione Hushabye, complained to Michael Aldridge, who was Hector, her husband, about the way he used to hunch forward just before a good laugh line she had. 'I don't like it,' she told him. 'It's not Hector.' He explained that he was doing it to avoid masking her at that important moment from about 250 people sitting above one of the vomitories. She then found, instead, a pretext for standing up before delivering the line.

The Chichester stage could be called democratic in that it works against the kind of performance calculated to dominate or dazzle or patronize the audience. The actor who wants to dictate to his audience needs to be in a playing area which is rigidly separated from the auditorium; Chichester encourages a more reciprocal and free-flowing relationship. And in a proscenium theatre, however many actors there are on stage, the one who is furthest upstage is always in the dominant position. He can address the others without turning away from the audience as they must to answer him. At Chichester some positions are better than others, and one of the best is the downstage point of the hexagon, with one's back to the centre of the audience, but there is never one that is better than all the others. And when the production does succeed in giving the audience the impression of sharing a space with the actors, of being wherever the action is meant to be occurring, it comes to matter much less that not all the actors' faces are visible all the time.

It might seem to follow from this that it is not a theatre for star performances, but the audience which has been built up is one which is attracted by star names, and whereas a more experimental and less hierarchical policy might attract more students, they cannot afford the prices it will go on being necessary to charge for the tickets unless the Arts Council subsidy is substantially increased. For their part, star actors are very glad of the opportunity to play meaty classical roles of the sort that are very seldom on offer in the West End, and without having to sign a long-term contract as they would with the RSC, while even the National, which depends more on stars, is reluctant to sign one up for a single production unless he will stay with it for quite a number of months. At Chichester the commitment need only be nine weeks of performances, and there are all the extra incentives of living in the country – perhaps taking a cottage at West Wittering close to the beach. Topol, for instance, a star who is in great demand and had been at Chichester in 1969, agreed to return in 1973, preferring to do the new Ustinov musical *R Loves J* there than in the West End.

4

Plays for Chichester

I remain convinced that only those forms of theatre
in which words are secondary – such as musicals,
dance drama, and Commedia dell'Arte – have much
to gain from the three-sided stage.

KENNETH TYNAN, reviewing the final production
of Olivier's first season, *Uncle Vanya*, in
The Observer

The decision about whether or not to mount a particular
play at Chichester has never been taken without knowing
how the leading parts are going to be cast; ideally it would
never be taken without knowing in some detail how it is
going to be directed and designed. As far as the spectators
are concerned, a play consists not just of the words they hear
but everything they see. Often the question of whether a
particular play is suitable for the Chichester stage or the
Chichester stage for a particular play is almost meaningless
unless the intentions of the director and the designer are
taken into account. Five plays by Shaw have already been
staged at Chichester – as many as by Shakespeare and more
than by any other playwright. But Shaw's plays are all
written with detailed and elaborate stage directions worked
out in relation to a proscenium theatre, and if the question
were asked 'Can they be staged without interfering with
the author's intentions?' the answer would have to be 'No'.
But then if the intentions of a play could not be communi-
cated without staging it in the way the author intended,
it would be impossible to put on an adequate production of
a Shakespeare play without building a Globe-type theatre.

That Shakespeare's stage directions are so exiguous and Shaw's so specific is a secondary consideration.

Shakespeare's plays and Shaw's are representative of two different kinds of theatre, and since the Chichester theatre and the Toronto theatre on which it was approximately modelled were both designed in reaction against the kind of theatre for which Shaw was writing, aiming to reinstate a relationship between actor and audience closer to that which prevailed in the Shakespearian period, it is not surprising that Shakespeare's plays can be accommodated more easily than Shaw's on the open stage.

For the director and designer working at Chichester plays can be categorized according to whether they need furniture and doors, as Shaw's do and Shakespeare's do not. Of course tables and chairs are sometimes necessary but they can be brought on and taken off in full view of the audience, as they were orginally, and if there are references to a door, as in the Porter scene in *Macbeth*, it does not need to be seen by the audience. But most of the action of most of the plays written during the last 300 years takes place in furnished rooms, and most often these plays are of three or four acts, with no alterations to the furniture or scenery except during intervals when the curtain would be lowered. In practice the proscenium and the curtain conspired to impose the Artistotelian unities of place and time. But Brecht reverted to the Shakespearian model, constructing his plays out of a series of almost self-contained scenes, moving freely from one locale to another and one time to another. Since 1956, when his company, the Berliner Ensemble, paid its first visit to England, a number of our playwrights, like Robert Bolt and Peter Shaffer, have followed suit, using what Brecht calls 'Epic' construction, and it is no accident that two of the new plays which have succeeded as well as any old plays at Chichester, Shaffer's *The Royal Hunt of the Sun* and Bolt's *Vivat! Vivat Regina!* have been written to this pattern. As in Shakespeare and most of Brecht, doors are unimportant and little furniture is needed. Changes of location do not call for complete changes of décor. A locale can be suggested by lighting, by a single prop or piece of furniture, or by a group of actors in a particular kind of costume. Just as the action of *The Royal Hunt of the Sun* moves between the Spaniards and the Indians, *Vivat! Vivat Regina!* alternates between the English and Scottish courts, so costume can almost replace scenery in locating each scene for the audience, and in both productions clever groupings of actors were almost architectural. A stage like Chichester really comes into its own when a series of scenic effects is created out of patterning costumed human bodies. But with a small cast and action set in a bedroom or drawing room this is impossible.

Does it follow that plays like this are unsuitable for the theatre? Tyrone Guthrie's answer to this question was categoric. In a lecture he gave on a visit to Chichester in May 1960, he said 'The sort of theatre it is proposed to build here is suitable for plays written before 1660 and suitable for most of the forward-looking plays of the present day, but unsuitable for most of the plays between 1660 and the present day. Totally unsuitable for, let us say, Sheridan, Wilde or Goldsmith, or for Somerset Maugham. Not totally unsuitable for most of Ibsen where the poetic element is much more important than the realistic. Not unsuitable for the more important and greater works of Shaw; *Heartbreak House*, for instance, or *St Joan* would be fine on such a stage as it is proposed to build here; *You Never Can Tell* would not, since that was a totally realistic comedy, and as such would be far better inside a proscenium. Now you may say, "Why build a theatre which is not suitable for any and every play?" The answer is another question: "How to build a theatre which is suitable for any and every play." Just as an all-purpose hall is a no-purpose hall, which is not very good for doing plays, not very good for concerts, is not very good for the Badminton Club, and not very good for the Church bazaar, so an all-purpose theatre is not a thing you can build. A play should be suitably presented in a theatre which offers the facilities which the author had in mind when he wrote it.'

Guthrie, in other words, did not believe that Shakespeare's plays could be suitably presented in a proscenium theatre, and at least part of his motive in devoting so much time to encouraging the creation of open-stage theatres in Toronto, Chichester and Minneapolis was to provide new stages on which he and other directors could do suitable productions of Shakespeare, Ben Jonson and their contemporaries. When Guthrie was thinking seriously of accepting the position of Artistic Director at Chichester, the only major theatres in England regularly presenting a classical repertoire were the Memorial Theatre at Stratford-on-Avon and the impoverished Old Vic in Waterloo Road, and there can be little doubt that what Guthrie had in mind for Chichester was a repertoire based mainly on Shakespeare and the classics, seasoned with some Shaw and some new plays, but drawing relatively little on the period 1660-1960. 1960, however was the year that Peter Hall was appointed as Managing Director of the Stratford Memorial Theatre, which was renamed the Royal Shakespeare Theatre the following year, and by the end of 1960 the company had secured a London base at the Aldwych, which, unlike the Stratford theatre, was to remain open all the year round. Even in 1962, when Olivier launched the first Chichester season, the Royal Shakespeare Company was the only other large scale company presenting a mainly Shakespearian repertoire, but once the National Theatre was also in existence, Chichester, having for two years been its summer home, then had, in effect, to become a rival. The theatre would only be full if some of the people who lived within range of the National Theatre and the Aldwych chose to spend at least a few of their summer evenings at Chichester. So Chichester must not merely offer samplings of the same repertoire.

Theoretically Guthrie's argument could be countered by saying that to present proscenium plays on an open stage was not doing any more violence to them than had been done to Shakespearian texts for three centuries in theatres which did not offer the facilities the author had in mind when he wrote them. But the obstinate fact remained that Guthrie, who had been the only professional man of the theatre whose advice had been influential in the shaping of the new building, had envisaged something quite different from the use to which it was to be put. Of the twelve plays

Olivier did in his two pre-National and his two National seasons, four were pre-1660, four were new and only four were written between 1660 and 1960. Of the thirty-two plays Clements did in his eight seasons, five were pre-1660 (four by Shakespeare and one by Jonson) and apart from the three English premières of plays by Anouilh and the musicalization of Peter Ustinov's 1956 success *Romanoff and Juliet*, the only two new plays were Ustinov's *The Unknown Soldier and His Wife* and Bolt's *Vivat! Vivat Regina!* Whether Bolt is a forward-looking dramatist in Guthrie's sense is arguable, but it is certainly not a claim that could be made for either Ustinov or Anouilh, who normally directs his own plays inside a proscenium, and writes accordingly. The remaining twenty-one of Clements's thirty-two plays were all written in the period 1660-1960 and they were all proscenium plays, except *Peer Gynt*, which Ibsen described as a 'poem' and wrote when he was in exile, with no immediate thought of having it performed. It is a play which could be staged very well at Chichester, though the 1970 production was disappointing. But in most of the other twenty the realistic element was far more important than the poetic. Even if you do not accept Guthrie's premise, which is based on a distinction between 'poetic' and 'realistic' plays, the fact remains that two-thirds of Clements's total output was of plays written for proscenium theatres, although the dramatic literature that is now available to us goes back over twenty centuries and the proscenium has been in existence for only three of them. There are Greek, Roman and medieval plays which it would be fascinating to see on the Chichester stage. Admittedly, when so much light spills into the auditorium, it would be extremely depressing for both actors and audience if half the seats were empty, but Olivier made Sophocles's *Oedipus Rex* into a great hit at the Old Vic in the 1945-6 season, and Peter Brook's production of Seneca's *Oedipus* was a success at the National in 1968 with John Gielgud. So even if the public can be attracted to pre-Renaissance plays only by star actors or a star director, there is no justification for excluding them altogether.

The failure to put on more new plays by 'forward-looking'

writers is much more serious. More than the director, the designer or the actor, the writer is the source of creative new ideas, and a country's theatre can be in a healthy state only when its bloodstream is well fed with playwriting talent. Currently England is very well off for young playwrights, but the Royal Court Theatre, the hothouse where so many talents have ripened, is a proscenium theatre which, as I have argued elsewhere,* has had damaging effects on the style of writers like Osborne, who have gone on thinking in proscenium terms. Both Ustinov's *The Unknown Soldier and His Wife* and Bolt's *Vivat! Vivat Regina!* may have gained from the open stage productions they received at Chichester, but neither Ustinov nor Bolt are playwrights who could be said to have suffered from having their work hemmed in behind a proscenium. In *A Man for All Seasons*, Bolt did try to strike up a more direct relationship with the audience than the proscenium normally allows by introducing a character, the Common Man, who talked straight out front, music-hall style. But Bolt did not go any further with this kind of technical experiment, and though it is not impossible that he might have written more plays and developed quite differently as a playwright if he had had a theatre like Chichester to write for, his commitment, like Ustinov's, is not primarily to the theatre, and there are other playwrights (like Peter Nichols) who in one play after another have tried different methods of breaking through to a more direct relationship with the audience, while there are some (like Arden) with a natural capacity for writing on a Brechtian scale and with a Brechtian sweep, but cannot do this for a picture-frame theatre.

At the moment, the Fringe provides the main arena for non-proscenium productions but the playwright can earn very little money there, though this has not discouraged writers like John Arden and John McGrath from ploughing a great deal of time into plays that will be staged only on the Fringe. But until the National is functioning inside its own building, Chichester is the one theatre where an open-stage production of a new play could bring the writer a

* *The Set-Up. An Anatomy of English Theatre Today,* London, Methuen, 1974.

reasonable financial return and, above all, a reasonable amount of public attention. And it is only by canalizing new talent that the Chichester theatre could have the exciting seasons it deserves.

Even if more new plays and more pre-Renaissance plays were included in the repertoire, the rival existence of the National and the Royal Shakespeare Company would make it unrealistic to draw as little on the 1660-1960 period as Guthrie would have liked. But with this period, as with any other, there is no litmus test which can be used to determine whether or not a play could be made to work at Chichester. In fact, some of the greatest successes have been achieved with realistic and even naturalistic plays that would at first have looked highly unsuitable for production there. At the beginning, Olivier described his feeling as being 'that my first job was to test the theatre out for the edification of other directors as much as for anyone else'. His first three plays were chosen to show off the amenities of the theatre with three contrasted styles. *The Chances* was mounted virtually without a set; the production of *The Broken Heart* he described as being 'as scenically ambitious as it could be without impinging on the lines of sight'. But neither of these achieved anything like as much success as *Uncle Vanya*, a play 'ostensibly and traditionally requiring all the realism that a picture stage could afford'. He himself preferred the production as it was at Chichester to what it became when it transferred, over a year later, to the Old Vic as part of the National's repertoire. For my part, I found that without losing any of the impact they had been making separately, the performances came together better, with less diffusion of effect, when they were seen through a proscenium, and that both the sense of place and the claustrophobia which need to be conveyed even in the outdoor scenes were realized better at the Old Vic. But if the characters seemed closer to each other there, possibly they seemed closer to us at Chichester.

In Guthrie's terms Chekhov's plays could be called more poetic than realistic, but Pinero's *Trelawny of the 'Wells'* is scarcely a poetic play, even if it did acquire a certain poetry in the Chichester production. Much of this came from wrestling with the very problems that made it apparently unsuitable. On the face of it, the most intractable difficulty was going to be the scene-changes. In *Uncle Vanya* Olivier and Sean Kenny had done the right thing partly for the wrong reason : 'one's pride would not admit the idea of black-coated figures coming on and fussing around the set in the intervals.'* In *Trelawny of the 'Wells'*, which has four acts, the first is set in the actors' digs and the second in a fashionable drawing-room in Cavendish Square. How was the transition to be achieved without an unacceptably early interval? The digs were suggested by a painted back wall, and when Rose Trelawny left for London at the end of the act, her fellow-actors crowded at the window to wave her good-bye, singing her song, 'Ever of thee I'm fondly dreaming'. Meanwhile, in the semi-darkness behind them, walk-ons costumed as local shopkeepers quietly removed the inelegant furniture. The back wall had been constructed in sections which now slid away or reversed to create the back wall of the sumptuous drawing-room, the shopkeepers were replaced by dignified footmen, who folded the carpet away to reveal a marble floor, and soigné guests made their appearance in black and white costumes. What could have disqualified the play from a Chichester production was transformed into an asset, and in fact the eye-catching deftness of the transformation so captured the imagination of the reviewers that they devoted more space to it than anything else in the production.

On the other hand, the play itself had in several ways to be remodelled for the production. Had it been a masterpiece, the shifts of emphasis and reversals of the author's intention could only have been damaging. As it was, only a few of them were; the majority were flattering. What suffered most was the climax of the final act, when there is a performance within the performance. The hero, Tom Wrench, is modelled on T. W. Robertson, the actor-manager-playwright who had been Pinero's employer when he started his career as an actor, and the play staged in Act

---

* Olivier in his Introduction to Leslie Evershed-Martin's *The Impossible Theatre*, Chichester, Phillimore and Co., 1971.

Four is based on Robertson's *Society*, which probably did more than any other play to establish the new school of realistic drama. It was very much a proscenium play, and at Chichester it was played back to front, with the upstage of the Pantheon Theatre represented by the downstage area, and actors with their backs to the audience – an idea perhaps borrowed from Anouilh's *Colombe*, where another play is staged back to front – but on a thrust stage, more of the actors' faces is visible to the audience, which also had a good close-up view of the energetic and rather thrusting technique of actors giving an old-style proscenium performance. But Pinero builds the act towards the climax in which the Vice-Chancellor interrupts the play from a stage box, and at Chichester the interruption could be represented only by some loud upstage thumping.

Where the production was flattering to the play was in making Pinero seem more self-conscious and satirical in it than he really was. Shaw praised *Trelawny of the 'Wells'* as being the one play in which Pinero was true to the real nature of his talent, which really belonged to the period he was depicting in it. 'The life that it reproduces had been already portrayed in the real sixties by Dickens in his sketch of the Crummles company, and by Anthony Trollope in his chronicles of Barsetshire. I cannot pretend to think that Mr Pinero, in reverting to that period, has really had to turn back the clock as far as his own sympathies and ideals are concerned . . . When he, as a little boy, first heard *Ever of thee I'm fondly dreaming*, he wept; whereas, at the same tender age, I simply noted with scorn the obvious plagiarism from *Cheer, Boys, Cheer.*' But to a modern audience, especially in a theatre of modern design, it would be impossible to present the nostalgia, the sentiment or the theatrical style of the play within the play without irony, and for the audience it is impossible to distinguish the irony of the production from the intentions of the author. It is difficult even to judge whether he intended any irony in Rose's farewell : 'Oh don't believe that, because I shall have married a swell, you and the old Wells – the dear old Wells – will have become nothing to me.' As an actress, perhaps, she could not be expected to miss the opportunity of an imposing exit line. But obviously Pinero was not treating Avonia Bunn's philosophizing with any distancing irony: 'We are only dolls, partly human, with mechanical limbs that *will* fall into stagey postures and heads stuffed with sayings out of rubbishy plays. It isn't *the* world we live in, merely *a* world – such a queer little one.'

Nevertheless, the experiment of presenting *Trelawny of the 'Wells'* on the Chichester stage was obviously well worth making, in the light-hearted way it was made. It was a play concerned with a phase of the theatre's development in which progress was being made from turgid rhodomontade and sets consisting of backcloth and borders to a new realism, so it was interesting to see it in a building which represents a much newer phase of the theatre's development. It happens to be one which rules out the realism that then seemed progressive. Tom Wrench says that when he writes a play there are to be no false doors and windows to detract from the theatrical reality. Both Robertson and Pinero would have disliked the painted back wall and the absence of doors in the Chichester set. But there are plays which become more interesting when they are not performed in accordance with the author's intention.

When Sheffield's Crucible Theatre was being planned, the Artistic Director, Colin George, was involved from the beginning, and it was possible for the architects and the members of the Building Committee to learn from the Chichester example, among others. The Sheffield theatre is open all the year round, playing mainly to a local audience, and the auditorium is smaller, seating only 1,008. Even so, it is on average very much less full than the Chichester theatre and one of the complaints patrons make is about the depressing effect of empty seats. On the other hand it is a great tribute to the design that it was only during the first three or four months that ticket-buyers were eager for the central seats. Now they are equally happy to be on the sides.*

Considerations governing the choice of plays for the repertoire must be different from Chichester's, but not so

---

* See Forbes Bramble, 'Crucible Theatre Sheffield – A Thrust Stage that Works', *Theatre Quarterly*, Vol III No 11, July-September 1973.

different as to be irrelevant. In the first year, according to Colin George, the most satisfactory productions were of 'traditional or classical work': *A Man for All Seasons*, *The Taming of the Shrew*, Dekker's *The Shoemaker's Holiday* and Aeschylus's *The Persians*. Plays with twentieth-century settings like Shelagh Delaney's *A Taste of Honey*, Stanley Eveling's *Mister*, Pinter's *The Birthday Party* and Coward's *Tonight at 8.30* caused problems which were never, in his opinion, satisfactorily solved. *A Taste of Honey* was the least problematic because the action was not confined to a single room. In the Coward play, one of the main difficulties was the distance that the actors had to travel in making entrances and exits. In the second season he was more confident in his use of the space, adapting it more freely to suit the requirements of the play. The shape of the stage was remodelled whenever necessary, and sometimes extended towards the vomitories. Plays with modern interior settings no longer looked lost in the surrounding space, which had been left unlit for *The Birthday Party* and decorated but left unused in *Mister*. In E. A. Whitehead's *Alpha Beta* the scale was reduced by building in a ceiling designed not to obstruct the stage lighting. The steps downstage centre were revealed as if they led down to the garden, and, upstage, the kitchen and entrance hall were shown dimly through a black scrim. Colin George took up Peter Nichols's suggestion that his play *The National Health* would be suitable, using the fully extended stage as the hospital ward. The fantasy scenes, which had been imported into the main acting area at the National Theatre with the aid of a lift, were situated at Sheffield on a raised balcony area at the back.

One advantage Sheffield has over Chichester is that many more productions are done, and lessons learned from one can be applied to the next. There is a bigger Arts Council subsidy than at Chichester and it is not quite so difficult to take risks, though virtually none of the plays done could be called experimental. But in this country we are still so inexperienced in our use of the thrust stage that to mount a new production, even of an old play, is always, in some sense, an experiment. There may be something Chichester can learn from Sheffield's example about the advantages of remodelling the stage and reducing its scale for intimate scenes in small rooms, but probably the main lesson to be learned is that continuity between experiments can lead to greater confidence in staging modern plays. Admittedly it is harder to achieve continuity in a series of nineteen-week summer seasons with guest stars and so many guest directors, but the problem needs more thought than it has been given.

5

Direction and Design

A director's work, like a writer's, often starts from a single image, and the seminal image for two of the best productions that have yet been done at Chichester, *The Royal Hunt of the Sun* and *Armstrong's Last Goodnight*, both had more of a connection with the circle than with the straight line or the rectangle. For *Armstrong's Last Goodnight* John Dexter thought first of a man swinging at the end of a rope and of clansmen sitting in a circle, cross-legged on the ground, like African tribesmen. (In writing the play John Arden had been influenced by Conor Cruise O'Brien's book *To Katanga and Back*.) Both ideas suggest a dynamic of movement and a method of grouping in which no one sector of the audience will be more favoured than any other. Dexter's production of *St Joan* in Olivier's second season was not quite on the same level of achievement but it also grew out of an idea which immediately threw up the possibility of cashing in on the potentialities of the theatre's shape. He started thinking in terms of a trial scene in which the audience could be involved directly as assessors. Sometimes actors would angle their lines outwards, challenging spectators to take sides in the debate. The object would be to make them feel as though they were actually inside the stone hall of the castle at Rouen where the trial takes place, and not to allow them merely to sit back, waiting to be entertained.

To say that the basic impulse behind a thrust stage production should relate more to the curve and the circle than to the straight line and the rectangle would be a simplification but I think a useful one, constituting a precept which has not been observed by most of the directors who have worked there. The first director to be employed more than once by Clements was Peter Coe, who was responsible for *An Italian Straw Hat* (1967), *The Skin of Our Teeth* (1968) *The Caucasian Chalk Circle* (1969) and *Peer Gynt* (1970). He does have a genuine interest in the opportunities that the open stage offers the director. He dislikes productions based on the convention of pretending that the audience is not there and, after working with Sean Kenny on *Oliver* (1960) and stripping all the masking out of the New Theatre to use the bare bones of the building as a background for the set, he directed *Macbeth* in Canada (1962) and was invited to succeed Michael Langham as Artistic Director of Stratford, Ontario, a position he would actually have taken up had Michael Langham not changed his mind about leaving. But most of the directors who have worked at Chichester have little commitment, experience or interest in open-stage techniques. Nor have they even learnt what could have been learnt from studying the best work done at Chichester, by Dexter, Coe and the Canadians. Clements has never been to Stratford, Ontario.

Writing in *The Observer* about the three productions of the Canadian company in 1964 (*Love's Labour's Lost, Le Bourgeois Gentilhomme* and *Timon of Athens*) George Seddon said 'Think of a cyclone. The centre of it – the back of the stage – is calm but away from it the swirling movement increases until at the perimeter it reaches gale force . . . There is no escaping this pattern, not only because a lot of actors merely standing round the edges merely obstruct our view but because, once you have accepted this form of stage you are committed to the necessity for movement . . . The basic test is whether a play demands this movement or is improved by it.' Subsequent experience has shown that it is not quite so simple : no one applying this would have thought that *Trelawny of the 'Wells'* or *Miss Julie* were suitable plays. And while it is very difficult to stage intimate scenes involving only two characters on such an unsheltered and wide-looking stage, it is not impossible, so long as the director is aware of the possibilities and the problems of giving the audience the impression of being present in the same room. But all too often directors try to approximate as close as possible to proscenium conditions, treating the shape of the stage and auditorium as disadvantages to be overcome. One director has usually started his rehearsals by telling his actors where to imagine that the proscenium is situated. Others, without going quite that far, have revealed that far too many of their preconceptions have been based on proscenium experience, and the resultant productions, like individual performances within them, have had a narrow focus aimed mainly at the central seats instead of radiating freely in all the necessary directions.

For the director, as for the actor, there is something of a feeling of naked exposure in working on an open stage. Instead of thinking in terms of a frame and a two-dimensional picture, he has to be aware that each stage picture he creates must be like a piece of sculpture in that it must stand up to being looked at from a variety of angles. With moves and groupings he has more freedom : more alternatives are open to him at each moment. But instead of being seen as part of the picture created by the scenery, everything he gets his actors to do will be seen in relief. For much of the time and for much of the audience the background to the action will be provided not by the set but by the audience on the other side of the acting area. The audience is therefore never going to forget that it is an audience : everyone will be watching and reacting in a somewhat different spirit, with less of a surrender to the illusion that the actors are actually the characters and the action is actually going on in pre-Christian Rome or in the Palace of the King of the Trolls.

This makes it harder for the director to do what must be done in any successful theatrical performance – to unify the individual spectators into a group which is reacting *en masse* to what it sees. It is distracting and destructive if either the actors or the spectators are aware of different reactions coming from different sectors of the audience, even if they are not all seeing the same stage-picture. In *Black Comedy* it was sometimes possible to involve the whole audience in the same piece of comedy business, as when Derek Jacobi moved in a semi-circle to take the electric light flex behind the rocking chair. Sector by sector the audience was given a chance to anticipate and relish the gag that was coming. Then, when the chair started to move, there was a big burst of laughter from the whole audience. But it is not always possible to prepare a joke in this way, and sometimes in *Black Comedy* it was necessary for Peter Shaffer and John Dexter to devise three simultaneous gags, one of which would be visible from the front and one from either side, but when the laughter came in one burst people were unaware that they were not all laughing at the same piece of comedy.

Generally the director is pressured by the stage conditions more in the direction of simplicity than of elaborateness. There is no possibility of giving depth to the scenery which has to be built against the back wall. But for this Olivier would almost certainly have staged *Uncle Vanya* with more than one wall and very much more scenic detail. Though the Andes in *The Royal Hunt of the Sun* had to be suggested by mime and movement, it was by no means a foregone conclusion that the set would consist merely of a large circular Spanish rosette emblazoned with a Christian cross, and it would almost certainly not have been if the play had been staged in a theatre of the kind Shaffer had visualized when he wrote it. Dexter's first impulse was not to have a set at all, but, according to Michael Annals, the designer, Shaffer felt the play needed a visual lift and asked for at least a big sun, the Inca symbol, to hang at the back. At first Annals was unable to think of any way of concealing it for the Spanish scenes. Dexter felt that a higher level was needed for the Inca to speak from but Annals could not see how to incorporate one. 'Then I got the idea of the folded cross which opens into a sun, with a space inside to use as a treasure chamber and gold bits the Spaniards could strip off at the end – destroying the Inca empire. It turned into a machine that worked for the whole play.' It provided a magnificent moment of theatre when it unfolded to convert the Christian cross into a resplendent pagan sun, revealing Robert Stephens as Atahuallpa, the Inca, at the centre of it, and it provided a cameo setting for scenes played on this high level, but it remained a neatly economic device.

The production as a whole was highly spectacular but

nearly all the spectacular effects were created not with scenery but with actors, groupings, choreography, movements, mime, costumes, props and masks. The jungle was evoked simply by shafts of light and bird noises. The Spanish army marched for miles without moving a step forward. The massacre of 3,000 Peruvians was recreated in slow movement by twenty actors, and then a large cloth, daubed with red to suggest carnage, was dragged emblematically across the stage. But thanks to architecture which pushed the action right out into the centre of the encircling spectators, the effects came into a focus that was quite unfamiliar. The theatre provided the possibility of creating a world in which the Peruvians could creep in through the vomitories or down the aisles, giving the audience all it needed of a feeling of physical involvement in the action without trying to make it forget that the whole thing was a theatrical performance.

The unfamiliar feeling of closeness to the spectacle made it easier for anyone to see exactly what he wanted to in the production. At the same time it could appear to be as full-bloodedly spectacular as any proscenium theatre musical or as austerely economical as an orthodox piece of Brechtian theatre. Ronald Bryden wrote in *The Observer* 'I enjoyed the spectacle enormously and would urge its sheer theatrical pleasure on all who, like myself, feel starved in our bare post-Pinter theatre of word and emblem of the living amplitude of a good spectacle'. Meanwhile Martin Esslin was able to point to the Brechtian alienation effects: the narrator who introduces his own *alter ego* as a boy, the use of mime inspired by Chinese and Indian theatre, the abandonment of realistic scenery, the use of masks, the stress on ritual, and the meticulous dating of key scenes, reminding the audience it was watching a representation of historical events valid only as a manifestation of social conditions prevailing in the past.

What was particularly interesting about the enthusiasm the production inspired was that it was unchecked by the very considerable reservations many of the more influential critics had about the play. For *The Times* it was 'hollow at the centre', while Bryden attacked the dialogue for borrowing unconsciously from Swinburne and damned the 'loftier flights of rhetoric' as 'contemporary equivalents of Chaste-lard'. The theatre would be expected to throw the play-wright's actual words into clearer relief than they could have in a proscenium theatre, to present an audience with the nearest three-dimensional equivalent to a radio play. But the reaction to Dexter's production of Shaffer's play was in fact only one of a great many pieces of evidence that have accumulated to indicate that the visual element at Chichester does not become subordinate to the verbal element. The director has to balance the two elements in a new way but the most effective Chichester productions have all been done by directors with a strong visual flair and a talent for collaborating very closely with their designers.

For the words of a play to have their full effect the ears and eyes of the audience need to be simultaneously focused at each moment not only on the right point but in the right way. In a production of *St Joan* at Minneapolis, Peter Dews saw a perambulating Inquisitor who took an ambitiously long move on his long monologue, riveting the attention of anyone who knew the play well not on the words but on how much he would need to hurry if he was to be back in position by the end of the speech. Of course there are weak plays and wordy passages in strong plays where the director may deliberately use movement to distract the audience from what is being said, but too much movement is as damaging as too little, and a good actor stationary in a good position can hold the audience's attention for as long as twenty minutes, as Margaret Leighton did in her death scene in *Antony and Cleopatra*. The position Peter Dews gave her was just downstage of the permanent structure, and having discovered how dominating this position could be he used it again the following year in *Vivat! Vivat Regina!* when Elizabeth had a fifteen-minute scene seated at a council table with Burleigh and Leicester downstage of her on the diagonals pointing to the vomitories. She was given one reflective move around the table in the middle of the scene but probably it would have held even without this.

The Chichester stage is wider than that of Toronto,

Minneapolis or Sheffield, so it is impossible to solve problems of reducing space simply by bringing the back wall forwards, and the most successful productions at Chichester have been the ones which called for a large space. It was fortuitous that Peter Dews found himself with such a large stage for *Vivat! Vivat Regina!* Sean Kenny had designed *Peer Gynt*, the first production of the 1970 season, and without consulting any of the other designers or directors, had extended the stage to bring the edge flush with the lowest step in order to incorporate a revolve (which was used only about three times). This was a big handicap for *Arms and the Man* and made it impossible to use the vomitories in *The Alchemist*, in which the perimeter of the acting area was used as a street, but by adding steps to the edge of the extended stage, Peter Dews was able to use the vomitories in *Vivat! Vivat Regina!* and the extra space on stage was a boon. When the production transferred to the Piccadilly, Eileen Atkins found during the early rehearsals on stage that it was much harder to feel royal when courtiers were crowding so close to her that they could almost read documents over her shoulder. Distance is nearly always necessary to give an impression of deference to royalty – and not only in the theatre – so some of the groupings were rearranged. But the production was never quite as effective as it had been at Chichester, where the diagonals from upstage entrances to vomitory exits allowed processional crosses a sweep that is unattainable in a proscenium theatre, and the space permitted great flexibility in the elaborate groupings of figures in bulky Elizabethan costume. As in Bolt's earlier historical play *A Man for All Seasons*, change of location does not call for a change of set. Peter Dews used the same council table for both Elizabeth's and Mary's courts, using it at different angles and sometimes straight, while the contrast between the Scottish and English costumes sufficed to change the locale for the audience.

In a play set in a modern furnished interior it is harder for the director and designer to make strong visual statements, and harder to focus the audience's attention to the required points at the required moments. When intimate relationships have, as so often, to be developed in a series of conversational scenes, it is essential to reduce the appearance of spaciousness. This had to be done in Pinero's *The Magistrate*, when the designer, Carl Toms, put a rail round the edge of the stage. He had the same basic problem in *Reunion in Vienna* and solved it by constructing the room for the first set on the diagonal. The hotel room did not need to look so small, so the next set was designed parallel with the back wall. Peter Rice had an even greater problem in designing *Arms and the Man*, needing to achieve intimate dimensions on a stage that was even bigger than usual.

Another problem in using furniture on the Chichester stage is that the rake of the auditorium is so slight. The angle of the rake, varying between 13° and 19° (compared with a variation between 21° and 28° at Sheffield) not only fails to concentrate the audience's attention down on the action as much as it should; it necessitates very careful planning of furniture and props. A high-backed armchair would have to be positioned so far upstage that an actor in it could make little contact with the audience, and stools, pouffes, low-sided chaises-longues and low-backed armchairs and sofas have to be glaringly recurrent in Chichester productions when so many drawing-room plays are done.

Another problem in creating a realistic room on the Chichester stage is that it becomes very difficult to use the vomitories. It is one of the conventions of the proscenium theatre that the arch represents an invisible wall through which the audience is watching the action. Sometimes there are even fire-irons to indicate the position of the fireplace and when footlights were still in use a red jelly would be used to throw up a glow on the hands that would be warmed in front of the imaginary fire. It is a very different matter to expect the Chichester audience to imagine that somewhere downstage of the hexagonal acting area is the wall of a rectangular room with a door in it represented by one of the vomitories. Act Four of *The Seagull* is extremely difficult for the Chichester stage because there has to be a door or French window leading to the garden, a door to the dining-room and another door to the room where Konstantin will shoot himself. When Nina comes in from the garden, Konstantin has to reassure her by barricading the door to the room where Trigorin and the others are eating dinner. Jonathan Miller and his designer Patrick Robertson situated the garden upstage right and the dining-room upstage left, making Konstantin go out through the stage right vomitory to shoot himself. A very loud shot then came from underneath the seats of the people sitting above it and the relationship between the two rooms was confused by the long walk the doctor had to take down the vomitory passage, opening and closing an invisible door before returning to reassure Mme Arkadina that the bang had been caused by a bottle exploding in his medicine case. An unsatisfactory solution to an almost insoluble problem.

It ought to have been much easier to stage Act One, which centres on the open air theatre Konstantin has had built by the lake, but in fact there was very little attempt to evoke either the sense of space or the sense of place that the play demands. Both upstage entrances were masked by gauze screens which were built so close to the wall that the movement of actors entering or exiting was cramped quite unnecessarily. They had to edge their way on and off in a way that contradicted the impression of being out in the open air. Nor did the birdsong sound-effects and the photographic projections compensate. Green leaf-shapes appeared first on the stage floor and then on the actors who moved into the area – a bizarre effect which was neither realistic nor surrealistic. The actress playing Nina, Maureen O'Brien, was put in a particularly difficult position when she had to ask 'What tree is that?' If there had been no suggestion at all of foliage on stage she could have made a definite gesture towards an imaginary tree, seeing it in her mind's eye and persuading the audience to do the same. But it would have been ludicrous if she had pointed to any of the projected foliage, and it was not her fault that the gesture she made was half-hearted and ineffectual.

It was also disappointing that we were given no feeling of being near a lake or that the audience watching Konstantin's play could see open spaces beyond. For Konstantin, to see a curtain rise on a room with three walls is to be reminded of the theatre his mother works in; his audience will be given an unimpeded view of the lake and the horizon

At Chichester this could hardly be suggested as it was in Stanislavsky's original production by detailed painting on a backcloth, and unless the curtain had been transparent, Konstantin's theatre could not have been brought any further downstage without masking. So it would have been difficult to give a sense of space upstage of it, but at least a generalized impression of open space could have been created by the acting – by the way the characters breathe and wander about and look around and relax.

The hexagonal shape has many advantages and many disadvantages. One is that it is difficult for the design to fight the dominant geometry and give each production a different appearance. Originally the galleried structure was intended to provide the basis of a permanent set which would be subjected only to relatively minor variations, but later it was made possible to remove the whole middle section of it, preparing the way for sets to become much more elaborate. A considerable proportion of the audience comes to at least two or three productions each season, and one of Clements's anxieties about keeping the stage more or less bare of decor was that this would induce visual monotony. Most of the plays in his repertoire could not possibly be made spectacular in the way that *The Royal Hunt of the Sun* was. But to use so much scenery so often is to oppose not only Evershed-Martin's intentions but the demands of the theatre he created.

6

The Olivier Régime (1) :

The First Two Seasons 1962-63

Critics have mostly blamed the theatre for the short-comings of the company, and every form of open stage for the shortcomings of this one. The enclosed stage suits the enclosed mind, apparently.

STEPHEN JOSEPH

If the Duke of Buckingham's adaptation of John Fletcher's *The Chances* had been presented in the West End, very few people indeed would have wanted to buy tickets unless there were some very starry names to attract them. Olivier had an excellent cast for his opening Chichester production including Athene Seyler, John Neville, Keith Michell, Rosemary Harris, Joan Plowright and Kathleen Harrison, but if there were nearly 5,000 people competing for the relatively few first night tickets that were not allocated to the press, it was not because of the play, not because Olivier was directing it, not because of the names on the cast list, and not even because a new open-stage theatre was opening, but because Olivier was opening it.

He had announced a nine-week season starting on 5 July 1962. The curtain was due to rise at seven o'clock. It was a fine summer evening and instead of collecting inside the foyer, most of the well-dressed audience stayed outside on the wide drive and on the lawn, looking at the imposing exterior of the first major modern theatre to be built in England since the war, with the soffit of the tiered audi-

torium projecting like the prow of a shallow battleship over
the impressive glass-fronted façade of the main entrance. At
four minutes to seven Olivier scored his first *coup de théatre*.
Above all the animated and expectant conversation, a fan-
fare and a well-trained, beautifully pitched male voice made
themselves heard over loudspeakers that no one had noticed.
Would the ladies and gentlemen be kind enough to proceed
to their seats? The performance would commence in four
minutes. The voice was extremely familiar. Olivier himself?
Surely not. But it was! But at a moment like this, how could
he be leaning over the shoulders of an assistant stage manager to speak into a microphone in the prompt corner? But
then perhaps the announcement was pre-recorded. More
fanfares, more Olivier announcements at intervals of a
minute. Charmed and almost flattered, the ladies and
gentlemen obediently proceeded to their seats.

Hazlitt had judged *The Chances* to be 'superior in style
and execution to anything in Ben Jonson', but most of the
Chichester audience found the intricate and episodic plot
extremely difficult to follow. The summary in the programme was laconically unhelpful. 'Two Spanish blades,
Don John and Don Frederick, on a romantic journey to
Italy, get into some trouble.' Nor was Olivier's production
calculated to make it easy for us to keep pace with the very
rapid succession of situational entanglements, swordfights,
seductions, deceptions, betrayals and quidproquos. He did
not seem even to be trying to stop our eyes from wandering
to the complex web of exposed girders in the roof, the bat-
teries of spotlights attached to them, and the more than
usually visible faces in the seats around us. It was an im-
pressionistic production, full of extravagant flashes of invention that briefly recaptured the wandering minds and
then let them wander off again. The stage, the projecting
platform, the catwalk, the on-stage staircases, and the
auditorium aisles were like a panoramic screen full of full-
length Van Dyck portraits that had fallen into the hands of
a group of cartoon film animators who had got drunk at the
end of a summer vacation course at an English university.
Malcolm Pride's elaborate costumes flashed out peacock
colours from their satins, velvets and braids. The men wore

plumed hats, spurred and be-ribboned boots. The women sported painted eyelashes, fanciful, feathery head-dresses, veils and bejewelled muffs. The production tumbled and exploded out of the vomitories and into every corner of usable space as if Olivier was making virtuoso fun of all the conventions of open stage theatre before the English audience had even had time to find out what they were. There was racing up and down suspended staircases and a chase along the catwalk and right round the theatre. The actors rode papier-maché hobby-horses like the ones used in Anouilh's *Becket* at the Aldwych and fought a duel in flamenco rhythm. The two blades chewed grapes through one of their main exposition scenes, and I was one of six or eight people who involuntarily added to the distractions when the seats underneath us rocked forwards, capsizing us onto the shoulders of the people in the row in front. Disapproving heads turned in the semi-darkness, and when we came back after the interval the loose seats were moored back in position with pieces of thick string.

Except for a Sunday night performance by the Phoenix Society in 1922, *The Chances* had not been staged for three hundred years. According to Olivier's programme note the original play was written either by Fletcher alone or by Beaumont and Fletcher jointly, but the consensus of scholars is that it was written by Fletcher with some contributions from another hand, but not that of Beaumont. It is impossible to establish exactly when it was written but it must have been about 1620. The first production seems to have been in 1638, thirteen years after Fletcher's death. The Duke of Buckingham, who lived from 1628 to 1687, is best known (as a dramatist) for his burlesque *The Rehearsal* (1671) and his adaptation of *The Chances*, brought out in 1682, took enormous liberties. According to the Reverend Dyce, 'for the last two acts of the original his grace substituted two from his own pen, which though written in very indifferent prose, and grossly indelicate, are by no means destitute of humour, and heighten perhaps the interest of the catastrophe'. Inevitably the styles of Jacobean comedy and Restoration comedy are mixed, and it is hard to be certain whether Olivier really wanted the mixture or what he thought he was going to do with it. The Jacobean style might have been expected to suit the Chichester theatre better, but it was the Restoration style that predominated both in the costuming and in the behaviour of the characters.

The plot is based on a novel by Cervantes. At the beginning, Don John (Keith Michell) is lumbered with a baby which is not his, while Don Frederick is lumbered with its mother, who is on the run. The ensuing confusions involve a vengeful brother, a misunderstood suitor and two girls both called Constantia, one of whom has a troublesome mother. There were some good lines. A girl declares 'A sin without pleasure I cannot endure'. A man's reaction on first catching sight of an attractive girl is 'Pray heaven she's a whore'. And one of the blades greets the landlady by enquiring 'Worshipful lady, how does thy velvet scabbard?' The comedy between the two of them and the landlady was consistently amusing but there was not much in the evening that worked cumulatively on the audience. Altogether it was like a series of verbal and visual jokes with little to connect them except the exuberance and the spanking pace that Olivier had imposed on the production. John Neville did not seem completely at ease, but Keith Michell played with enormous panache and relish, and enough underlying humour to make it acceptable. Rosemary Harris, who is always convincing, produced a pleasing lisp, and Joan Plowright's vivacity went a long way towards making her flat Lincolnshire vowel sounds acceptable. At least they added to the comedy. After the skipping curtain calls and the National Anthem, sung in unison by the cast, there was a firework display outside, and everyone who was thinking about the Artistic Directorship of the National Theatre knew that Olivier had substantially increased his chances of being appointed to it.

The Bishop of Chichester had been present, and in the following morning's papers, one of the reviewers described the play as having 'comedy bawdy enough to disturb a bishop's composure'. The production had reminded Alan Brien of 'that ghastly overwound clockwork ticking which shakes the chorus in a Slade and Reynolds musical'. For

Robert Muller it had 'wave upon wave of seventeenth-century Errol Flynnery', and he summed it up as 'a piece of inconsequential bawdy, briefly and undeservedly rescued from the merciful clutches of obscurity . . . We are served with lute-song and lechery, generally enjoyable and played all out on a single note of flamboyant vulgarity.' The reaction was typical: even the people who disapproved vehemently, as many did, had found a good deal in the evening that was enjoyable.

John Ford's *The Broken Heart* is a better known play. T. S. Eliot judged it to be inferior in construction to *'Tis Pity She's a Whore* but superior in quality, and he picked out as 'perhaps the purest poetry to be found in the whole of Ford's writings' the lines:

> *Remember,*
> *When we last gathered roses in the garden,*
> *I found my wits; but truly you lost yours.*

But Eliot's essay and the play itself are unknown to the majority of theatregoers and it seemed perverse to open a new theatre with two such out of the way pieces. If Olivier didn't want to do yet another Shakespeare play, there were plenty of plays by Marlowe, Jonson and Webster. Or if it had to be a lesser-known playwright, why not Tourneur, Middleton, Marston or Chapman? If it had to be Fletcher, there was more fun to be had out of *The Wild Goose Chase*; and *'Tis Pity She's a Whore* had only just been done at the Mermaid, providing quite enough Ford for most appetites. But at least the new production of *The Broken Heart* would bring the bonus of an appearance by Olivier himself.

The set was very much more elaborate than it had been for *The Chances*: Kenneth Tynan and Irving Wardle both compared it with a three-tiered wedding cake. Roger Furse, who had designed all Olivier's Shakespeare films and *The Prince and the Showgirl* (which co-starred him with Marilyn Monroe) now succeeded in making the Chichester arena look like a film set. He devised a complex structure, slender columns supporting a projecting platform with a pillared balustrade on the downstage edges of it, and, upstage, a

pedimented colonnade, suggesting a Greek hillside temple
but containing a second platform level with the tops of the
columns. This provided three main acting levels, which were
connected by staircases, which were to be used as much for
elaborate tableau groupings as for movement from one level
to another. There were doors that could enwrap the ground-
level columns like the walls of a room and the main acting
area had an oblong depression in it, like a shallow swimming pool. Two paintings of classical statues stood on either
side of the back wall.

The voice which had again been heard over the loudspeakers ceremonially summoning the spectators to their
seats, spoke at the opening of the play, when Olivier
appeared as the prologue at the top of the wedding-cake to
promise us a solemn evening :

> *The title lends no expectation here*
> *Of apish laughter, or of some lame jeer*
> *At place or persons; no pretended clause*
> *Of jests fit for a brothel, courts applause*
> *From vulgar admiration: such low songs,*
> *Turned to unchaste ears, suit not modest tongues.*

He spoke the prologue simply and extremely well, but any
implicit promise of straightforwardness in the production
was disregarded. The frenetic cavortings of *The Chances*
ought to have purged his system of any compulsion to over-
exploit the stage, distracting from the spoken word with
superfluous movement, but now the audience, which could
not have followed the opening exposition without concentrating quite hard, also had to watch two actors marching
up and down the stage as restlessly as if they were liable to
be fined for standing still.

The play is set in Sparta and requires a prevailing mood
of Senecan stoicism. The climax comes during a feast, when
Calantha, the King's daughter, successively hears of three
deaths – that of her lover's twin sister, her father, and her
lover. She dances on, giving no sign of emotion, only to die
later of the broken heart that provides the title. But the
acting and the costumes were equally lacking in the restraint, simplicity and austerity that are needed. Disdaining

both Greek classicism and Spartan severity, Roger Furse's baroque creations in silk jersey gave the characters a Pompeian look, and the performances – partly because the cast had not correctly gauged the amount of projection that the theatre needed – seemed ornate and declamatory. Tynan wrote his review in the form of an open letter to Olivier: 'A lot of vocal brandishing took place in a vacuum. "Vehemence without real emotion," said G. H. Lewes, "is rant; vehemence with real emotion, but without art, is turbulence." One noted both kinds of emotion in your *Broken Heart*.'

Nor could Tynan have returned a more unfavourable verdict on his performance. 'Surely Bassanes is a stupid, self-deluding dotard at whose ridiculous jealousy we are supposed to laugh until, in the course of time, it becomes pathetic. You played him from the first as a sombre old victim bound for the slaughter, too noble and too tragic ever to be funny. Ford's comedy was thus robbed of its essential comedy.'* But possibly Olivier had taken his cue from Eliot's essay, which argues that 'Ford misses an opportunity, and lapses in taste, by making the unloved husband, Bassanes, the vulgar jealous elderly husband of comedy: Penthea is a character which deserved, and indeed required, a more dignified and interesting foil.'† Olivier's attempt to make Bassanes more interesting may not have succeeded – the performance had too much of the surface of his Titus Andronicus without the substance – but though unmemorable in itself it probably helped Rosemary Harris to the heights she reached as Penthea, a noble Spartan whose twin-brother loves her excessively and perhaps incestuously, preventing her from marrying the man she loves and forcing her to marry the aging Bassanes, who literally drives her mad. Rosemary Harris, who was alone in not apparently trying to move the audience, was alone in succeeding.

If the third production had not been more successful than the first two, it is doubtful whether the theatre would still

* Kenneth Tynan's review in *The Observer* reprinted in *Tynan Right and Left*, Longman, 1967.
† 'John Ford' in T. S. Eliot's *Selected Essays*, Faber, 1932.

be a theatre today, but *Uncle Vanya* was a triumph. Theoretically it might have been the least likely of the three plays to succeed on the open stage, but unlike the other two it was easy to follow, and the cast-list was extremely attractive. Having Olivier and Michael Redgrave in the same production would alone have been enough to make it a major theatrical event, but there were also Sybil Thorndike in a small part (the Nurse), Lewis Casson in an even smaller one (Telyeghin), Fay Compton as Vanya's mother and Joan Plowright as Sonya. Joan Greenwood turned out to have been badly miscast as Yeliena, but her presence was glamorous, and her husband, Andre Morell, turned in an effective, if depthless, performance as Yeliena's unsympathetic husband, the Professor.

Retrospectively it seems impossible that it could have been anything but a success; after the first night it seemed far from impossible. In the *Daily Express* Clive Barnes complained that 'The new theatre, used as a simple arena, backed by a utilitarian set by Sean Kenny, did little for the play, so the production emerged as a series of pictures torn out of their frame.' In the *Daily Mail* Robert Muller pronounced it 'the wrong play for the wrong stage . . . The audience saw the actors lost and separated against a sloping blur of pink faces . . . each time an actor turned in the middle of a speech his voice was blotted out.' In the *Evening News* Felix Barker said 'The intimacy we expect from a tender fragment by Chekhov is exchanged for a sort of global perspective'. In *What's On in London* Kenneth Hurren wrote 'This moody masterpiece exposes the disadvantages of the arena stage quite disastrously', and in *The Queen* Clancy Sigal said 'the open stage is like a bomb thrown in the midst of Chekhov's delicate tapestry'. But J. C. Trewin hailed it as 'one of the indisputable triumphs of our period' and *The Times* critic thought 'It is doubtful whether the Moscow Art Theatre itself could improve on this production except in the atmosphere and sense of enclosure to be had from a box stage'. Though Harold Hobson in the *Sunday Times* had reservations about the compromise of the permanent set – 'the garden looked like a drawing-room and the drawing-room like a garden; and both were indistinguishable from the dining-room' – his verdict on the production as a whole was warmly enthusiastic. 'There are things accomplished, emotions probed, resources of richness, courage and integrity throbbingly presented which I have never seen more than hinted at in any other production of this Chekhov play.'

In spite of the lighting, which sometimes made it difficult to see the actors' eyes, the individual performances came over powerfully. Sybil Thorndike and Lewis Casson usefully prepared the way for what was to come, doing far more than the ambiguous, indoor-outdoor furniture could to suggest years of hard wear in the service of an inconsiderate master. As Vanya, the younger and more self-pitying victim of the same unconcern, Michael Redgrave gave one of his finest performances. He may have been less successful than Scofield was eight years later at the Royal Court in transforming an attractive face into one that could plausibly belong to a man consistently unsuccessful with women, but he succeeded almost completely with his voice and his body. His movement became unco-ordinated; turned-in toes made his loping walk unsteady. His tight, nervous voice rose in pitch when he flew into hysterical catalogues of grievances against life in general and the Professor in particular. At the climaxes he became almost inarticulate, gasping and quivering with rage and flailing self-righteously with gawky arms. But he did not alienate too much sympathy to be very touching in his crestfallen silence at the moment of arriving with flowers for Yeliena and finding her in Astrov's arms. And he succeeded in the notoriously difficult task of making it credible both that Vanya would shoot at the Professor and that he would miss. By building up the right neurotic momentum to the climax of releasing all the long-inhibited aggressions, Michael Redgrave made us accept both the uncontrollable anger and the erratic aim.

Olivier was almost equally successful in suggesting the eroding effects of his character's earlier life, and the essence of the contrast between the two men emerged far more clearly than it usually does through the handling of their contrasted attitudes to Yeliena. The cumulative effect of Vanya's disappointments has not been to make him any less of a

romantic. Astrov is a less disappointed man but more disillusioned. The idealist in him has been defeated, but with
women he is a realist. Vanya hopes passionately for a long-
term relationship with Yeliena; Astrov hopes for nothing
beyond a few pleasant moments of physical contact. As
Chekhov put it in a letter to Olga Knipper, 'he talks to her
in that scene in the same tone as of the heat in Africa, and
kisses her quite casually, to pass the time'.

Joan Plowright's Sonya was all the more poignant because
she did so little to subdue her natural vitality and optimism,
which were therefore seen fighting against impossible odds.
This was a girl with no faith in her own face but spirited
enough to be rallied very easily when the beautiful Yeliena –
well-meaningly but stupidly – encourages her to believe that
what she feels towards Astrov may not be unrequited. And
her likableness made her seem all the more pathetic when
she found out the hard way that it really was every bit as
hopeless as she had feared. She played the final scene un-
forgettably, quite without self-pity or sentimentality, the
desperate optimism making her voice tough and abrasive as
she bullied herself to believe what she was saying – that it
was important to go on living and working, that Vanya and
she would finally be rewarded for all they had done.

It is not hard to understand why it had seemed a good
idea to cast Joan Greenwood as Yeliena. It is easy to miss
the comedy underneath the girl's boredom and self-indulg-
ence and an actress whose forte is comedy might have been
expected to unearth it. But mannerism is always limiting
and vocally she had become far too mannered. As in *The
Broken Heart* she seemed incapable of directness and failed
to suggest what was underneath the surface of behaviour.
In fact she herself looked bored and self-indulgent.

Backstage the actors had to work under very difficult conditions. There were thirty-seven in the company during the
first season and forty-one during the second, but the theatre
contained only ten stone-walled dressing-rooms, badly venti-
lated, poorly lit and without adequate mirrors. There was
no green room and the backstage corridors were narrow.
Actors had the hardest time of all when they had to make

quick changes. In some dressing-rooms five of them were crowded together. But adverse conditions – so long as they do not continue for too long – can sometimes increase the feeling of team-spirit, especially when everyone involved believes in the importance of what is happening. For over a hundred years there had been discussions about the importance of having a National Theatre and campaigning to initiate the processes that would bring one into existence. Now the foundations were actually being laid – not of the building but of the company of actors and the artistic policy. At the same time the Chichester theatre was becoming a success in its own right. The advance booking for the first season had been just over £30,000; before the second season opened on 24 June 1963, over £50,000 worth of tickets had been sold.

John Dexter's production of *St Joan*, which later became the first production to follow the inaugural *Hamlet* when the National Theatre opened at the Old Vic in the autumn, made the best use that had so far been made of the Chichester stage. There was no appearance of restlessness but there was a good surging speed and sweep to the progression of the action. Without the interruptions of scene-changes it moved forcefully and logically from Joan's first appearance at de Baudricourt's castle to the victory at Orléans. The effect of bringing the play out of the picture-frame stage was to open it up, letting the weight fall squarely on the words and the acting, which was very good, without touching the heights that Redgrave, Olivier and Plowright herself had reached in *Uncle Vanya*. But there are a lot of words in the play, and one's valuation of the final result had to depend on one's valuation of Shaw's writing.

Desmond MacCarthy's review of the original production at the New on 26 March 1924 argued that the reason Shaw lacked a vivid historical imagination was that he had no real love for the past. 'I do not believe he cares a dump for things that are dead, gone and changed. The first thing he invariably does when his setting is in the past is to rub off his period the patina of time (*vide Caesar and Cleopatra*);

he will scrub and scrub till contemporary life begins to gleam through surface strangenesses and oddities. He is confident that he has reached historic truth when he has succeeded in scratching historic characters till he finds beneath a modern man in fancy dress.'* The modernism that Shaw imposed on this medieval material in the twenties was itself dated by the sixties, and this mattered much more on an open stage. As Dexter's designer, Michael Annals said of the play, 'it should be presented as if it had just been written . . ., To satisfy contemporary taste, decor must break down illusion. You have to give audiences something they can recognize as real, even to the extent of letting them into the secret of the actual mechanics.'

If the dynamic of the play had been genuinely theatrical, this could have worked as an advantage. Michael Annals's set dispensed with all the historical clutter that usually diverts the audience's attention and within his spare, stone-surfaced set, Dexter's production was so clearly articulated that it inevitably highlighted all the shortcomings of Shaw's technique of characterization, which was to clothe abstract arguments with human traits and habits of speech, making frequent use of insubordination and nicknames.

Joan Plowright and John Dexter had worked together on Arnold Wesker's *Roots* : and in more than one sense her St Joan was rooted in her Beatie Bryant. But her capacity for blazing indignation and for showing a nascent individuality bursting through the mud of social habit and prejudice were more moving in *Roots* than they could be in *St Joan*, partly because the saint's enemies are too unreal to give her a good fight. Dexter did not underestimate the importance of making the church look like a fortress of common-sense, but while Shaw does full justice to the beliefs of the men who act as its spokesmen, he is totally uninterested in their guts. Cauchon's benignity is generalized and the Inquisitor's deadliness is entirely rhetorical. If the actors sometimes sounded as though they were over-projecting, the basic fault was Shaw's. The most nearly real of Joan's relationships is with the Dauphin, and after she has helped him to his coronation at Rheims cathedral she is basically alone.

* Desmond MacCarthy, *Shaw*, MacGibbon and Kee, 1951.

Dexter's production succeeded best of all in showing the isolation she suffers. As Peter Dews was to find later with *Vivat! Vivat Regina!* it is not difficult in this theatre to use space and staircases to contrive groupings that highlight the physical and spiritual isolation of a central character.

The acoustic problem was minimized. Strategically placed sounding boards helped to carry the sound forwards, as the two massive staircases helped to push the action forwards. Scenically the only difficulty Dexter failed to resolve was provided by the scene on the banks of the Loire. The flag has to indicate that the wind has changed direction, and in order to achieve this mechanical trick, Dexter set the scene too far upstage for contact with the audience to be easy. John Clements, who had played Dunois with the Old Vic at the New in 1947, was to complain later that the scene had been 'stuck up on a mantelpiece'.

Several critics praised the trial scene, which had Joan encircled by her captors, though it was a pity that the faces of the judges were not visible. *The Times* critic found that 'the static scenes in Warwick's tent and the extended preliminaries to the trial have been opened out in a way that animates the argument'. Both Philip Hope-Wallace and W. A. Darlington thought that the closely argued scene between Cauchon and Warwick did not hold as firmly as usual. But J. C. Trewin praised the way Dexter had joined the Epilogue to the end of the trial scene by making twenty-five years pass as Brother Martin moved down the steps with no light except on the cross he was carrying. Joan's last walk down the staircase, together with the soldier on leave from hell, was also picked out for praise. On the thrust stage, as in the old proscenium theatre, movements down a staircase can be extremely effective.

Olivier's decision to revive *Uncle Vanya* for the second Chichester season provoked a major quarrel with Evershed-Martin, who thought it was quite wrong to repeat something, however successful, from the previous year. The theatre could be open only for a limited summer season and three new productions each year would have been few enough. But Olivier was now under enormous pressure, planning for the opening of the National Theatre in October at the Old Vic, where he wanted to put *Uncle Vanya* into the repertoire in November. Astrov was the only part he played himself during the second season at Chichester. Evershed-Martin was not unaware of the size of Olivier's problems, but he had himself committed so much time and energy to the Chichester project that, having succeeded, he did not want the new theatre to be treated as secondary to any other theatre, however important. But Olivier had been given complete artistic control, and this naturally gave him the right to programme his own seasons without consulting the Board.

The production of *Uncle Vanya* was much better than it had been the previous year, because Rosemary Harris took over the part of Yeliena from Joan Greenwood and penetrated far more deeply into the reality of what has made such a beautiful girl into such a joyless woman. The bored wife became less frivolous and quirky, more human, more a victim of a bad marital mistake in a society in which it could not easily be corrected. Possibly Olivier would have cast Rosemary Harris in the part the previous year but for the fact that she had large parts in both the other plays. The rehearsal schedule had been an extremely taxing one. Apart from having to learn lines, the actors had worked from eight in the morning till midday, from two till six and again from eight till midnight. So no one was required to play leading parts in more than two out of the three productions. But now, with Rosemary Harris's performance to play against, both Olivier's and Redgrave's became even richer than they had been before.

The part of the Professor was taken over from Andre Morell by Max Adrian, which made the old man less of a heavyweight bully and more of a spoilt son grown old. Otherwise there were no cast changes, except in the very small part of Yefim, which was taken over from Peter Woodthorpe by Robert Lang. Later on, when the production moved into the National's repertoire, Wynne Clark, Keith Marsh and Enid Lorimer were to take over from Sybil Thorndike, Lewis Casson and Fay Compton, but these three veterans returned to Chichester for the second season, so the casting of the production then was stronger than it had ever been before or was ever to be again.

John Arden's *The Workhouse Donkey*, the first new play to be launched at Chichester, was written for the Royal Court, though it is hard to see how such a big, bustling, sprawling play could have been accommodated on such a small stage. Arden's plays are Brechtian in some ways and Jonsonian in others, and none of them is easy to fit into a proscenium frame. For a year (1959-60) he held a playwriting fellowship at Bristol University where there is a small experimental theatre with an open stage. He wrote *The Happy Haven* for it, and found the play worked much better than when it was done later at the Royal Court. 'I suspect that one of the reasons . . . is simply that the audience was frozen off by the proscenium arch, and the parts of the play that were meant to come out at the audience completely failed to do so.'* But he does not like theatre-in-the-round, so Chichester ought to have been the ideal theatre for him. 'I do like a background behind the actors because I like them to be related to an architectural point. You can group actors in relation to a stage-with-corners quite easily, but when the stage is round, there is bound to be an amorphous quality about the visual side of the production.'

The title of *The Workhouse Donkey* probably refers partly to Apuleius's *Golden Ass* and partly to the medieval Feast of Fools. Though it was only in the back of Arden's mind – he remembered it consciously later – he knew of one occasion when a naked girl was brought into York Minster on a donkey's back. He believed that 'one of the prime functions of theatre has, since the earliest time, Aristophanes and beyond, been to inflame people's lusts in something like the same sort of way as the tragedies produced a purgation of the spirit'.† There is a striptease scene in *The Workhouse Donkey*. 'The difficulty was to get the girls who were play-ing the parts of dancers to look first of all attractive and provoking to the audience, then attractive and provoking

* Interview in *Encore*, July-August 1961.
† Interview in *Encore*, September-October 1965.

to the other characters on the stage, and then to look as if they were really girls who were just doing this for a living, and a rather dreary kind of living when it's all added up.' This gives a valuable pointer to the kind of style necessary to make the play work. The actors must be able alternately – in an almost measured progression – to relate inwards to each other and outwards to the audience, to swing between naturalistic identification with the character and critical detachment, commenting à la Brecht on the social situation. Here, too, the shape of the Chichester stage ought to be ideal, encouraging the actors to angle some lines outwards and some inwards.

But the audience was not ideal, even in 1963, when it was a good deal less staid than it was to become. Arden wanted a Dionysiac abandonment of all restraint. 'I would have liked the striptease scene to go on a good deal longer and have become a good deal more indecent . . . I felt on the first night that this is the sort of scene that ought to be extended into the audience. I don't quite know to what extent but I was reminded of a pantomime in Dublin where an individual dressed as a gorilla bounded on to the stage and did a lot of knockabout with two comedians . . . and raced about the audience, plonked himself down into a fat woman's lap and took her hat off, deposited her hat on a bald man, then flung its arms round another bald man and nuzzled him in the face . . . and just as you were beginning to wonder how far it was going to go, the gorilla suddenly bounded back on to the stage, unzipped the costume, and it was an attractive chorus girl in a little dress.' Previously her antics had been embarrassing, but then, with the tension released, everybody cheered and clapped. But it is questionable how much tension of this kind could be set up at Chichester, though, as Arden argues, 'The legitimate theatre began like this . . . Greek comedy was more like pantomime than anything else in the modern theatre. And yet it was also a serious literary form in which important social and religious questions could be brought forward.' He goes on to quote Tyrone Guthrie's remark 'The theatre is a temple and a brothel'. But even in this Guthrie-inspired theatre, the audience would not want the brothel elements to be given what Arden would consider to be their fair share.

The main character, Charlie Butterthwaite, a wily old Labour councillor, is an Aristophanic creation, vulgar, vivacious, bubbling over with a vitality that is always edging onto the obscene. His opponent, Colonel Feng, the local chief of police and an incarnation of Puritan restraint, is an almost tragic figure. Arden has compared him with Malvolio 'a strong unbending character who really belongs to tragedy'. When situated in a comic world he must end up being humiliated.

The play represents one of the most whole-hearted attempts in contemporary dramatic literature to depict an English local borough as a kind of modern city-state. As in Arden's 1959 play *Serjeant Musgrave's Dance* the Yorkshire town is represented as virtually self-governing, and the large cast of characters is grouped schematically* : we find a group of Labour councillors, a group of Conservatives. Labour is in power at the Town Hall but the play's battle for power centres on the new police chief as both factions try to get him on their side, or, failing that, to get rid of him. The electorate is represented by a corrupt doctor, his attractive daughter, and the manageress of the local night-club. The social element missing from the microcosm is the working-classes.

There is a lot of bad blank verse in the play, and little of Arden's best writing, but like *Bartholomew Fair*, it is bursting its seams with raw life, accurately observed and vividly reproduced. Frank Finlay's performance as Charlie Butterthwaite produced a delighted whoop of recognition from Mervyn Jones.† 'I know Butterthwaite. It is a measure of the class and regional limitations of our theatre that he has never been put on the stage before, but here he is, and if Arden had done nothing else, he would deserve our thanks.'

In *The Scotsman* Ronald Mavor praised Stuart Burge's direction for using all three dimensions (as though most directors didn't, or couldn't). Roger Furse again provided a set on three levels, and Stuart Burge had a municipal band playing in the upper gallery. Underneath, to quote Bernard

---

* See Ronald Hayman. *John Arden*. Heinemann.
† *Tribune.*

Levin's review, 'he swirled a huge cast around with great fluency and spontaneity, yet with firm control. The open stage is made to work for the play and is not there to be apologized for.'

7

The Canadian Interlude

There are so many new Shakespeare productions in England every year that the most successful way of celebrating his quatercentenary in 1964 was to invite companies from abroad. The World Theatre Season was inaugurated at the Aldwych during the RSC's March-June recess with companies from Paris, Berlin, Rome, Dublin, Warsaw, Athens and Moscow, none of which staged a Shakespeare play, while the company from Stratford, Ontario was brought to Chichester to give a three-week season in April, consisting of two Shakespeare plays, *Love's Labour's Lost* and *Timon of Athens*, and Molière's *Le Bourgeois gentilhomme*. Both guest seasons were important, and the English theatre has been immeasurably richer for the fact that the World Theatre Season went on to become an annual event. It would be richer still if companies from Canadian and American open stage theatres were regularly invited to Chichester. Their influence could then hardly fail to rub off on English shoulders.

The theatre at Stratford, Ontario, is bigger than the Chichester Festival Theatre but the contact between actors and audience is closer. When Stuart Burge went to Ontario later in the year to direct *Richard II*, he said 'My first impression on stepping on to the stage was an extraordinary sense of contact with the auditorium, much more than at Chichester'. And Michael Langham, after a preliminary visit to Chichester, made no attempt to hide his disappointment from the Canadian press. 'Chichester may have been inspired by Stratford; its auditorium and stage may have a superficial resemblance. But there the likeness ends. Partly because of the structure of the building, partly because of the limited funds with which it was built (the equivalent of what Stratford spent on heating and air-conditioning alone) the Chichester theatre creates a theatrical experience which fails to match the electrifying excitement of Stratford.'

The Chichester auditorium is flatter. At Stratford, as Michael Langham said,* 'By steeply raking the auditorium it has become possible to make significant movements not only from side to side or in awkward inside-out triangles, but from front to back. In fact there are no sides or front. The lines shift according to the viewpoint, allowing a greater plasticity, an infinitely greater variety of relationships and groupings to shade and emphasize the text.' The main acting area at Chichester is also flatter, and twice as broad, making it more difficult to concentrate and focus the action. Nor is the stage high enough, but neither is Stratford's. Langham says 'Ideally the level of the stage should present the actor so that the greatest impact from him is felt in dead centre of the auditorium, not, as so often happens, in the front three rows. At Stratford he's in line with rows B, C, and D, so for some productions I raised the whole platform by a step to reach more towards the centre.'†
Only a limited amount of remodelling could be done at Chichester, but Langham made three important suggestions: that the stage should be topped by one more level, which would automatically create a smaller playing area; that the stage should be raised from the level of row D to that of row H; and that a new V-shaped back wall should be built to improve the acoustics and give an illusion of intimacy. He hoped that the changes he introduced would be retained permanently. They were not, though it was recognized that he had improved the general standard of audibility and that his triple-pillared balcony provided both a useful setting for more intimate scenes and a useful recessed area. It also allowed more vertical deployment of actors than had been seen previously.

The season began with Langham's production of *Love's Labour's Lost*, designed by Tanya Moiseiwitsch. The visual

---

* Interview in the *Sunday Times*, 5 April 1964.
† *Theatre Quarterly*, July-September 1973.

element was favoured at the expense of the verbal. In *Plays and Players* Peter Roberts complained that 'the elaborate conceits of the early Shakespeare were machine-gunned round the auditorium at a pace that hardly gave the audience time to reflect on its beauty – or preciousness'. Several critics described the production as balletic : *The Times* reviewer wrote 'Its spirit is that of a ballet with language operating as the musical accompaniment. Sometimes, as in the riddlesome scenes between Boyet and the girls, the rhythm of the lines precipitates its own dance steps, and a constant virtue throughout is the care for visual balance and contrast – the dazzling change from drab costumes as the four girls flood the stage in white satin; the great moment when "the scene starts to cloud" and a multi-coloured riot instantly evaporates into elegaic gravity. In general the sense of ensemble is dominant and one remembers the chorus of derisive moues from the girls and the fantastic Muscovite invasion of the courtiers more than any separate performances.' Generally he felt that 'the play's airborne gaiety and rapid transitions of mood lend themselves naturally to the open stage's enrichened vocabulary of movement . . . all depends on atmosphere, pace and attack.' Ronald Bryden's reaction in the *New Statesman* was similar : 'Michael Langham has realized the stage's limitations : in fact it is a rostrum or series of rostrums, and he clears it for each speaker in turn to hand down his lines as from a pulpit, turning the play into an intricate, dancing game of King of the Castle'.

'Intimacy' was not a word that had often been used in praise of the Chichester stage, but now, in *The Guardian*, Christopher Driver came out with the supreme tribute : 'No form of entertainment between the arrival of the proscenium arch and the invention of broadcasting has achieved such intimacy.'

The audience responded enthusiastically, and on the first night there were six curtain calls, which themselves became the basis almost for a separate performance. In *Punch* Basil Boothroyd (who had his doubts about whether it was right to leave the audience to visualize the park without any scenic help) thoroughly approved of the curtain calls. 'A proscenium stage would defeat all these splendid patterns of flowing movement, never more successful than in the calls at the end, when the players surge in and out of the exits in a rushing confusion that resolves into a design, breaks, resolves itself again and with its purely physical ingenuity crowns the evening.'

But if the Canadian critic Jacob Siskind is to be believed, what Chichester audiences were being given was inferior to the original production. 'The show as seen here lacked the warmth and the charm of that presented in Stratford . . . It is the stage here that is at fault . . . The production limped across the staircase here at Chichester and it is a libel on the original Michael Langham conception . . . With people walking or striding across the stage, or onto it, instead of floating by, as they seemed to in the original production, the show lost the fairytale quality that made it such a delight.'

Predictably, many of the English critics objected to the Canadian accents, and, less unreasonably, to the speech-patterns, which had been evolved for a more popular audience, less familiar with Shakespeare's idiom. Michael Langham was by no means insensitive to Shakespeare's constructional ability. As he said, 'the use of the open stage reveals a stage craftsmanship of a precision and brilliance he is seldom credited with'. But the open stage, properly used, also allows the phrasing and the rhythms to emerge more clearly than they can from behind a picture-frame, and the Canadian productions failed to take advantage of this. Part of the trouble was that they concentrated on the visual and kinetic aspects that could appeal to an audience unwilling to listen hard or think hard; but they also coarsened and sentimentalized many of Shakespeare's points. In *Love's Labour's Lost* this was most obvious in the treatment of Moth, Don Armado's page, who was given spectacles and the sort of cuteness that appeals (or is expected to appeal) to the public which patronizes old-fashioned American musicals. In Jean Gascon's production of *Le Bourgeois gentilhomme* Douglas Rain's homely characterization of M. Jourdain looked as though it had been angled to appeal to the same taste, and in Michael Langham's modern-dress production of *Timon of Athens*, which had John Colicos in the lead and music by Duke Ellington, there was none of the uncomfortable satirical pungency that Guthrie had been able to infuse into the best of his modern-dress Shakespeare productions, though there were some highly effective moments when the bustling movement on stage was frozen to allow one actor in a spotlight to deliver a soliloquy.

The possibility of applying the brakes and narrowing the focus suddenly was one of the main lessons that could have been learnt from the Canadians.

8
The Olivier Régime (2) :
The National Theatre Company Seasons 1964-65

The Workhouse Donkey had played to an average of seventy per cent capacity and some of the matinees had been very sparsely attended, but Olivier boldly started his third season with another boldly chosen new play, Peter Shaffer's *The Royal Hunt of the Sun*, which was to have been produced by the RSC at the Aldwych. Peter Hall had hesitated and finally decided not to risk it; Olivier decided to do it at the National. It was an expensive production, with a cast of thirty-three actors – Shaffer would have liked more – and it might not have been economically feasible to do it as one production out of three in a nine-week summer season if it had not been destined to go into the National's repertoire at the Old Vic. But this was arranged before it was settled whether or not it would open at Chichester. When it did, it was an immediate success, arousing much more interest than the other new production of the season, Marston's *The Dutch Courtesan*. The third play, Olivier's *Othello*, had already been seen at the Vic, but it was still being so avidly discussed that people would gladly have travelled much further to see it than the sixty-three miles from London to Chichester.

It was hard to evaluate *The Royal Hunt of the Sun* because it was hard to separate the text from the concept or either from the production. Writing in the *Daily Mail* on 8 July 1964 Bernard Levin saluted it as 'the greatest play of our generation . . . I do not think the English stage has been so graced nor English audiences so privileged since

Shaw was in his heyday'. A second viewing merely con-
firmed him in his opinion. On 13 July he called it 'the finest
new play I have ever seen'. But Benedict Nightingale, who
reviewed it in *The Guardian*, did not admire the actual
play : 'Ultimately it has to rely on its appeal as a spectacle.'
And when Bernard Levin came to write about it again six
years later in his book *The Pendulum Years*, he did not
repeat his superlative judgment, merely bracketing it with
Osborne's *Inadmissible Evidence* as summing up the tensions
of the sixties. *The Royal Hunt of the Sun* had been 'saying
farewell to the faith that was disappearing or already gone',
while *Inadmissible Evidence* was 'looking ahead in some
disquiet to the emptiness that was to follow'.

Certainly Peter Shaffer's play is about faith. It had been
conceived several years earlier when he had to spend a few
weeks in bed, and took the opportunity to read H. M.
Prescott's *The Conquest of Peru*. He was fascinated by the
story and, above all, by the confrontation it embodied between two contrasted ways of life – Catholic imperialism
and Inca 'communism'. 'The Inca civilization had no concept of romantic love, no private property in our sense of
the term, no possibility of moving from where one started
either physically or in status. A man was allotted a fixed
portion of land from birth, he married at twenty-five,
whether he liked it or not, he stayed in his place of birth all
his life, retired and was pensioned off at fifty. A complete
communist state.' His first draft contained a lot of historical
narrative, but, as the play evolved, it became more and
more of a conflict, physical, psychological and ideological
between two men, Pizarro, the Conquistador, leader of the
Spanish expedition, and Atahuallpa, who to the Incas was
a god, the ruler, the giver of life, the source of all benefits,
the embodiment of the sun. 'And the theme which lies
behind their relationship is the search for God – that is why
it is called "the Royal *Hunt* of the Sun" – the search for a
definition of the idea of God.'

The narrative element by no means disappears altogether.
He needed a narrator and used the character of Martin
Ruiz as an old man. Ruiz was page to Pizarro on the ex-
pedition, so we get two actors playing the part, one very

young, and two attitudes to Pizarro's behaviour, one hero-worshipping, the other retrospectively critical. Something of Prescott's style survives in the narrative links, which are ponderous but more solidly, straightforwardly and, on the whole, simply written than the rest of the dialogue. It is ultimately the texture of Shaffer's prose that lets the play down. To take the weight of the enormously ambitious subject, and to control the resonances emerging out of the wide-ranging references in Shaffer's highly serious attempt to work out a dialectic between his two contrasting civilizations and their values, nothing less than poetry would be powerful enough. Not verse, necessarily, but at least a concentrated and reverberating prose poetry like that of John Whiting in his best plays. Language like this could have also been tilted more easily to suggest the sixteenth century. Shaffer's prose is workmanlike but at worst portentous and at best undistinguished.

> You have no eyes for me now, Atahuallpa : they are dusty balls of amber I can tap on. You have no peace for me, Atahuallpa : the birds still scream in your forest. You have no joy for me, Atahuallpa, my boy : the only joy is death. I lived between two hates : I die between two darks : blind eyes and a blind sky. And yet you saw once. The sky seems nothing but you saw. Is there comfort there? The sky knows no feeling but we know them, that's sure. Martin's hope and De Soto's honour and your trust – your trust which hunted me : we alone make these. That's some marvel, yes, some marvel. To sit in a great cold silence, and sing out sweet with just our own warm breath : that's some marvel, surely. To make water in a sand world : surely, surely . . . God's just a name on your nail : and naming begins cries and cruelties.*

If Michael Langham had treated Shakespeare's poetry as if it were a score for a ballet, here was prose that could best be treated as a score for a spectacular piece of theatre. Even *The Times* critic, who found the play 'hollow at the centre' conceded that 'its externals are magnificent – not only in the prodigal displays of treasure and the blazing feather costumes, but in the exotic movement of the production and

* Peter Shaffer. *The Royal Hunt of the Sun*. Hamish Hamilton, 1964.

in the panache of the writing'. He warmed particularly to the final sequence, when 'a ring of celebrants converge chanting on the dead King, wearing fantastic golden masks fixed in expressions of expectation that miraculously grows to bewilderment as the sun comes up and the body remains inertly supine on the floor. It is a superb effect.' In *The Observer* Bamber Gascoigne was full of admiration for the courage of 'daring to present the solemn Inca rituals, the long journey by 150 Spaniards through a steaming jungle and then over the Andes, and the subsequent massacre of 3,000 Indians'. In the *Sunday Telegraph* Alan Brien was no less complimentary about the mimed sequences. Though they dispensed with both props and scenery, he found them 'as exhausting and as exhilarating as any Hollywood sequence filmed by cameras hanging over the edge of a real precipice. The butchery of the 3,000 unarmed and blinkered Peruvians by the grubby white gods from beyond the ocean is enacted in slow motion by a score of actors like a ritual dance of death. Nearly all the incidents are choreographed with simple, stylized movements.' John Dexter, who directed with Desmond O'Donovan, had been in Japan and been deeply impressed by the Noh theatre. The slow funereal gliding walk he gave to the Incas, their feet scarcely leaving the ground, was taken directly from the Noh theatre. When Dexter asked his movement director, Claude Chagrin, whether she could teach the actors to do it, she said it would take two years. He gave her six weeks, and the results were quite passable. For all the limitations of the writing, the play was important because it ventured so far away from naturalism and broke so much new ground in doing so. Or if the ground was not wholly new, at least it had been neglected in post-war British theatre. Shaffer's impressions of the Chinese Classical Theatre from Formosa, which Peter Daubeny had brought to London in 1957, mingled fruitfully with Dexter's impressions of Japanese Noh theatre, to form a post-Brechtian version of total theatre, drawing on a wide mixture of stylistic resources, just as Jean-Louis Barrault had in his forties and fifties productions of Claudel.

By going so far beyond naturalism the play also provided some superb acting opportunities especially for Robert

Stephens as Atahuallpa. Very little is known about the Incas and this would be a disadvantage if naturalistic criteria were to hold, but he made it into a great advantage. It is believed that their speech used to hit the consonants hard, sighing away on some of the diphthongs,* that they were very influenced by birds, and may sometimes have imitated bird sounds in their speech. The first time Robert Stephens attempted a bird-cry in the rehearsal room, the other actors laughed, making Dexter so angry that he threatened to send them home and go on working just with Stephens. This was what acting was all about, he said, and if they couldn't understand that, they had no right to be in the theatre. One of the main virtues of the play is its ambitiousness, which forces everyone working on it to take risks of the sort that no naturalistic play demands or even allows, and breakthroughs can hardly ever be made without taking the chance of seeming ridiculous. Had Robert Stephens been scared of mockery or had Dexter allowed the amusement of the others to inhibit him, he would never have won his way through to the extraordinarily impressive performance he gave, full of intuitive understanding of a generous and sincere man who spanned between the animal and the divine, making bird noises and genuinely believing himself to be a god.

After the failure of his first two Jacobean revivals, Olivier had to be more careful about his third, and in John Marston's *The Dutch Courtesan* he had at least the security of knowing that Joan Littlewood had made a considerable impact with it at Stratford East in 1959. This could have been regarded as a reason for not reviving it again so soon, when so many interesting Elizabethan and Jacobean plays were being neglected, including Marston's *The Malcontent*, which is a better play, as most critics agree. *The Dutch Courtesan* is not even characteristic of Marston: T. S. Eliot's view is that the theme could have been handled better by either Dekker or Heywood.

So what was there to recommend the play? It is fairly well constructed and provides the possibility of introducing

* See Ronald Hayman, *Playback 2*, Davis-Poynter, 1974.

some lively knockabout comedy into the sub-plot about the tricks that Cocledemoy plays on the middle-class citizen Mulligrub. It contains some pleasing verse, a villainous courtesan who speaks broken English and some vigorous invective. Cocledemoy's most picturesque threat is 'I'll make him fart firecrackers'.

There are also some good acting parts. Malheureux is reminiscent of Angelo in *Measure for Measure*, a melancholy, self-righteous man who falls in love with Francischina, the courtesan. She offers herself to him on condition that he kills his friend Freevill, who is on the point of abandoning her to marry the virtuous daughter of Sir Hubert Subboys. John Stride and George Innes did reasonably well as the two young men, but Billie Whitelaw found the Dutch accent a big handicap. In *The Guardian*, Philip Hope-Wallace complained about 'the continuous strain of hearing. Billie Whitelaw affects an au pair girl voice which is surely too thick and must surely be totally incomprehensible to those who are sitting behind her when she talks . . . According to where your seat is placed, a play in this arena theatre comes and goes like a conversation on a bad long-distance wire.'

Very few productions which have originated at Chichester seem better when they transfer to London, but *The Times* critic reacted more favourably to *The Dutch Courtesan* at the Old Vic. 'Rescued from the desert expanses of the Chichester open stage and now supported by lightweight settings that manage to look both realistic and impressive, this production arrives at the National Theatre much improved. It has had time to mature and its comic detail has developed an economy and a precision which compare starkly with one's slap-happy recollections of the original production. Of course, this change is partly a consequence of moving into a theatre where no effect needs to be wasted.' But far less would have been wasted at Chichester if the adaptations made by the Canadian company to the stage had been retained.

Othello too was less satisfactory in Chichester than it had been in London. The production had been conceived for the Old Vic stage and in re-rehearsing it for Chichester,

Dexter for once failed to make the most of the space. It is also arguable that Olivier's Othello was essentially a proscenium performance. Its basic impulse was forwards and outwards, rather than sideways or inwards; it failed almost completely in relation to the surrounding performances, giving the impression of having been conceived, evolved, polished and lacquered without any reference to what the other actors were doing. Jonathan Miller, who was later to direct Olivier in *The Merchant of Venice*, maintained that 'this performance has nothing to do with *Othello* as Shakespeare wrote it and remains a large indigestible lump in the middle of the play'. Later, after seeing it again at Chichester, he added 'John Dexter's production seems to be arranged around Olivier like a garnish round a joint'.

Because of the physical strain on Olivier the performances were spaced out to give him two free evenings between each performance, and the play was done only sixteen times during the season. 21,760 tickets were sold and almost as many applications for seats were turned down. Fifty five-shilling tickets were sold on the day of each performance and before the first performance there was an all-night queue, headed by two Dutch boys who waited for three days. Olivier received an enormous ovation : when he took his solo curtain there were cheers from all over the auditorium, many people were stamping and some were standing on their seats.

The critics were divided about whether the show was better or worse than it had been in London. According to *The Observer*'s critic 'even the devotees of the peninsular stage at Chichester will admit that the National Theatre *Othello* has lost considerably in its transfer from the Old Vic. In terms of production the change is most noticeable whenever several people stand about listening, as in the Council scene before Othello leaves Venice. The most natural shape for such a group on the Chichester stage is a circle of actors facing inwards, but if this remains static the main speakers will be permanently masked from large sections of the audience. The director's solution is usually to keep things moving.' There was also a diffusion of emotional intensity. 'At the Old Vic I several times felt the most sweet and powerful sensuality between Othello and Desdemona. At Chichester these moments had vanished.' Perhaps they were still there, he conceded, but 'I think it is more probable that I was never quite at the right angle to catch them . . . Olivier's performance was still magnificent but even it reached me with less force than before and certain of his more ambitious "effects" seemed to have hardened into a false mould.'

The Times critic, on the other hand, found the Chichester production 'a good deal more solid than the original'. He admitted that there were problems of masking and acoustics, but he argued that 'the disadvantages are outweighed by other open-stage characteristics, permitting both elaborate crowd movement and the concentration of a sacrificial altar – which lends itself beautifully to the play's requirements . . . The necessary absence of properties matches the free unlocalized setting of the play, and scenes like the carousel and the lantern-lit slaying of Roderigo have been recharged with energy and the sense of danger.' He found that Maggie Smith's performance as Desdemona had 'grown in positive character' and that Frank Finlay's Iago had 'lost many of its original grotesque features'.

Meanwhile fund-raising was still continuing. The original building contract had been for £95,000, but since it was obviously not going to be difficult to finance them, improvements costing about £10,000 were incorporated. A great deal remained to be done, though, and the fund-raisers went on organizing coffee-mornings, fêtes and flower-shows. Alan Draycott, one of the original donors of £1,000 and now a member of the Board of Management, was a race-horse-owner and in 1963 at the meeting in Fontwell Park, a horse called Tommy the Greek was raffled in aid of the theatre, raising £2,000, and racehorses were again raffled at Fontwell Park in 1964 and 1965. Gifts were still coming in, too, and there were contributions from the Festival Theatre Society, taken partly from members' subscriptions, partly from the proceeds of fund-raising events. By the end of June 1964, £166,837.11.0 had been collected.

But it was becoming clear that the National Theatre

company would not be able to go on playing at Chichester
each summer, much as the actors would have liked to. The
Arts Council was pressuring it to do more touring, and in
March 1965, at the Festival Society's annual general meeting, Evershed-Martin made the first public statement about
the uncertainty of the theatre's future : 'It may be that the
National will not be with us for a great deal of time in the
future and that we may have other ideas.' He also mentioned the possibility of an autumn season on the same lines
as the Canadian company's spring season the previous year.

The appointment of John Clements as successor to Olivier
was announced by the *Portsmouth Evening News* on 8 July,
and by most of the national papers the following morning.
Olivier was then fifty-eight, Clements was fifty-five and
playing Mr Barrett of Wimpole Street in the musical *Robert
and Elizabeth.* He had a house in Royal Crescent, Brighton,
three doors away from the Oliviers' house, and they often
travelled up to London together. Olivier introduced him as
'the finest man in England for the job, a noble actor-
manager'. It had obviously been a great strain on Olivier
to be responsible for Chichester as well as for the National
Theatre and it was remarkable that the arrangement had
continued as long as it did, even if he did not himself act or
direct during his fourth season. 'Something had to give,' he
said. 'I have never been able to give Chichester thought
outside the Festival season. I tried to twin up the two jobs
but it was not possible.'

The language and the dramatic texture of John Arden's
Armstrong's Last Goodnight, the first play in Olivier's final
season, could hardly be more different from that of *The
Royal Hunt of the Sun.* But there is one striking similarity
which may help to explain why these two plays had two of
the most impressive productions that have ever been seen on
the Chichester stage, and to indicate one direction in which
playwrights could be briefed if the management were interested in commissioning serious new work. Both scripts are
basically concerned with a confrontation between two different modes of civilization, one of which is much more
advanced than the other and therefore more willing to con-

done the use of immoral means in pursuit of a politically and socially desirable end. And in both plays the conflict is worked out primarily in terms of a battle between two male personalities. One man has the primitive virtues of humane warmth and directness. The other is more sophisticated, more disillusioned, more dishonest, defeating his opponent by treachery. (It was curious that Robert Stephens, who had been the noble primitive in *The Royal Hunt* should be the devious victor in *Armstrong's Last Goodnight.*)

Not that Johnny Armstrong of Gilnockie is either innocent or incapable of treachery. Like Goetz von Berlichingen in Goethe's play, which Arden had adapted as *Ironhand*, he is a robber baron, and when we first see him he is vowing friendship with Wamphray, only to disarm him while he is asleep in the forest and leave him to be slaughtered by the father of the girl he is reputed to have raped. But Armstrong is amiably incapable of suspecting duplicity in other people. Compared with his adversary, the mature intellectual Sir David Lindsay, he is a child. Arden was taking liberties with history in making Lindsay − the author of the play *The Thrie Estaits*, which had already played such an important part in the Chichester theatre's pre-history − into an emissary sent by the young king, James V of Scotland, to negotiate with Armstrong, because his border raids are so troublesome. But the idea is germane to the development of an extremely interesting plot structure, much more complex than that of *The Royal Hunt*. While Armstrong is temperamentally a lover of brawling and disorder, Lindsay loves peace and the rule of law, and he is capable of high moral seriousness.

> *I will gang towart his house*
> *As ane man against ane man*
> *And through my craft and my humanity*
> *I will save the realm frae butchery*
> *Gif I can, good sir, but gif I can.*

As an intellectual, Lindsay is an idealist; as a practical politician he tries to be more Machiavellian. The English are paying the Scottish Lord Maxwell to encourage the raids of the robber barons, and to get Maxwell on his master's side, Lindsay persuades the young king to imprison Lord Johnstone, Maxwell's enemy. But when both Scottish lords gang up against Lindsay, he is himself in danger, particularly as he has been unable to use the powers of reason to make the King appoint Armstrong as his officer, which would put him on his best behaviour, or to persuade Armstrong to desist from the border raids, which give him so much childish pleasure. Having alienated all the Scottish factions, Lindsay flirts with the intellectually appealing idea of a free confederation of the English and Scottish borderers, and he goes as far as making overtures to the English. But if Armstrong is an anachronism representing a primitive anarchy which has to be wiped out in the interests of political unity, Lindsay is ahead of his time, trying to apply rational diplomacy to a political structure which is not ready for it. In the end, to win back the King's goodwill which he has almost lost, he stoops to ambushing Armstrong in a manner thoroughly unworthy of the standards he has set himself. Like *The Royal Hunt*, *Armstrong's Last Goodnight* ends with the contrition of the victor.

Trained as an architect and always alert to the problems he was posing his designers, Arden had conceived the play for a proscenium theatre, but had thought in terms of the medieval convention of 'simultaneous mansions'. The King's palace was to be represented in miniature, stage left, with Armstrong's castle stage right. Upstage centre the forest, representing the wild land of the Borders, was to be suggested by a single tree. At Chichester, René Allio's beautifully simple set preserved the basic idea, but without using a cyclorama to fill in the background, as would have been inevitable in a Victorian or Edwardian theatre. Allio built a tilted platform over the whole acting area, raising it and angling the actors into a better relationship with the auditorium. It was probably the best set ever designed for the Chichester stage.

But what made it so effective was Arden's dialogue, which is extraordinary in its density and its visual suggestiveness, needing no more help than Allio provided with his bare stage and his bulky costumes. As in a Shakespeare play, the verbal imagery and the action combined to create a compelling sense of locale. Shakespearean, in fact, is the only word to describe Arden's power of using words, rhythms and sometimes rhymes to convey a vivid impression of the profusion of thickets and bracken in a forest or the bleakness of the empty hills. When Wamphray dies, pinned against a tree by his enemies' spears, the father of the girl bids him a stony farewell:

> He will remain here on this fellside for the better
> nourishment of the corbies. Ride.

And the Chichester stage has never seemed wider than when Arden's words reinforced the optical illusion in the scene when Lindsay was helping his secretary, mortally wounded with a gully knife still sticking in his side, to stagger back to Edinburgh.

LINDSAY: Ye canna mak the journey in that condition, Sandy –

MCGLASS: I can. Observe me, sir: I'm maken it. Observe, I'm upon the road. (*He staggers round the stage, supported by Lindsay. As he goes, he sings*):
O lang was the way and dreary was the way
And they wept every mile they trod
And ever he did bear his afflictit comrade dear.
A heavy and a needless load.
A heavy and a needless load.

The problem of presenting a primitive society is inseparable from the problem of contriving a language to write in. In *The Royal Hunt* Michael Annals's enormous feathery costumes for the Incas and Robert Stephens's imaginatively bird-oriented speaking had valuably supplemented Shaffer's dialogue, but it is the language itself that must do most of the work if the audience is to be transported effectively into the past. Arden's compromise recreation of sixteenth-century Scots was brilliantly worked out, but unfortunately the Chichester acoustic increased the audience's difficulties, which would have been considerable anyway. The play had been premiered at the Glasgow Citizens' Theatre, and there the actors had apparently had less trouble in making the language intelligible. According to Christopher Small, writing in the *Glasgow Herald* on 8 July, 'the sort of Babylonish dialect which Mr Arden concocted for his sixteenth-century Scots to sound in the main convincing on native tongues, has evidently been too much for most of the English players, and their efforts alternately to dodge it and to tackle it lands them not seldom in mere unintelligible jabber.'

At Chichester the difficulty the critics had in following the dialogue made them unappreciative of the poetry in it. As in most of Arden's plays, a great deal of his inspiration came from the ballads. There is a ballad about Johnny Armstrong, and the whole theme lends itself eminently well to treatment in ballad terms, whereas the ballad element seems much more forced and foreign in the world of *The Workhouse Donkey*. The declaration of desire that Lindsay's mistress makes to Armstrong is full of simple, salty images that derive from the ballad tradition, but it combines them with elaborate metaphysical conceits. As pastiche of sixteenth-century verse, this is very good, but it is more than mere pastiche.

> *When I stand in the full direction of your force*
> *Ye need nae wife nor carl to stand*
> *Alsweel beside ye and interpret.*
> *There is in me ane knowledge, potent, secret,*
> *That I can set to rin ane sure concourse*
> *Of bodily and ghaistly strength betwixt the blood*
> *Of me and of the starkest man alive. My speed*
> *Hangs twin with yours: and starts ane double flood:*
> *Will you with me initiate the deed*
> *And saturatit consequence thereof –?*
> *Crack aff with your great club*
> *The barrel-hoops of love*
> *And let it pour*
> *Like the enchantit quern that boils red-herring broo*
> *Until it gars upswim the goodman's table and his door*
> *While all his house and yard and street*
> *Swill reeken, greasy, het, oer-drownit sax-foot fou –*

Arden said that his linguistic model was Arthur Miller's play *The Crucible*, with its compromise reconstruction of early American speech. *The Crucible* makes less demands on the audience's capacity for intense concentration and quick guesswork, though the language sometimes borders on the poetic, but the richness of Arden's rhythms and imagery make them incomparably superior to Miller's. Arden had steeped himself far more deeply in sixteenth-century literature. Ballad simplicity also works in a valuable way against the massiveness of the theme. Where Shaffer's language was liable to become inflated, Arden's is constantly swung back towards solid, physical facts, and in this way it saved itself from being eclipsed by the visual and theatrical effects of the Chichester production by John Dexter and William Gaskill. At the end of the play, for instance, when the trap is finally sprung on Armstrong, the young King condescendingly wanders downstage with the robber baron, who is flattered to be offered a drink out of the royal flask. Behind them, one by one, Armstrong's men are gagged and dragged silently off-stage by barefooted Highland soldiers, leaving their leader alone and unarmed. This is superb theatre, especially on an open stage, with the audience so close to the ambush, but the impact does not overpower that of Armstrong's starkly simple dying song, sung without even his piper to accompany him.

> *To seek het water beneath cauld ice*
> *Surely it is ane great follie*
> *I hae socht grace at a graceless face*
> *And there is nane for my men and me.*

The collaboration of the two directors was very successful. They did not discuss the text before starting rehearsals. Dexter first took about four days to block the moves. Then, after a run-through, Gaskill took over for a week, working mainly on interpretation. After looking at the results to-gether, they divided forces, not working together again until the final phase. They also had Arden working directly with the actors – 'because he's so accurate, especially on the speaking. He has a marvellous ear and speaks the lines better than any actors, attacking them with that peculiar, hard, astringent North country delivery.'*

Dexter and Gaskill were thinking partly in terms of film

---

* William Gaskill. Interview in *Encore*, September-October 1965.

images. 'Albert Finney used to work in baggy trousers to get the feeling of, you know, the bent knees, the images that are so characteristic of Japanese films, and we tried to move very quickly, which is a very Oriental thing. And we talked constantly about the Oriental and the Negro; always, to get any response out of the actors to a different society, one has to think beyond the British Isles and beyond Europe to something which is absolutely alien. And I think Albert Finney rather conveys this in his performance. He has been criticized for pulling faces, but it's absolutely deliberate – it's meant to convey a certain kind of culture, like the grunting and grimacing of Mifune in Kurosawa films.' Something of this must have come through in performance. In her review in *The Observer* Penelope Gilliatt spoke of 'an almost cinematic shot of a girl lugging the corpse of her untrue lover into the woods'. She also singled out both of the images that had been starting points in Dexter's mind – 'a hanged body that turns like a salmon on a hook' and 'a ring of soldiers with jagged black hair sitting in a Japanese-looking squat with one knee up and one on the ground'.

But it was a great tribute to Arden's play that several of the critics who had seen both productions preferred the Glasgow one, which had not had the advantages of a large budget, a long rehearsal period or star performances. Ronald Bryden 'harked back longingly to that first, less lavish staging. Physically it had nothing to match René Allio's splendid rough furs and buff-coats, the lighting and sounds which turned the bare Chichester platform into high moorland at dawn, horns winding down the fells. But at least it saw that the play's key relationship – that with Armstrong failing – is Lindsay's with his young Highland secretary. As played in Glasgow by Leonard Maguire and John Cairney, this was richly touching: a father-son affection of equals, in which all the subtlety of Lindsay' tact, humanity, Scots egalitarianism and civilized self-doubt could display itself. Reduced to a functional English office-friendship by Robert Stephens, it left his Lindsay an uneasy, immature posturer, as inept in political relationships as in personal ones.' Christopher Small also criticized Robert Stephens as playing 'lightly, with cynicism, rather than the compassionate worldly wisdom that Leonard Maguire showed us in the same part of a man trying with his humanity as well as his cunning to unravel rather than cut the Gordian knot'.

Albert Finney's performance in the leading part was also subjected to unfavourable comparisons. According to *The Times* critic, 'the towering Iain Cuthbertson . . . brought out its violent innocence and terrifying comedy. Albert Finney's performance is less varied, and the speech defect seems more a physical accident than a symbol of primitive mentality.' Benedict Nightingale's verdict in *The Guardian* was similar : the Chichester production 'had more polish, more attention to detail, but less sheer emotional impact. The Armstrong clan in particular is curiously lacklustre and muffled beside the bluff Davy Crocketts we saw in Glasgow. I also admit to preferring Iain Cuthbertson as Johnny Armstrong to Albert Finney. Mr Finney emphasises the sullen, brutish side of the character . . . He misses warmth and generosity of heart.'

Trelawny of the 'Wells', which opened a week later on 13 July, could hardly have provided a greater contrast, giving the audience something it could lap up, enjoying every mouthful without any mental exertion. To be sure, it is also a play about a confrontation between two sets of values, old and new, but its horizons are much narrower, and purely theatrical.

The central, highly romantic story of the young actress who fails in her attempt to marry into society is devised as an argument in favour of realism : she returns to the theatre a changed woman, incapable of acting in the old artificial way. Nothing less than realism can feed her talent now. Pinero obviously intended his hero's play, which is called *Life*, to stand for T. W. Robertson's play *Society*, which had been launched by Sir Squire Bancroft in 1865, and when we see *Life* being rehearsed in Act Four, the dialogue he writes for it is an affectionate pastiche of the sort of dialogue he had to speak himself as a young actor. He also shows an old theatrical couple of the same vintage as his former employers reduced to working as small-part character actor and wardrobe mistress :

> And so this new-fangled stuff, and these dandified
> people, are to push us, and such as us, from our
> stools!
> Yes, James, just as some other new fashion will, in
> course of time, push *them* from their stools.

There is also a pleasantly ironical treatment of the juvenile
lead who at first protests indignantly at being cast as the
Demon King in the pantomime and later finds that some of
his lines have distinct possibilities.

> *I'm Discontent! From Orkney's isle to Dover*
> *To make men's bile bile-over I endover.*

But if Pinero was not quite capable of the irony that
Desmond O'Donovan's production was imputing to him,*
at least he was capable of making the nature of theatrical
magic into the subject of a theatrically magical effect. The
formidable Vice-Chancellor, Sir William Gower, grand-
father of Rose Trelawny's suitor, at first disapproves vehemently of his grandson's liaison. But in Act Three he discovers
that her mother had acted with Edmund Kean. Abruptly
his hostility melts. Kean was 'a *splendid* gipsy' and when
Rose shows him a chain and a sword-belt that Kean had
used, the old man handles them like holy relics, putting the
chain over his own shoulder. And at Chichester we felt as if
we were under the same spell as the Chancellor, even more
strongly than we could have been in a proscenium theatre.

The National Theatre's casting was impeccable. Paul
Curran was the old Chancellor, (played in the original production by actor-playwright Dion Boucicault). Graham
Crowden energetically threw his eccentrically comic personality into the part of the comedian, Augustus Colpoys, while
Robert Stephens's crumpled sincerity pleasantly filled out
the role of the T. W. Robertson character, Tom Wrench.
Louise Purnell was delightful as Rose Trelawny, accurately
described as looking divine in washed muslin, and, as a
coarser but warm-hearted fellow-actress, Avonia Bunn,
Billie Whitelaw was equally irresistible. Edward Pether-
bridge applied a pleasantly light touch to the part of the

* See page 51.

juvenile lead, Ferdinand Gadd, (originally played by Gerald Du Maurier) and as the aging theatrical couple, displaced from their positions of supremacy, Gerald James and Wynne Clark were humorously robust.

The final production of this exciting season was a well-devised double-bill consisting of Strindberg's *Miss Julie* and Peter Shaffer's new farce *Black Comedy*. This may have seemed an unlikely coupling, but after a gruelling theatrical experience in which a pet bird has its head chopped off and a high-born young lady is driven to suicide by the servant who has just slept with her, an audience is urgently in need of the release that farce can provide. It was noticeable, especially in the first few minutes of *Black Comedy*, that gratitude was making the laughs even louder and even longer than they would normally have been, in spite of the fact that tension had already generated a certain amount of laughter during *Miss Julie*. There is, of course, a strong element of comedy in it, which Strindberg intended to provoke laughter, but Maggie Smith, who played Julie, was at first disconcerted by the reaction.* Later on in her career she could have handled the laughter with more confidence, as she did, to some extent, later in the run, but this was a difficult phase in her development from an actress whose forte was comedy and revue to an actress of tragic stature. She had herself been incredulous when told she was required to play Desdemona opposite Olivier's Othello, and now the role of Miss Julie seemed like a crucial challenge.

Her entrance could hardly be better described than it was by Bryden. 'She started well, with a light, steel-backed run down to the stage, one arm swinging with nervous, calculated abandon. She had the unease of a thoroughbred, wheeling and sniffing round the kitchen in oblique, fascinated circles which brought her closer and closer to Albert Finney's valet. On this stage, he had the place of command, could sit and wait for her. That was the first mistake – Strindberg makes her enter upstage, already dominating him.'† Though Michael Elliott, the director, has since

* See Ronald Hayman, *Playback 2*, Davis-Poynter, 1974.
† Review in *The New Statesman* reprinted in *The Unfinished Hero*, Faber, 1969.

worked a great deal at the University Theatre, Manchester, and become more expert in the use of an open stage than most Chichester directors, in this production he did not use the space as well as he would later have been able to. The conflict of the play involves a complex balance of power between mistress and servant. By setting the play in the kitchen – long before 'Kitchen Sink' became a catchphrase – Strindberg was deliberately giving the valet a territorial advantage : there is no position and no chair which belongs naturally to Miss Julie. Sexually attracted by Jean, she has to find a variety of pretexts for prolonging her visit to this room where the cook, his fiancée, is on home ground.

Himself the son of a maidservant, Strindberg was neurotically involved in the play's sexual battle – arguably too involved to get the balance right. In the original private performance in Copenhagen, when his first wife, who had been a baroness, played Julie, she gave the critic of *Dagens Nyheter* the impression of being too cold to seduce a man like Jean. At Chichester Maggie Smith did not seem too cold but too passive to do the seducing. Albert Finney was consistently given the stronger, more central position and Michael Elliott also failed to solve the problem posed by the distance that the group of servants had to travel when they entered for their rather awkward scene in the middle of the play, which is introduced partly in order to have something happening on stage during Julie's and Jean's absence in the bedroom.

Like *The Royal Hunt of the Sun*, but in a totally different way, *Black Comedy* shows the results of the impact that the Chinese Classical Theatre had on Peter Shaffer. There was a cryptic note in the programme : 'In one of the most celebrated scenes in the repertoire of the Chinese Classical Theatre, two swordsmen fight a duel in a completely darkened room. The scene is performed with the stage fully lit.' As always happens, the secret of the play's central device was given away by the reviewers, but the relevance of this note was puzzling to the first night audience until the play started in complete darkness and we heard the voices of a young couple talking confidently and moving about the onstage room as if everything were normal. We could even hear sounds of furniture being moved about and of a drink being poured – the clink of a glass and the hiss of a soda syphon. The dialogue continued through the darkness for well over a minute until they put a record on the gramophone and the sound ran down as if there had been a failure of electricity. Suddenly the stage was flooded with bright light and the boy and the girl stood still as if they were suddenly in darkness

> God! We've blown a fuse!
> Oh no!
> It must be.

And he gropes his way across to the light switch, moving blindly. The play's convention had been established.

Though Shaffer had conceived the idea several years previously, he remained in doubt about whether it was worth trying to write it up until he had a meal with Kenneth Tynan, who was looking for a play to go with *Miss Julie*. When Shaffer outlined the idea to him, he was extremely enthusiastic about it and persuaded Olivier to commission the play though, like most actors, he had misgivings about the possibility of performing farce on an open stage. Shaffer had only a week to write the first draft. He then went down to Chichester to work on it with Dexter, afterwards taking another week to rewrite part of the second act. He had meanwhile had a valuable object lesson on how people behave in the dark when he was staying at Dexter's house. Arriving alone, at night, while Dexter was rehearsing several miles away, he found the house in darkness, failed to make the electricity work and waited dispiritedly for Dexter to return.

A play written in this convention could reveal so much about the characters that it would be more embarrassing than funny. Part of the idea's appeal was that it would be dangerous. As Shaffer said, 'I think danger is the most important element in farce. Not merely physical danger (like falling down a trap-door – as they do in *Black Comedy*) but the sort of danger where a leading character realizes that if they open that door, his marriage is at an end . . . I think most farce is a study in frustration. The hero of *Black Comedy* is merely trying to marry his girl-friend, impress his future father-in-law and sell his sculpture to a millionaire. He is prevented and frustrated in all these aims.' But of course there are frustrations, dangers and embarrassments far more interesting than these. As Penelope Gilliatt complained in her *Observer* review, 'there is something else in all games with darkness that might have been developed here, something hallucinatory and out of joint that could have made the play much more startling and touching than it is about people whose usual links with one another have suddenly become damaged and suspect. *Black Comedy* would have lost no comedy if it had had the nerve to be more black; as it is, the play seems a blinding idea not very boldly pursued.'

Part of the trouble was that a brilliant idea was being worked out in terms of a conventional situation and conventional characters – the spoiled deb, the peppery colonel, the camp antique dealer, the repressed spinster, the well-read German refugee, the millionaire art collector. But there was a great deal in the production that was fresh and irresistibly funny. With her quacking debby voice, her bottom stuck out as she groped her way up and down a staircase, and her dialogue bristling with words like 'sweetipegs' and 'sexipegs', Louise Purnell was delightful as the fiancée, and Graham Crowden was hilarious as the Colonel. His comic business with the rocking-chair was improved by a first night accident when it pitched him forwards and settled on top of him. Another lucky accident gave Derek Jacobi, who missed his footing, a most impressive slide down the staircase without seeming to touch it. As the harrassed young sculptor he had also worked out an amusing way of walking in the darkness, moving sideways for safety and testing the floor as if sections of it might have been removed. The audience enjoyed itself enormously and the word-of-mouth reports circulating about the production were so enthusiastic that there were regular all-night queues for the fifty tickets not put on sale until the day of the production, and a foreign visitor is known to have paid £25 for two tickets on the small but thriving black market.

Deprived though it was of his personal presence, Olivier's final season was the best that Chichester has ever had. With a new play as ambitious and interesting as *Armstrong's Last Goodnight*, a triumphant revival of a Pinero play that might have seemed either too proscenium-oriented or too theatrical in its subject-matter, and a new farce of such immense audience appeal, the programme had a balance and an excitement about it that has never since been equalled or even emulated. Though Clements has employed some ex-National Theatre stars, including Maggie Smith and Robert Stephens, he has neither put on a new play by Arden or Shaffer, nor had a play directed by Gaskill or Dexter, though Dexter obviously feels such a pull towards open stage conditions that in his National Theatre production of Peter Shaffer's 1973 play *Equus* at the Old Vic, he put some of the audience on stage behind the acting area.

9

The Clements Régime (1):

1966-68

In the press conference held after Clements's appointment had been announced, he was asked whether he liked the shape of the new theatre. His stonewalling answer was that there might be room for experiment. He would study this problem. His main interest was in the possibility of a provincial survival of the old actor-manager pattern and his aim was to appeal to the same level of public taste. He is quoted in the *Sunday Telegraph* of 11 July 1965 as saying 'In the old theatre the actor-managers once dominated – then they dried up, and there was nobody but Olivier, me and Rix. This provincial thing is a new form of it. The wishes and ambitions once inherent are still present, but there were difficulties in realizing it because of the economics of it.' He said that he hoped to present some new plays 'if one can find them' and mentioned the possibility of a longer season.

Later he announced his intention of making the season 'above all a festival of acting' and soon he had evolved the formula which he was to apply methodically to his programme-planning throughout his eight-year régime, with only minor variations. Each year (except 1973) there was a classic – Elizabethan, Jacobean, Restoration or 18th century – and in the first and fourth seasons there were two. Each year without exception there has been a 'modern classic' by Chekhov, Shaw or Thornton Wilder. In five years out of the eight there has been a 'new play', if the category can be stretched to include English premieres of Anouilh. He has done two plays by Pinero, one by Eden Philpotts and one by Robert Sherwood. His first musical production *The Beggar's Opera* (1972) was followed by *R loves J*, the musical adaptation of Ustinov's *Romanoff and Juliet* in 1973. He planned a Goldoni play but replaced it with a Labiche when Danny Kaye let him down. He has produced one play by Ibsen, one by T. S. Eliot and one by Christopher Fry. His contract with the Chichester management gave him a percentage as well as a salary, and his company, John Clements Plays Ltd, was to have first refusal of the West End production of any play that transferred. For six successive years, 1966–71, one of the four Chichester productions did transfer to London, where it was presented or co-presented by his company.

His first season would have lasted sixteen weeks if the opening had not had to be postponed from 24 May to 1 June. In the fifteen weeks it ran, about £133,000 was taken at the box office and the plays were seen by about 138,000 people. He described in an interview* how he planned his first season. 'I started out by thinking of actors, as I did with my season at the Saville ten years ago. I wanted the opening to be a gay, colourful evening. Suddenly the picture came into my mind of Alastair Sim, Margaret Rutherford and Bill Fraser in the three main parts in *The Clandestine Marriage*. They seemed ideal for Lord Ogleby, Mrs Heidelberg and Sterling and the whole project had the kind of smell that I like. I also thought it was high time Celia Johnson played Madame Ranevsky in *The Cherry Orchard*. The problem was to find the right actors for the other parts but I think we've got a very fine cast together. Macbeth I'd played in America in 1962. The day after my Chichester appointment was announced I met Michael Benthall at a British Council reception and he said I must do it at Chichester. And *The Fighting Cock* also was suggested to me.' His stars may have been of a different vintage from Olivier's, but he did collect an impressive number of well known names for his first season including Hugh Williams, Margaret Johnston, Tom Courtenay, John Laurie, Zena Walker and Sarah Badel. Hugh Williams was living in

* *Plays and Players*, June 1966.

Portugal but he was enticed back to the English theatre by
the prospect of appearing again with Celia Johnson who
had starred with him in the West End production of his
own play *The Grass is Greener*.

The Clandestine Marriage by George Colman and David
Garrick had first been produced at Drury Lane in 1766, so
this was its bicentenary. It had caused a rift between its two
authors when Garrick refused to play the part of Lord
Ogleby, an amorous old beau, though he had apparently
written it for himself. Certainly it provides plenty of acting
opportunities and Alastair Sim's performance made the
most of them. As Sheila Huftel wrote in *The Scotsman*,
'Sim does not aim at comedy and pathos; but at comedy
and tragedy. His determination to strike a gallant attitude
is in constant battle with his limbs that cannot bend.'

Desmond O'Donovan, who had done so well in bringing
Trelawny of the 'Wells' out of its proscenium, had been
invited to direct, but he had much more difficulty with *The
Clandestine Marriage*. His original intention had been to
treat it unromantically, highlighting the materialism of the
characters, the extent to which nearly all of them are
financially motivated. And indeed the comedy had been
inspired by Hogarth's *Marriage à la Mode*. Sterling is a
successful, money-conscious London merchant, whose clerk,
Lovewell, has been clandestinely married to his younger
daughter. Anxious to improve his social position, Sterling
has engineered an engagement between his elder daughter
and Sir John Melvil, nephew of Lord Ogleby – they seize on
the opportunity the marriage provides of an easy way out
of their financial difficulties. By any standards it is a highly
money-conscious play, but in spite of the current tendency
to focus on social and economic factors, the production that
emerged was, in John Russell Taylor's words 'a little too
pretty-pretty for modern tastes, which would prefer a little
less of the frills and fancies and a little more emphasis on
the sharp social satire at the expense both of the nouveau
riche merchant class and of the game but tottering aris-
tocracy'. Nevertheless there was plenty to enjoy in the
evening, and the audiences were well pleased. The pro-

duction played to capacity business all through the run.

The decision to do Anouilh's *The Fighting Cock* (*L'Hurluburlu*) was taken within twenty-four hours after the script had been brought to Clements by Sarah Badel, whose father, Alan Badel, had scored a major success as Hero in Anouilh's *The Rehearsal.* It ran for 364 performances in the West End in 1961-2, and opened in New York in 1963, with Badel in the same part. *The Fighting Cock* had been written in 1958 and it is about General de Gaulle's self-imposed exile from French politics, which continued until the Algerian situation provoked him into returning. Ronald Bryden summed the play up as 'treating Mongeneral's relationship with France on a level of "Can this marriage be saved?" It decides that it couldn't, which may be one reason why the play has taken so long to arrive here.' But it had arrived in New York in 1959 in a production by Peter Brook.

Though Anouilh's attitudes are not to be equated with those of his General – *hurluburlu* means scatterbrain – he had not quite come to terms with his own inclination towards authoritarianism. As with the General in *The Waltz of the Toreadors*, he is ambivalent but more sympathetic than adversely critical. If no man is a hero to his valet, an aging general cannot but be slightly ridiculous in the eyes of his family, and cannot be expected to accommodate himself easily to modern life and changing values. Still, as a soldier he won his way into a position where he could expect his orders to be obeyed, so he must be entitled to some respect. Perhaps he demands more than he deserves, but doesn't he receive less? Even if he seems old-fashioned in his ideas about honourable behaviour, isn't there something attractive about the straightforwardness of his principles? Of course he hasn't quite lived up to them in his relationships with women, but men will be men. And how can adequate moral standards possibly prevail in the easy-going anti-authoritarian society of today? Anouilh seems to share a great many of the General's feelings about the indiscipline of the young. The modern world is crawling with what he calls maggots:

Don't you see where all this has got us? To music without the effort of making it, to sport you sit and watch, to books that nobody bothers to read – (they digest them for you – it's easier and it saves time), to ideas without thinking, to money without sweat, to taste without the bother of acquiring it (there are glossy magazines that take care of all that for you). Short cuts to the good life. Cheating – that's our great aim now. I'll tell you, Doctor. It's a maggot's eye view. The worms have brought us round to their wormy ways.

So he enlists the help of local aristocrats and dignitaries to get rid of the maggots and reinstate the old absolutes – 'austerity, discipline and hard work'. Anouilh's sympathy is clearly with the General when he is knocked down by the arrogant son of a war-profiteer. Tarquin Edward Mendigales has gone to bed with the old man's daughter and given his wife a clear view of how tedious her life has become, but hits back hard at the old man's righteous indignation. And again at the end, when the General's private campaign has predictably flopped, when his daughter has left home and his wife is on the point of leaving him, when he has been worsted in an undignified fight with the milkman, we are meant to sympathize with what he says. He is left on stage with his young son, philosophizing and preparing to take part in amateur theatricals :

No Toto, we're going to do something which is also very important. We're going to act our parts just like we do in life. In life, we must have courage, we must have our little supply of Ministafia, and we must act our parts with a smile. 'Man is an animal, inconsolable and gay'. I'll explain that to you too, one day. The main thing is to be able to look yourself in the face in the morning, when you shave.

Ministafia is red blotting paper which he used to chew as a boy to give himself courage.

Anouilh, then, does not make it at all easy for director and actors to achieve balance and focus. Like his other plays *The Fighting Cock* is rich in moments of infallible theatrical effectiveness. The audience will be entertained, amused and often touched, identifying with one or other of the characters. But what does it all add up to?

It costs John Clements no great effort to make himself

convincing in high-ranking military roles, but his performance was too straightforward. That Anouilh makes the
General deplore the national habit of celebrating the fall of
the Bastille indicates the possibility of a bizarre comedy
which was missing in this production, as indeed was all
satirical edge. What was surprising was that the character
of Mendigales, who is the butt of Anouilh's most unam-
bivalently satirical writing, made such a forceful and likable
impression. In fact John Clements's step-son, John Standing
who played the part with enormous charm, almost ran away
with the show. 'I predict a great future for Master John,'
Collie Knox enthused in the *Evening Argus*. 'We have at
last found a young Rex Harrison.'

After *Uncle Vanya* had been produced in 1962 and repeated
in 1963, it was perhaps rather soon to put another Chekhov
play into the Chichester season, and *The Cherry Orchard*
was in any case a strange choice. Act Two, which is set in
a field with an old bench in it, should be easier to stage at
Chichester than inside a proscenium, but all the other three
acts need an indoor atmosphere. Act One hinges on the
family's delight at returning to the old house where the
children have grown up. The lay-out of the house is important, and so is the furniture. Gaev makes a speech to the
book-case. Alan Tagg is much too good a designer to be
unaware of what is required, but all he could provide was
a back wall with a book-case slightly raised on a railed
platform, and shabby furniture dotted about the acting area.
In the last act, after the house and its cherry orchard have
been sold, we need a fairly solid impression of the place
they are having to abandon, and the recurrent Chekhovian
claustrophobia never crystallizes into clearer theatrical expression than in the final moments of the play, when the
frail old servant, forgotten by the family, is locked into the
empty house with no chance and very little desire to get out
alive. It would be difficult to stage this scene at Chichester,
and Lindsay Anderson did not succeed in satisfying B. A.
Young of the *Financial Times*: Firs 'had only to turn round
and go off through one of half a dozen spare exits.'

The *Cherry Orchard* could be staged successfully at

Chichester, but not without devising a convention which would have to inform the style of the whole production. It will be interesting to see whether Chekhov plays are done in the open-stage auditorium of the National Theatre when it moves into its new building. But a director there will presumably have the advantages of a long preparatory period to confer with his designer and of working with a permanent company. If Lindsay Anderson were invited to direct *The Cherry Orchard* again there, he might do it very differently. By 1966 he had done several productions on the small stage of the Royal Court, including Sunday night productions – which had to be done without much décor – but he had done only two plays (*Billy Liar* and *Andorra*) in larger theatres and he was not yet used to handling stars. Like some other directors who have a particular flair for casting, he is at a great disadvantage when he is not free to cast his own productions, and the company Clements had picked gave him a mixture of contrasted acting styles. Celia Johnson had played Olga in *Three Sisters* in 1951 and given an excellent performance as Mrs Solness in *The Master Builder* at the National Theatre in 1964, but side by side with Hugh Williams (who played Gaev, her brother) it was almost inevitable that she would come across as a woman who has spent more time making tea in Kensington than making love in Paris. She was accused of lacking insouciance; the virtues she finds it easiest to convey are self-control, decency, dignity, honesty, fortitude and reliability. Ranevskaya needs to be more passionate and more feckless. If she and Hugh Williams evoked the world of drawing-room comedy, Tom Courtenay, as Trofimov, could not fail to suggest an Angry Young Man no longer quite so young or angry, while a Lopakhin with an Irish accent and a Firs with Scottish speech-rhythms helped to destroy any sense of place or time. The performance that was most richly redolent of Russia at the turn of the century was Bill Fraser's in the small part of Simeonov-Pishchik. Looking back over the reviews one finds general agreement that he provided the most moving moment of the evening when the impoverished old landowner realized that he would never again see Ranevskaya and her family.

The reviews also show that although this was Chichester's fifth season, critics (and presumably audiences) had still not accepted the theatre's shape. 'Things fall apart,' wrote B. A. Young, the *Financial Times* critic. 'It is the theatre's fault. There are too many directions in which people might come on and off, and Mr Anderson uses them all lavishly.' Surely, then, Mr Anderson should have been blamed, and Mr Tagg, who designed it for him. Perhaps they would have come nearer to evolving a solution to the visual problems if they had started, as Olivier and Kenny apparently did, from thinking in terms of the scene changes.* In *Trelawny of the 'Wells'*, too, the scene changes had been the biggest problem, and the solution (which was found quite late in the rehearsals) helped to define the production's style. Nor was there any break in the continuity of the action. As Olivier is well aware,† in producing Chekhov for British audiences today, it is essential to move briskly from Act One to Act Two and, after the interval, from Act Three to Act Four. Whatever the disadvantages of Sean Kenny's décor for *Vanya*, at least there was no interruption of the action, but Lindsay Anderson and Alan Tagg failed to find a satisfactory way of moving from the old nursery in Act One of *The Cherry Orchard* to the field of Act Two. For B. A. Young Act One went 'extremely well' but the atmosphere ebbed away afterwards because 'the visible transformation of the room into the countryside destroyed what had been built up'.

Several critics objected to the invisibility of the orchard, though this does not pose the same kind of problem as the tree in Act One of *The Seagull*.‡ In *Punch*, Jeremy Kingston complained that 'Gaev (Hugh Williams) stands at what is referred to as the window and describes the avenue glittering between the cherry trees: in fact he is staring into an aisle between rows of pink faces'. The one critic to make out a strong case in favour of the production was Ronald Bryden,§ who did not find that the atmosphere was dis-

* See page 40.
† See Ronald Hayman, *Playback*, Davis-Poynter, 1973.
‡ See page 63.
§ This was the year he joined *The Observer* as drama critic.

sipated or the play's structure loosened by the staging. 'On the contrary, I found that it enabled Anderson to bring out Chekhov's vaudeville design of a string of disparate grotesques romping on and off again, and its inability to conjure up the gleaming acres of blossom beyond the windows becomes a positive, startling virtue. One realizes, for the first time, to what extent the orchard is purely an idea, different things to different characters. To Madam Ranevsky it is beauty, childhood, innocence; to Lopakhin, it is the deadly charm of unproductive inertia; to Trofimov, it is the ghost of thousands of dead serfs.'

In 1956 Michael Benthall produced *Macbeth* at the Old Vic with Paul Rogers in the lead. When the production went on a tour of the United States, Clements took over the leading part, and ten years later, Benthall's Chichester production was partly conceived as a reproduction of the Waterloo Road original. As Clements said in an interview with *Plays and Players*, 'We didn't so much change as develop that production. The Chichester stage enabled us to use height as you can't with a proscenium. We told Alan Tagg that we wanted an indeterminate historical period, but primitive, barbaric. There's nothing sophisticated about these people. One of the difficulties is that Shakespeare wrote about them in sophisticated Elizabethan poetry.'

Clements said a great deal more about his and Michael Benthall's intentions in an interview with Sheila Huftel,* explaining why they had cut out the cauldron scenes and reduced the role of the witches. 'Shakespeare called them the weird sisters – not witches. That is why we took out the hubble-bubble of the cauldron scene, which I believe was elaborated by Middleton . . . there are almost identical passages in his play *The Witch*. Lady Macbeth is the spur; but the horse is already running long before he feels the spur . . . It is the suddenness of the murder that unnerves him; something welcomed in theory but baulked in practice. After it, as I see it, instead of shrinking and disintegrating, he gets bigger and more powerful. To be untouchable; to

* Published in *The Scotsman*, 10 September 1966.

be safe . . . He is in blood stepped in so far that he must go on. (That is why I die with blood on my hand) . . . Macbeth is greatest at the end when he rejects all metaphysical aid. "Hang out our banners on the outward wall" is a shout of defiance to God . . . After the murder Macbeth is shattered. Lady Macbeth has to take back the daggers. She has to drag him off, otherwise those knocking at the gate will find him with his hands covered in blood. The time he has to change into his nightgown is just the time it takes Macduff to discover the body. Yet Macbeth comes back, fully in control, goes into Duncan and foolishly spoils Lady Macbeth's careful plan by unnecessarily killing the grooms. Then he makes a rabble-rousing speech that is totally false . . . I see the play as a piece of music, a vast concerto for two pianos, and this demands bravura acting.'

Some critics, like Irving Wardle of *The Times*, saw in the production almost exactly what Clements intended them to see, while others, like Ronald Bryden of *The Observer*, saw the opposite. For Wardle, Clements started as an uninteresting man of action and acquired substance as a result of his crime. 'In the final scenes, instead of shrinking into a monstrous wreck of his earlier self, he reaches his tragic peak – gaining renewed courage when he loses supernatural protection . . . and going down under his assailants while staring fixedly at a bloodstain on his hand.' Bryden's reaction was 'He has a bold new conception of Lady Macbeth. The usual error is to give her the stronger will. Here the will is Macbeth's, hers the appetite that works on it. She is the jackal leading the lion to kill, quickly gorged and sickened by the blood which whets his hunger . . . In complement Clements's Macbeth is strong, decisive, a burly jovial captain given away only by the heavy fixity of his eyes. Banquo's murder ordered, he towers over his wife in tongued scarlet, impatiently turning her questions. No doubt which is leading devil here. But after the banquet he can only decline, the eyes growing more dull, the voice more hollow. The shape of the play is lost, the gradual moulding by passion and events of a wavering, ambiguous character into a hard, irrevocable outline of damnation.' But he did respond to the intention behind Lady Macbeth's feigned faint. 'Macbeth, voicing unctuous remorse for killing the grooms, raises his bloody hands. The circling crowd below, searching for the killer, falls silent. He has drawn suspicion on himself. Glancing quickly round, his wife pitches to the floor.'

Alan Tagg's massive rocky set provided height which helped to clarify moments like this by isolating the hero in clear focus, well above the crowd. There were steps curving upwards away from the stage on either side, with a midway landing on them for intimate scenes. But, as Philip Hope-Wallace pointed out, more effort could have been made 'to exploit this three-dimensional approach'.

Harold Hobson ranked Clements with Olivier as 'one of the two great Macbeths of our time', and for Michael Aldridge, who played Banquo, he was 'the best Macbeth I've ever seen'. Ronald Bryden was less impressed: 'I don't think he's beaten the odds against him – the clipped Restoration voice, the soldierly precision.' And Hilary Spurling of *The Spectator* preferred the silences to the speeches. 'This is an earthbound Macbeth with no streak of the fiend; human and pitiable rather than tragic. We feel for him not in the speeches particularly, more in his heavy brooding pauses; and in the dreadful clunk, clunk, clunk of his boots coming out from Duncan's chamber after the murder, down three steps and stopping . . . Michael Benthall, who directs, has a splendid sense of masculine adventure, blowy nights, dark lanterns, thunderclaps, the clank of iron swords, and everywhere wild thanes out among the heather.'

Margaret Johnston's melodramatic Lady Macbeth came under heavy fire. B. A. Young said 'She spoke most of her lines in a high sing-song, her deep-set eyes fixed on the roof of the theatre'. The balance between her and Macbeth was inevitably upset. What Clements had intended could not come across, even for Irving Wardle: 'Instead of a man with imagination and a woman with none, we are confronted with a brisk unreflecting soldier and a hysterically neurotic wife.' This altered the motivation for the murder. 'The hold she has over Macbeth is that of the neurotic blackmailer. He carries it out partly through ambition but largely to stop her from retiring to bed for a month.'

Clements's first season certainly succeeded in pleasing the public. There were overnight queues at the box office for his *Macbeth* and whereas the total advance sales for Olivier's first season had been £30,000, with Clements's second season, this was the amount of money taken at the box office from sales to members of the theatre society, who had priority booking privileges. When tickets were put on sale to the general public, £100,000 had been taken before the first night of the season, though about £30,000 of this came from bookings for Danny Kaye's appearance in Goldoni's *The Servant of Two Masters*, which was cancelled when he decided not to come.

Meanwhile money was still being spent on the theatre itself. During the winter of 1966-7 £50,000 was spent on a new scene dock, six new dressing rooms, a wardrobe and a laundry, the money coming partly from the Arts Council, partly from donations, subscriptions and fund-raising activities like the racehorse raffles. It is arguable whether increased scenic flexibility was an improvement, but it was made easier to take down sections of the back wall. However it is more difficult and more expensive to make alterations to a theatre built of concrete and steel than to one of bricks and wood, and there was no way of eliminating the awkward steps leading to the scene dock. The theatre had been designed for productions that would not depend on scenery, and no adaption was going to be more than a compromise.

The 1967 season, which lasted sixteen weeks, from 30 May to 19 September consisted of Eden Philpotts's *The Farmer's Wife* (which had been premiered in 1916) Farquhar's *The Beaux' Stratagem* (1707) Shaw's *Heartbreak House* (written 1913-16 and produced in 1921) and Labiche's *An Italian Straw Hat* (1851) which replaced the Goldoni play. So all four plays came within the period that Guthrie had proscribed, 1660-1960. Clements, who had wisely become acquainted with the stage as an actor before directing on it, now directed both *The Farmer's Wife* and *Heartbreak House*.

The Farmer's Wife would infallibly appeal to a wide

public. It makes no more intellectual demands on the audience than *The Archers,* but columnists could be counted on to bracket the production with the National Theatre's revival of *Hobson's Choice* as part of a 'regional revival'. The plays of Brighouse and Stanley Houghton had been produced by our first repertory theatre, Manchester, after it opened in 1908. Though set in Devon, *The Farmer's Wife* was premiered at Birmingham, which opened five years later. When it was revived in 1924 at the Royal Court, it ran for 1,324 performances.

David Benedictus* explains its appeal in terms of the sex war. 'Women love it. They love to see women blatantly using the sneakiest methods to humiliate their eternal enemy. They love to see a man of substance pleading for a wife.' The man of substance is Samuel Sweetland of Applegarth Farm, a widower who relishes the idea of 'a female or two going round my brain like the smell of a Sunday dinner'. He has two pretty daughters and the younger had thought that the boy who wants her was courting her sister :

SIBLEY :   What we're doing, Dick – is it honest?
RICHARD :   As honest as sunlight.

It is very much a parlour play, and Peter Rice's set closed up the open stage with miniature walls. But far from feeling excluded, the first night audience applauded almost every exit, responding delightedly to each hobbling reappearance of Michael Aldridge in ill-fitting livery as the misogynistic gardener, Churdles Ash, the part Cedric Hardwicke had created.

> What are women made of nowadays?
> The same old beastly stuff as they always was.

He comes out with a series of home-made proverbs like 'Them as skims the cream off women stays bachelors' and 'Beer drinking don't do 'arf the 'arm of love-making'. But probably Michael Aldridge's best moment of all was in his paralysed reaction to the news of Samuel Sweetland's long-delayed success in becoming engaged. After standing with

* *Plays and Players,* August 1967.

his hat in his hand for an interminable-seeming silence, he let it fall to the floor. Slowly, carefully, stepping on it, first with one foot and then the other, he ground it into the floor, shrugged, and finally came out quietly with the words 'Go on'.

Diana Churchill was miscast as the housekeeper, and though a programme credit was given to a 'dialect coach', there was no uniformity or even consistency about the Devon accents. Doris Hare, Irene Handl and Margaret Courtenay played the three women who refused to be taken as the farmer's wife. As Thirza Tapper, Irene Handl discovered a deliciously genteel way of coping with lines like 'Hark, do I hear a galloping horse?' and 'You are the first man, Samuel Sweetland, who has accepted my sex challenge'. She even had to say 'This is so sudden'.

Earlier on in his career as an actor-manager, John Clements had enjoyed a tremendous success with Farquhar's *The Beaux' Stratagem*. At the Phoenix in May 1949 he had presented his own production of it, starring himself and his wife, Kay Hammond, and it had run for 532 performances – a record for a classical revival which has never yet been broken and probably never will be, now that the classics can hardly ever be produced except in repertoire. Possibly he was wise not to direct it again himself, but after William Gaskill's revolutionarily and definitively realistic production of Farquhar's earlier play *The Recruiting Officer* at the National in 1963, it was odd that Clements should choose William Chappell to direct, casting Fenella Fielding as Mrs Sullen. Chappell had trained as a dancer and worked as a director mainly in revue, musicals and light comedy. Fenella Fielding can seldom find the courage to be simple and put aside her mannerisms. But perhaps Clements was deliberately opting for the old style, full of artificial flourishes and revue-type comedy.

Four years later, when Gaskill was directing *The Beaux' Stratagem* at the National, he started by writing to the actors, asking them not to think of the play in terms of accents, 'because I knew that was the first thing they would do, playing peasants – put on funny voices . . . What you should actually work at in Restoration comedy is to make people say it as if it was them speaking, which is not easy. You've got to tell them, this is *you* saying it: it isn't Millamant.'* When necessary in rehearsal he would make actors paraphrase the text in their own words: in this way they became familiar with the characters' motives and the progression of their speeches from one point to the next.† This is to start from the playwright's words and to work outwards; the old-fashioned approach was to start from a set of superficial notions about the style, the movements and the manners of the period and then impose them on the characters. The actors would not always understand the meaning of what they were saying, but they could become louder and faster when in doubt, and the audience anyway would be distracted by bows and curtseys, flourishes with fans and comic business with snuff-boxes.

After the progress that had been made at the Royal Court, the RSC and the National in the direction of giving a playwright's words their full value and regarding plays as statements about social behaviour, it ought to have been impossible to start working on *The Beaux' Stratagem* (which is a probing and well-written play about particular people at a particular place in a particular time) from the viewpoint of theatrical style and amusing comedy business, but the Chichester production struck Mary Holland as 'a mincing, teasing, china brittle exercise in coyness', while Irving Wardle complained about Chappell's 'old-fashioned reduction of the characters to laughable bumpkins and gallants, treating the exploits of the fortune-hunters as a leisurely metropolitan affair, lingering over episodes with Palm Court accompaniment from a scratch trio'. Nor did Chappell even secure uniformity of style. John Standing (as Aimwell) played in the grand manner, while Anton Rodgers (as Archer) was trying for a more straightforward *verismo*. Maureen O'Brien (as Dorinda) could not adapt her style to that of Fenella Fielding's arch Mrs Sullen. Once again it was left to Bill Fraser to turn in the most striking performance – as Gibbet,

---

* Interview in *Theatre Quarterly*, January–March 1971.
† See the interview with Maggie Smith and Robert Stephens in Ronald Hayman, *Playback 2*, Davis-Poynter, 1974.

the highwayman. Playing in an eye patch, he kept getting tangled in his cloak and dropping his blunderbuss.

If Shaw wrote the last act of *The Doctor's Dilemma* to prove that he could handle a death scene, *Heartbreak House* was his attempt to prove he could create the kind of theatrical poetry that Chekhov conjured out of prose. But though the play contains some of his best-written dialogue, it falls short of the poetic. Like Shaw, John Clements is essentially prosaic, and in directing *Heartbreak House*, as well as playing Captain Shotover himself, he was reaching out very ambitiously towards the poetic. Chekhov is the least didactic of playwrights and when his dialogue is inconsequential it is because his characters each have preoccupations that are tangential to those of the others. Shaw's habit of mind was incomparably more schematic. Even in writing what he styled 'a fantasia in the Russian manner on English themes' he could not avoid repeating what he had done before with cartoon representatives of the conflicting sections of society. Boss Mangan, the tycoon, is a reprise of Undershaft in *Major Barbara*, while the Burglar is only a variation on Doolittle in *Pygmalion*. As in so many of his other plays, the predatory bourgeois women and the time-serving bourgeois men, do not behave like real-life bourgeois but talk like Bernard Shaw. The Wilde-like aphorisms are sometimes brilliant

> There are only two classes in good society in England : the equestrian classes and the neurotic classes. It isn't mere convention : everybody can see that the people who hunt are the right people, and the people who don't are the wrong ones.

But the attempts at apocalyptic poetry are dispiriting – and in the wrong way.

MRS HUSHABYE : What can it have been, Hector?
HECTOR : Heaven's threatening growl of disgust at us useless futile creatures. (*Fiercely*) I tell you, one of two things must happen. Either out of that darkness some new creation will come to supplant us as we have supplanted the animals, or the heavens will fall in thunder and destroy us.

LADY UTTERWORD : (*in a cool instructive manner, wallowing comfortably in her hammock*). We have not supplanted the animals, Hector. Why do you ask heaven to destroy this house, which could be made quite comfortable if Hesione had any notion of how to live? Don't you know what is wrong with it?

HECTOR : We are wrong with it. There is no sense in us. We are useless, dangerous, and ought to be abolished.

Hector's dialogue would be more acceptable if it were put into the mouth of Captain Shotover, but as Desmond MacCarthy objected when the play was revived during the second world war, 'Neither the denizens of *Heartbreak House*, nor those of Horseback Hall, behaved like the characters in this play when the catastrophe came. On the contrary their sons, in a spirit that was half joy of life, half willingness to die, volunteered at once; their women (enjoying themselves, but that is neither here nor there) ran hospitals and did war work.' But already, in his review of the original production, he had made the essential point : 'Mr Shaw does not know what heartbreak is.' Ellie Dunn is not heartbroken at all, only disillusioned, first to discover that the romantic-seeming Marcus Darnley is only a friend's flirtatious husband and later to discover that the Captain's mystical insights are produced by rum. In spite of himself Shaw is offering us a microcosm of English society, an all too deliberate and wakeful attempt at a nightmare vision of the ship of state foundering – the captain 'is in his bunk, drinking bottled ditchwater, and the crew are gambling in the fo'c'sle'.

Shaw's text, in short, is much less worthy of reverential handling than Farquhar's, but at Chichester it received much more. Technically Clements was quite canny in the way he brought the action further and further out into the arena, and the final act, which is set in the garden, was less effective when the production transferred to the Lyric. But the overall effect of pulling the play out of the proscenium was to highlight its weaknesses. Its appeal is more conversational than visual, and the text emerged with unflattering clarity. It was not even cut, and the performance, which started at 7.00, ended at 10.40. For once there was no thought of 'the last bus to Bognor' – a phrase which trumps many discussions about pace and timing in the Chichester theatre.

Instead of existing and talking, the characters all use their dialogue to explain themselves. Hesione Hushabye is made to say 'But I warn you that when I am neither coaxing and kissing nor laughing, I am just wondering how much longer I can stand living in this cruel, damnable world'. This is not an easy line for an actress to substantiate by her onstage behaviour, but Irene Worth came closer to success than anyone else I have seen, moving slinkily and easily between extrovert friendliness and neurotic withdrawal, between teasing and scolding. Bill Fraser and Michael Aldridge again proved themselves invaluable. Ronald Bryden described Fraser's Mangan as 'a bulging, macassared profiteer who sees himself in the admiring mirror of Kipling, while showing us a Georg Grosz cartoon'. Meanwhile Michael Aldridge succeeded in making Hector Hushabye less of a cartoon than Shaw wrote. Sarah Badel was better cast than she has usually been at Chichester as the innocent-seeming victim of an arranged marriage who matures quickly into a calculating little arranger, while John Clements, disguising his face better than his voice, made a considerable initial impact, but became less funny as the evening wore slowly on, partly because his speeches were becoming longer and more portentous, partly because there was little development or variation in his performance.

During the final month before the first night of *Heartbreak House*, he had not only been running the theatre, directing rehearsals, preparing his own performance and keeping an eye on his production of *The Farmer's Wife*, he had also had to cope with the crisis Danny Kaye caused by withdrawing from *The Servant of Two Masters*. After several meetings with the director, Peter Coe, he had agreed to do twenty-nine performances as Truffaldino, agreed to accept the normal top Chichester salary of £75 a week and booked all nine bedrooms at the Millstream Hotel, Bosham, for himself and his retinue. Then, eleven days before rehearsals were due to start, he telephoned Clements to say that since

Israel was now at war with the Arab countries, he had decided to go out to entertain the troops. 'I feel I can be of moral assistance.' He offered to make good any financial loss incurred by the theatre in refunding ticket money and to fly to Chichester every Sunday to give concerts. There was no evidence that any of the Israeli leaders were eager to have him there, and most of the soldiers did not understand English. Peter Coe flew to Las Vegas, where he was appearing in cabaret, in a last minute effort to persuade him to change his mind, but in vain. Fenella Fielding, who was to have been his leading lady, told the press 'I feel outraged on behalf of my profession and the public'.

Clements and Coe then had to decide between recasting Truffaldino and choosing another play. Apparently either Alec Guinness or Albert Finney would have been acceptable substitutes for Danny Kaye, but none of the well-known comedy actors who wrote or telephoned to offer their services seemed adequate, so it was decided to scrap everything that had been prepared and find another play for the company that had been engaged. It was sensible to look for an ensemble play rather than one which depended on a star personality. And with so little time in hand Peter Coe felt it must be a play he knew already.

The choice fell on *An Italian Straw Hat*, the farce by Eugène Labiche and Marc-Michel, which had been seen in a Theatre Workshop production twelve years previously. W. S. Gilbert had made two versions of it, one with music, one without, and in 1927 René Clair had made it into a silent film. It seemed to be a play that would suit both the audience and the theatre. In essence it is a chase. A bridegroom on his way to the church is delayed when his horse eats the straw hat of a young lady who is out with an officer and who will be compromised if she returns to her husband without it. Prodded by the irascible officer, the groom then sets out to find a duplicate hat, pursued by his bride, his father-in-law and the entire wedding party in eight cabs. From a milliner's boutique he goes on to a Baroness's musical soirée and a flat where a man is sweating in a Turkish bath. Movement matters more than dialogue or character, and Peter Coe took full advantage of the opportunity of letting the action spill all over the auditorium. (In most theatres the actors cannot move about the auditorium without becoming invisible to large sections of the audience.)

Taking his cue either from the nuptial theme in the play or from the critics who had said that Roger Furse's 1962 set for *The Broken Heart* looked like a three-tiered wedding-cake, Peter Rice deliberately cultivated the wedding-cake image, painting the timber white and adding eight flights of stairs, as well as a spiral staircase. As in *The Workhouse Donkey*, there was a band on the top level. In corporal's uniform Bill Fraser marched his squad of soldiers round the gallery; on the middle tier of the cake the bridal suite awaited the couple, while the action swirled all round, characters haranguing each other on the main stage while the wedding party waited impatiently in the aisles.

Peter Coe's idea of treating the characters like marionettes was useful for hustling the action forwards when it was flagging, but the more mechanical the plot of a farce is, the more important it is for the characters to seem real. And, as Philip Hope-Wallace pointed out, the effect of 'respectability in disarray is quite impossible to establish when the general mode of conduct is like chucking-out time at the Moulin Rouge'. The crowd movement was effectively and amusingly choreographed, but, with his cheeks rouged to make him look like a toy soldier, John Standing found it impossible to be convincing as the bad-tempered officer, while Sarah Badel's bride was a painted doll that squeaked Papa. Fenella Fielding appeared under a green wig as the affected baroness who mistakes the groom for an Italian tenor, and her voice is well suited to ambiguous lines like 'I know I do my best work in the bath – so free and untrammelled'. David Bird scored heavily because he was allowed to be human as the unhappy corporal book-keeper who was never given time to change out of his wet underwear, and Michael Aldridge had some extremely funny moments as the bride's horticulturist father wandering in and out with a pot of myrtle. The translation by Lynn and Theodore Hoffmann was full of awkward would-be colloquialisms like 'Shut yerself up, yer little pipsqueak', but there were plenty of visual distractions. In spite of having to work so quickly, Peter Rice used his costumes to provide some striking effects including the black and white wedding group and the soirée dressed in orange and magenta.

The first night audience received the production rapturously and on the final night of the season the ovation culminated in an impromptu celebration. Coloured lights were switched on all over the theatre and balloons were dropped on the audience. Fenella Fielding sang the chorus from her song and the company, after singing *La Marseillaise*, spilled out into the auditorium, shaking hands with delighted playgoers.

One man who was not happy with the trend of current developments was Leslie Evershed-Martin. In the speech he gave at the annual dinner of the theatre society on 29 March 1968 he did not try to conceal his misgivings. 'We have got to remember that box office is not everything. Very popular theatre is not necessarily the finest theatre. We have got to keep on thinking back to the early days and what sort of theatre we said this would be . . . and I look forward to the day when the theatre, the stage, the plays and everything connected with the Festival Theatre will be unique. We have not had this yet except in one or two instances.' He also complained about the habit of clapping entrances and exits. 'I think it is nicer if everyone is so involved they do not want to disturb what is happening.' John Clements was not present at the dinner. One of the local newspapers' reports on Evershed-Martin's speech provoked a letter from the poet Ted Walker, arguing that the theatre's policy could only 'aggravate that special type of philistinism that one meets everywhere in England – that the arts are kept for certain, special occasions instead of being an integral part of everyday life . . . I'm . . . dismayed that the annual festival mounts plays sometimes which, however well acted and produced, are *bad plays* and have been considered bad plays for 200 years or more.'

Clements was not deflected from continuing on exactly the same course. He invited Peter Ustinov to direct his new play *The Unknown Soldier and His Wife*, playing the lead himself, and invited Alec Guinness to direct T. S. Eliot's *The Cocktail Party*, playing the lead himself, as he had at the Edinburgh Festival premiere in 1949. (Rex Harrison played it in the West End.) The second half of the season was to consist of *The Tempest*, with Clements as Prospero, and Thornton Wilder's *The Skin of Our Teeth* with Millicent Martin in Vivien Leigh's old role of Sabina. These stars and these plays attracted higher advance bookings than ever before – £105,000. The takings for the whole season were about £165,000 – representing a twenty per cent improvement on 1967, though the season was only one week longer – 17 weeks.

Success as a raconteur has been bad for Ustinov the actor, and success as both raconteur and actor has been bad for him as a playwright. He was at his best in the fifties, writing *The Love of Four Colonels* and *Romanoff and Juliet* which were produced in 1951 and 1956, and in the film *We're No Angels* (1955) he turned in a more impressive performance than Humphrey Bogart – not only funnier but more solid and interesting. One cannot help liking a performer who obviously enjoys life as much as he does, but he was never self-disciplined or self-critical, and his ever increasing fluency and facility have made him self-indulgently eager for quick returns. He has earned a great deal of money and he likes to win immediate love and laughter from each audience he meets.

His performance in *The Unknown Soldier and His Wife* was never boring and consistently funny but often unsubtle. His direction was slack and indulgent but quite imaginative in its exploitation of the space, situating a steam bath in the stage trap and a cinema screen on the back wall and letting searchlights rove over the auditorium. But his writing was not consistently funny, usually unsubtle and often boring, though the basic idea was an imaginative one. His Unknown Soldier was the Common Man recruited as private soldier by the power-fixated warmongers in successive phases of civilization. Simon Ward played the perennial victim. After a prologue at the cenotaph, we see him as a Roman legionary implausibly using flower power to pacify hordes of barbarians, and then dying at the point of a spear intended for a subversively blasphemous artist. In the retinue of a nobleman on the crusades he is killed by a blow intended for his lord, and as a soldier of Louis XVI he dies as a victim of the revolution. Each death leaves a pregnant wife pensionless and unprotected, providing a series of opportunities for Prunella Scales to be touchingly stoical. But as in Shaw's comic-strip history plays, the victims are less interesting than the villains, and Ustinov had written a series of fat parts for himself as an opportunistic churchman. As a Roman priest he rigged the auguries. Then we saw him as St Benedict, drunkenly distilling his liqueur, and as a periwigged eighteenth-century cleric sipping chocolate in the boudoir. He delivered a Puritan sermon on the danger of debauching babies by exposing them to naked nipples, and finally we saw him as a modern Archbishop never more at home than when in front of the television cameras and disconcerted when the camera pans away from him during the interment of the Unknown Soldier to focus on the young wife who is finally giving birth behind a tomb.

The other actors had to play the other archetypes – the bullying sergeant, the self-intoxicated general, the courteous enemy leader, the scientist who invents ever more efficient means of killing. The idea is full of possibilities, but there are also pitfalls and Ustinov seemed not so much to be falling into them as jumping in joyfully. The archetypes become clichés; the spectacle of the same destructive patterns being repeated in successive eras of history became less tragic than tedious; and instead of finding a style that could assimilate both the seriousness and the farce, he milked each moment for its maximum yield without regard for what was to come next. Even the overall structure seemed unplanned : he spent so long on early history that he had to scamper through the later periods in order to catch up with the present.

In *The Love of Four Colonels* the parodies of different theatrical styles helped to shape and discipline the writing; in this play the writing is extremely flabby. There are epigrammatic squibs, mostly rather damp, like 'It takes so much longer to understand one's actions than to perform them', or 'My son, there is nothing more pernicious than the weakness of the strong'. There are punning anachronisms like 'For coarseness of expression this varlet takes the wafer', and there are dramatizations of corny jokes, as when a depraved crusader is castrated off-stage by a Saracen and his yell turns to a falsetto scream. But we are also submitted to a lot of flatulent philosophizing about the silliness of war. As Philip Hope-Wallace pointed out, the play had very little to say beyond what was going to be said later on in the season by Thornton Wilder in *The Skin of Our Teeth* – that it's all happened before and we shall probably survive to see it all happen again. *The Unknown Soldier and His Wife* even shares Wilder's sentimental optimism, suggesting that perhaps the time will come when the Common Man will refuse to fight, that if only the private soldiers would all go on strike, there could be no war. It is this attitude, together with the cosily comic treatment of the villains, that precludes all serious treatment of its theme.

For most actors most plays become unimportant once the curtain has fallen on the final performance : they forget the lines they worked so hard to learn and never again look at the script. For Alec Guinness *The Cocktail Party* has never ceased to be important. 'It changed a lot of things in my life. You could say it was the seed of my conversion to Roman Catholicism a few years later.' After playing the Unidentified Guest in *The Cocktail Party* at the Edinburgh Festival in August 1949, he played it again on Broadway in January 1950, and when he crossed the Atlantic on the same liner as Eliot they talked a great deal about the play. So after a thoughtful four-month gap between his first two involvements with the play, he then had an eighteen-year gap before his third, in which he went on – intermittently at least – thinking about the play.

'I am quite happy working on this type of stage,' he said, 'but some plays are made for it and others present problems. This one presents problems.' One of the main problems was that although the theme was taken from a play by Euripides and the dialogue written in verse that was influenced – as was everything Eliot wrote – by the Elizabethan and Jacobean playwrights, these elements were carefully concealed behind the surface of a drawing-room comedy. The

Chichester audience had Christopher Fry's programme note to explain how the *Alcestis* had provided the starting-point for the story, but none of the original audiences or critics had recognized its source. In fact Eliot had considerable difficulty in convincing those who knew both plays that there were parallels. And he did not want the audience to be conscious that the dialogue was written in blank verse. But to take the play out of the proscenium frame is to change the balance between naturalistic and non-naturalistic components. Unable to think of the characters as real people in a real drawing-room, the audience is more aware of words, rhythms, imagery and symbolic patterns.

Another problem for both director and designer was to create the intimacy of drawing-room conversations on this wide stage. Michael Warre put very large doors in the back wall, and painted in a good deal of detail, effectively making the whole area look smaller than it was. (When the production transferred to the West End, although reviewers thought it was the same set, it had in fact been redesigned and simplified.) And Guinness, partly through skilful direction, partly through the concentration behind his own performance and the effect it had on the other actors on stage with him, managed to infuse both intimacy and intensity into the two-handed and three-handed scenes which make up most of the action. In Edinburgh and on Broadway his first appearance as the Unidentified Guest had given the audience no clue that Sir Henry Harcourt-Reilly might be a psychoanalyst or psychiatrist; but now his make-up and beard gave him a strong resemblance to Freud himself. Though this may seem unsubtle, the actual performance was precise and delicately shaded. The sudden, brief song and dance he performed with his walking stick seemed to stick out from the surface of his normal restrained demeanour like a gargoyle in a cathedral, but to be equally well integrated. The original director had been very much less assured and stylish in his modulations. He had felt obliged to work for a streamlined continuity, to conceal constructional irregularities. Guinness was professional enough to capitalize on them not only in his own performance but in his production. A farcical element, present in the writing but invisible in the earlier production, came into clear focus. Even Eliot's technical inadequacies as a playwright were turned to advantage. He always found it very difficult to get his characters on and off stage. (In his next play, *The Confidential Clerk*, he contrives an exit for Sir Claude by making him say that he wants to be alone with his pottery.) At Chichester the drawing-room set for *The Cocktail Party* could have only two doors, and Alec Guinness took the opportunity of giving a farcical turn to the awkward comings and goings of the characters at the first of the two cocktail parties in the play. The actual shape of the theatre was forcing him to stylize, but he did so with a very light touch. As Frank Marcus said, pushing the characters out on an open stage 'makes them more rather than less two-dimensional, but it serves a useful purpose in the more formal symbolic passages. His greatest achievement, however, is that he creates a texture of lightness, almost of gaiety, which deflates any latent pomposity.'

In Eliot's previous play, *The Family Reunion*, there are some extremely difficult transitions for the uncles and aunts who are treated sometimes as individuals, sometimes as a chorus. In *The Cocktail Party*, the party guests, Julia Shuttlethwaite, Alexander MacColgie Gibbs and Sir Henry Harcourt-Reilly never have to speak in unison, but there are passages in which their function is mainly choric. For these, in the Chichester production, they donned dark glasses, but, as J. W. Lambert put it, 'To manage on the stage their modulation from upper-middle-class inanity to a businesslike conspiratorial authority needs tact – and gets it : Nan Munro's Julia Shuttlethwaite clucks around her class like a socially agile Lady Bracknell, calms into a celestial district visitor; Hubert Gregg's Alexander Mac-Colgie Gibbs, tipping his bowler, tripping off to the kitchen to whip up his inedible specialities, settles cunningly back into the deft Establishment fixer of some celestial old-boy network.'

Euripides's Alcestis dies so that the gods will prolong the life of her husband, the King, and Heracles, the son of Zeus, goes down to the underworld and wrestles with death before bringing her back to life. In *The Cocktail Party* Sir Henry

Harcourt-Reilly is the Heracles figure. (Except for the S every letter of the Greek name is contained in the English one.) But the Alcestis role is divided between two women, one of whom is set by the priest-like psychiatrist on a course that leads to her death. The play's concern is with the life and death of the spirit, and the situation that Harcourt-Reilly has to change is one in which both women and the man they share are in a state of spiritual desolation or death-in-life. 'What is hell? Hell is oneself. Hell is alone.' (Eliot had wanted to refute the proposition '*L'enfer, c'est les autres.*' 'Contre Sartre', he had once whispered at a rehearsal when this line was spoken.) So Celia Copplestone becomes a missionary and dies a martyr's death, crucified near an ant-hill, but her death gives the others a new start in life. The husband and wife are reunited; the opportunistic young man who has gone out to a film career in California is given something to remember. And in the Edinburgh production the natives who killed her

> *Had erected a sort of shrine for Celia*
> *Where they brought offers of fruit and flowers,*
> *Fowls, and even sucking pigs.*

These lines appear in the text published in November 1949 but were cut out of subsequent editions. The preface to the August 1950 edition says 'certain alterations in Act Three, based on the experience of the play's production were made', and Alec Guinness used the text of this edition.

But the whole structure is too schematic, as if humanity should be categorized into those capable of martyrdom; those capable only of the muddles and compromises of an ordinary marital relationship; and on a still lower level of consciousness, the unredeemable who pursue only their own affairs. The verse is very much thinner than that of *Murder in the Cathedral* but the play is equally non-visual. Eliot was trying to smuggle new elements invisibly into the drawing-room comedy without upsetting its conventions, trying politely to reform what could only be revolutionized.

If the Chichester stage helped to throw the poetry and the symbolism of *The Cocktail Party* into unprecedentedly clear focus, how was it to affect *The Tempest*, in which, more than in any of Shakespeare's other plays, the symbolic design is dominant and the balance between poetry and drama comes down on the side of poetry? There can be little conflict, since Prospero can use his magical powers to anticipate and stultify all the actions of his enemies, and the only interaction between the characters is devised to exteriorize a steady internal impulse towards reconciliation.

From the statement David Jones made about his production before it opened, it was clear that he did not view Prospero either as a god or as a playwright saying farewell to the powers that his art had given him. But he did not seem to have any clear alternative ideas of what he might stand for. 'He is an intensely human man who tries to take on the forces of evil and anarchy in the world single-handed, and who comes to realize that his own nature is as flawed as that of those who have wronged him. In that recognition lies his salvation.'

Except for the shipwreck prologue, the whole of the action of *The Tempest* is set on an unlocalized island during the course of a single afternoon. The downstage point of the Chichester hexagon can readily suggest the prow of a ship, and the stage itself an island, so it would have been interesting to see the play performed on bare boards, as it was originally. Instead, David Jones trustingly put himself into the hands of Ralph Koltai, whose décor and costumes dominated the production without providing what Jones said he wanted : 'a space that gives the marvellous words of the text room to breathe'. Koltai's designs for the previous year's all-male *As You Like It* at the National Theatre had been brilliant, wittily providing a forest made of thin transparent tubes which did nothing to dehumanize the comedy or restrict the actors. The clothes were modern and mostly made of shiny white and silver plastic materials; the furniture consisted of perspex cubes, and the whole series of visual jokes integrated beautifully with Clifford Williams's effervescent production. In *The Tempest* the same formula was applied to a very different kind of comedy. Almost everything was blazing white, with some blacks and off-whites. The main acting area was a huge saucer, with an immense white mobile disc upstage of it and a large globe which opened up at one point to reveal Ferdinand and Miranda inside. 'It looks like a smart piece of fibreglass sculpture,' said Philip French in the *New Statesman*, 'or a giant Brobdingnagian ashtray built by Claes Oldenburg to replace Nelson's column.' Ariel's tight-fitting one-piece silver garment was modern, and Prospero had a perspex wand, but most of the costumes were traditional in their shapes; they were made of modern materials, like Prospero's plastic robe. The logs and the daggers, however, were painted white.

Designer and director seemed to have done their work on separate planets. As Irving Wardle wrote, Koltai 'has furnished an environment appropriate for ritual purification and white magic. But the production itself signally ignores this invitation. For magic it relies on tricks of lighting and electronic sound effects (crassly juxtaposed with pastiche seventeenth-century music) and there is little sense of ordeal either for the lovers or the courtiers.' Other reviewers were equally critical of David Jones's failure to utilize the space provided by the set and the theatre. 'I had high hopes early on,' wrote Michael Billington, 'when Prospero advanced to the promontory of the Chichester stage and raised his wand as if to summon Ariel from the roof of the auditorium, and felt singularly let down when the airy spirit came tripping on behind his master's back. Similarly the Masque arranged by Prospero for Ferdinand and Miranda began promisingly but ended not with a sudden eruption of pagan ritual but with a handful of extras leaping around in modern fish-net shirts.' 'Why has Mr Jones taken so little advantage of his open stage?' asked B. A. Young. 'All he uses is a couple of entrances at the back of the stage and an occasional, not very effective, appearance on a platform above them . . . In spite of the fantastic garbs of Iris, Ceres and Juno, I have never seen their interlude go for less. As for the groupings of the cast, it is too full of pointless or unimpressive moves. When the banquet-laden table is conjured up, the shipwrecked grandees simply stand about as if they were waiting for someone to say grace.'

Clements's Prospero reminded Philip Hope-Wallace of a ringmaster bestriding the stage with boots and a whip, while

three other leading critics were prompted to use the word
'Victorian'. Irving Wardle called him a 'grizzled Victorian
sage . . . missing the mystery of the part' and complained
of his 'morally self-righteous approach to Caliban'. Frank
Marcus said he 'deals with his spirits like a firm Victorian
headmaster with his pupils. He seems slightly ashamed of
his magic and treats it as an off-beat, rather childish hobby.'
Michael Billington also compared him to a Victorian
schoolmaster.

The production and the performances failed to offer any
new insight into the play, unlike Peter Brook's seventy-five
minutes of acting exercises based on *The Tempest*, which
arrived later on in the month at the Round House. Taking
some of his cues from Jan Kott's book *Shakespeare Our
Contemporary*, which puts Caliban virtually on the same
level of importance as Prospero, Brook used both improviza-
tion and lines from the text to show the birth of Caliban
and the way Prospero educates him. But he also used wordless sounds, rhythmic repetitions and possibilities of weaving
lyrical patterns with the actors' bodies and movements to
create a sense of wonder and a genuinely felt celebration of
the brave new world that Miranda discovers. Without
attempting to arrive at a finished production, the evening
showed up the shortcomings of what had been done at
Chichester, cruelly whetting the appetite for something we
are unlikely to see – *The Tempest* at Chichester directed
by Brook.

Tyrone Guthrie considered Thornton Wilder to be the
greatest living playwright and he has had many unlikely
champions, including John Whiting. But when Peter Coe
directed *The Skin of Our Teeth* as the final production of
the 1968 season, Ronald Bryden dismissed it as a 'vulgarization of every expressionist technique of the inter-war theatre
into the commercially upbeat, sentimental razzmatazz of the
Broadway musical', going on to compare it with Giraudoux's
neglected *Sodom and Gomorrah*, 'in which mankind, parti-
cularized in a single couple, destroys the world over and
over out of indomitable egotism. In its black, sophisticated
truth, it makes *The Skin of Our Teeth* look cheap.'

In an essay published in 1942, the year the play had its Broadway première, Wilder made out a case for 'generalized truth'. 'The myth, the parable, the fable are the fountainhead of fiction,' he maintained, going on to suggest that characterization was 'like a blank check which the dramatist accords to the actor'. His first play *The Trumpet Shall Sound* (1926) had been about God's infinite capacity for forgiveness, and *The Skin of Our Teeth* is about man's infinite capacity for survival. History, for him, was the history of the human family. As Irving Wardle has put it, 'It is a strange view of history that ignores everything above the level of domestic mediocrity and annexes every crisis in human survival in the name of the average American family. Wilder may invite his public to consider how insignificant a place they occupy in the universe; but what he shows on the stage is a universe belonging exclusively to them.' Generalization, in fact, leads him to simplification, and congenital optimism to sentimentality.

In *Our Town* (1938) the action had spanned thirteen years, and glimpses into the past and future of the characters had been introduced during interruptions of the action by a Stage Manager who chatted to the audience; in *The Skin of Our Teeth* (as Wilder wrote it) the actors themselves keep interrupting the play they are performing – also called *The Skin of Our Teeth* – to talk to each other and the audience. But in Peter Coe's new production, Wilder's 'history of the world in comic strip' became 'the longest running TV serial in the world, the Homo Sapiens story'. Peter Coe himself rewrote and updated the script, importing television cameras and showing a harassed floor manager trying to pilot a mutinous cast through a series of technical breakdowns during a transmission going out live from the stage of the Chichester Festival Theatre. A control room was built into the gallery above the stage, television commercials were shown in the interval and an elaborate counterpoint was evolved between the technical breakdowns that the show has to weather and the worldwide catastrophes that mankind survives by the skin of its teeth.

Perhaps it was too soon after *The Unknown Soldier and His Wife* for another cartoon strip history. Even the use of archetypes was very similar. George and Maggie Antrobus are Adam and Eve, and then every father and mother in history. George represents the progressive intellect: he invents the wheel and the alphabet, and discovers that tomatoes are edible. Maggie is the eternal mother, the incarnation of domesticity, while Sabina combines the roles of seductress and skivvy. Mr Coe might have presented her as a French au pair girl except that she also represents the Common Man. She has a choric relationship to the audience. She refuses to play scenes that aren't nice, and sometimes endearingly interjects 'I don't understand a word of this play'. The son, Henry, is the Cain figure, and the play came closest of all to *The Unknown Soldier and His Wife* in the last act when he was seen commanding the enemy forces. Perhaps this gave Ustinov the idea.

But a new element was provided by the local allusions. There were television stills of current events in Brighton and Bognor Regis. The Ice Age of Act One was not seen descending on New Jersey, and whereas Wilder's Act Two ended with the arrival of Noah's flood at Atlantic City, the Chichester audience saw it arriving on Brighton beach. In the final act, the siren signalling the end of the world war was the lunchtime hooter from Shippam's potted meat factory.

The production was full of surefire shock effects. Dinosaurs and mammoths ten feet high lurched down the aisle in Act One to escape from the spreading ice, and the refugees included masked African gods and concentration camp victims with crushed cardboard faces. Microphones on long booms dipped over the stage, there was a fortune-teller spotlighting members of the audience, a mushroom cloud was projected and there were references to student power. But it was not so easy to anglicize the homely American idiom of the family, and the casting of Millicent Martin as Sabina upset the balance of forces in the eternal triangle she is meant to create with George and Maggie. As Harold Hobson wrote, 'Unfortunately it is the skivvy part of the character, rather than the siren, that Millicent Martin embraces with enthusiasm. With admirable but mistaken courage she conceives her as a Cockney slut, and even when she wears a shimmering bathing suit in a beauty-contest she remains curiously glacial. It was not thus that Vivien Leigh, with provocative duster and flauntedly short skirts (an enormous excitement twenty-three years ago), played her.'

10
The Clements Régime (2):
1969-71

I can think of nothing that would have made Brecht angrier than the treatment his play *The Caucasian Chalk Circle* received at Chichester and the reactions the production prompted. 'The part of the judge, Azdak,' wrote B. A. Young, 'can be a real star vehicle; and when you have an actor like Topol playing it, it's hard to avoid total surrender to his talent.' Brecht did not want his audiences to surrender but to remain alert and critical, and the notion of putting on one of his plays just because an actor wanted to appear in it would have been anathema to him. It is a weird notion by any standards, especially when the character that the actor wants to play does not appear until after the interval, but Topol, who had already played Azdak in Israel, said it was his favourite role in all drama. It also gave him a chance to reappear in front of audiences that knew him only from *Fiddler on the Roof* and would have been quite unable to recognize him as this lecherous drunk, even if he had not chosen to have his head shaven all over.

Peter Coe's production seemed to appeal to the critics who dislike Brecht, outraging those who take him seriously. The argument of the play is that areas of land, like children, should belong to those who can best look after them. The prologue shows members of a goat-breeding collective disputing with fruit farmers about a tract of land in Georgia which had been used as pasture for the goats before the German invasion, but could now be more productive if it were irrigated. After the land is given to the fruit farmers, a Georgian folk singer is invited to tell the old story of the chalk circle, which will justify the decision. The play which follows is meant to be acted by the peasants of the two collectives. It shows how a kitchen-maid saves a small boy abandoned by his mother when his father, a feudal governor in old Georgia, is murdered by rebellious barons. Eventually the mother starts legal proceedings to get her child back, but the only judge is Azdak, a jokey ex-scribe appointed by the soldiers to replace the judge who has been hanged. He is corrupt and venal but his sense of justice comes into play when he is confronted with the cruel governor's wife and the gentle kitchen-maid. He draws a circle on the ground, puts the child inside it and tells the women to pull it out. When the mother grabs the boy fiercely, he awards him to Grusha, the kitchen-maid, who loves him too much to hurt him.

Without the prologue and the summing-up in the epilogue which were both cut in Coe's production, the play has less point, and without such alienation effects as stylizing some of the movement and putting masks on the cruel characters, including the Governor's Wife, it can become a tear-jerking fable. In the RSC's 1962 production Paul Dessau's astringent music was scrapped in favour of new songs by Dudley Moore performed by Michael Flanders from a wheelchair at the side of the stage. Peter Coe went still further, inviting Joe Griffiths to perform his own songs. Irving Wardle called him a 'guitar-thrumming troubadour who injects the show with the reedy indulgence of pop folksongs', and summed up the style of the whole production as 'taking a middle course which one might call pantomime naturalism'.

In Brecht's own staging of *The Caucasian Chalk Circle* there was a superb scene – which later influenced Peter Hall in his production of *The Government Inspector* – when a large crowd of peasants packs into a small room built well to one side of the stage, milling around the bedside of an apparently dying man. To conceal the boy's identity and give him security, Grusha marries the man in a bedside ceremony, only to find that he has been faking illness to avoid enlistment in the army. Even this sequence misfired in the Chichester production, and Coe must have cast Heather Sears as Grusha without reading Tynan's review of the Berlin production* : 'Angela Hurwicz is a lumpy girl with a face as round as an apple. Our theatre would cast her, if at all, as a fat comic maid. Brecht makes her his heroine . . . London would have cast a gallant little waif, pinched and pathetic : Miss Hurwicz, an energetic young woman too busy for pathos, expresses petulance where we expect her to "register" terror, and shrugs where other actresses would more likely weep. She strengthens the situation by ignoring its implications : it is by what it omits that we recognize hers as a great performance.' Ronald Bryden's verdict on Heather Sears was 'She makes the kitchen girl a kind of wistful Cinderella'. Or as Irving Wardle put it, 'Grusha the dim-witted victim of animal instinct is not shown – and a whole dimension of character, as well as social comment is missing.'

There were those, including Ronald Bryden, who enjoyed Topol's performance. He called it technically monotonous but concluded 'In energy, gusto, and sheer frontal attack on the audience, it is magnificent'. John Barber found it guilty of 'some exaggeration and shouted mugging' and in *The Guardian* Robert Waterhouse said he 'overacted with abandon'. Several critics were impressed by the physical risks he took and the blood that appeared on his hairless head. B. A. Young reported 'He hurls himself about the stage or is hurled about by his tormentors with the abandonment of an all-in wrestler'. But in both Ernst Busch's Berlin Azdak and in Hugh Griffiths's at the Aldwych, one of the most essential qualities was the slyness, and this was missing. As Martin Esslin† said, Azdak is 'a very intelligent man whose roguery stems from the recognition that in a rotten world one has to be rotten to do good. Topol, who bawls the text out at the top of his loud voice, does not only not suggest this sardonic, bitter, penetrating intelligence, he does not seem to understand the lines he is speaking.'

Pinero's first farce, *The Magistrate*, written in 1885, was a

* Reprinted in Kenneth Tynan, *Curtains*, Longmans, 1961.
† Review in *Plays and Players*, July 1969.

great success at the Royal Court in 1895, when audiences had been dwindling. At Chichester in 1969 audiences were not dwindling: advance bookings for the season had been a record-breaking £115,000. But *The Magistrate* was one of the greatest successes of the Clements régime. With his heavyweight casting, his feeling for the Victorian period and his talent for organizing a production as if it were a military operation, he can do this kind of play supremely well.

Some reviewers compared Pinero's farce with Feydeau's, which is undeniably more efficient and quicker-firing, but it probably owes a good deal to Pinero's, as his does to Labiche's. As in *An Italian Straw Hat*, much depends on frenetic activity inspired by an urgent need to keep up a façade of respectability, and as Alastair Sim said, the play was suited to the Chichester stage in so far as the spectators were put into the position of eavesdroppers. John Clements's production took time to let its Victorianism solidify. As he said to an interviewer,* 'We have the whole of the Victorian period to bring to life; its measured pace, its people, and their attitude to it and one another . . . In the few lines before the plot involves them, we can afford to let the play breathe.' In fact there are quite a lot of lines before the plot involves them, and some of the exposition at the beginning of each act might well have been pruned, but the meticulous accuracy of the performances by Alastair Sim, Patricia Routledge, Michael Aldridge and John Clements himself not only prepared very well for the comic climaxes, it prevented the pace from dragging. Alastair Sim, in particular, strengthened a great many weak jokes by underplaying the build-up and then speaking the punch line very softly.

> When he died, she came to England, placed her boy in school in Brighton, and then moved about quietly from place to place . . . drinking . . .
> Drinking?
> The waters

It is a proscenium play which needs doors and depends on furniture almost as much as *The Cherry Orchard*. But

* Caryl Brahms, *The Guardian*, 31 May 1969.

Clements was aware by now of the importance of very quick scene changes, and the squad of stage-hands who rushed on to move the furniture was so speedy that it was usually applauded. Clements wanted the scenery to look painted, like Victorian scenery, and to look dusty. This forced Carl Toms, the designer, to use brighter colours than he wanted to, and to be less realistic. A predominance of sepia tones would have been subtler.

But the comedy came deliciously to life. Mrs Posket provides the springboard for the plot with her determination to conceal her age. She is described as 'the daughter of a superannuated general who abstracted four silk umbrellas from the Army and Navy Stores and on a day when there wasn't a cloud in the sky'. What she does is to subtract four years from the age of her nineteen-year-old son, and the boy himself is among those deceived. This would have been even funnier if a bulkier actor than Christopher Guinee had been playing the part, but there was plenty of entertainment in his drinking and card-playing, in his simultaneous relationships with his music mistress and the housemaid. The scene which may have been seminal for Feydeau's *Hotel Paradiso* comes when his magistrate step-father accompanies him to a bachelor dinner in a dubious hotel and two other couples appear there on the same evening: the boy's ramrod godfather, Colonel Lukyn with his friend Captain Vale, and Mrs Posket with her sister Charlotte, who is Vale's fiancée. A police raid on the hotel leads to a highly theatrical hide-and-seek scene on a darkened stage, with the audience closer than in any previous production to both hunter and hunted as the sergeant smugly listens to the pounding heartbeats of his cramped and cowering victims. After a night in the police station the Army officers seem crestfallen. 'I have been washed by the authorities' snaps the Colonel, and Michael Aldridge had a very disconsolate moment as the Captain when asked whether he was bathed too. 'In Lukyn's water'.

But it was Alastair Sim's evening. In Ronald Bryden's description in *The Observer*: 'Flashing haunted stares and grins of ghastly falsity, trembling jerkily as a skeleton emerging from a cupboard, he wrestles his Calvinist conscience over his minuscule peccadillo with the gloomy, majestic intensity of a Prometheus gnawing his own queasy liver. His weak, appalled murmur of "Horrible, horrible!" as he reviews the events of his night out throbs with the despairing quaver of a hill-strayed sheep.' He had a superbly stricken moment when he tried to shake his adored step-son and succeeded only in shaking his own jittery body. Night after night Maggie Smith used to watch from the wings, marvelling and wondering how he did it.

She had just had a baby. She was to have rejoined the National immediately afterwards but when Clements heard from Olivier that she was not going to, 'I leapt to the telephone and said "Would you like to come to Chichester?" She said "Yes, I'd love to". I said "What do you want to play?" She said I've no idea. And I racked my brains and said "Do you know *The Country Wife*?" She said "No, I don't". I said "Read it tonight". She rang me the next morning and said "Yes please".' But it was not really a good part for her. Margery Pinchwife is an innocent, ingenuous country girl who almost accidentally learns how to use her native wits to elude the clutches of the man who married her because he thought her too ignorant to be difficult. It was an ideal part for Joan Plowright who had made a great success in it at the Royal Court, where it was her first lead, in 1956. Maggie Smith naturally seems more knowing, more sexually sophisticated and quick-witted. But of course she is too good a comedienne not to give a very funny performance, and she was particularly good in the letter scene. As Felix Barker described it, 'Sprawling over the table, mob cap, bent head and flowing dress somehow all congealed in a riot of animal enthusiasm, she scrawls across the page. All we seem to see is a quill emerging from the flurry of white to stab the inkwell.'

But all her best moments came when she was either alone on stage or doing something independently of the other actors. As Ronald Bryden saw, 'The production has been assembled as a vehicle under her, with little regard for the play's real shape and no attempt to integrate the cast's wildly varied styles. It's an *ad hoc* ragbag, deliberately loose enough to accommodate the Sparkish of Hugh Paddick, camping in his best *Round the Horne* manner; Gostelow's Pinchwife, a broad, sturdy, Molière caricature; and Patricia Routledge's Lady Fidget, an artful but private miniature, built on a tiny facial tremble betraying the tension between lust and gentility.' There was also Keith Baxter's minutely naturalistic Horner and Renee Asherson's demurely restrained Alithea.

Even a director in control of his own casting would find *The Country Wife* a difficult play, partly because of the complex interweaving of the three main strands in the plot and partly because Wycherley borrows from such a variety of sources, including Terence, Molière and possibly Juvenal.* But a clear pattern does emerge. If Pinchwife is exorbitantly mistrustful, Sparkish is absurdly gullible, while Horner, like so many Restoration rakes, provides the playwright with a means of indulging his own sexual fantasies at the same time as tilting satirically at the hypocrisies woven into the fabric of normal social behaviour. Lady Fidget and Mrs Squeamish are as eager as Margery Pinchwife is for extra-marital sex, and far more dependent on Horner's stratagem of pretending to be a eunuch, for this serves not merely to make their husbands suspicious but to make the relationships socially acceptable. But the acid at the centre of Wycherley's comedy was covered with several layers of sugar-coating in Robert Chetwyn's Chichester production. As Hugh Leonard put it, 'He has given us a romp, a bedroom farce in which not one face is pock-marked or grimy, nor one dress-hem splashed with the mud of the London streets in which it has trailed . . . Movement and the use of music combine to soften the play's over-riding misogyny; there is no hint of real squalor, either moral or physical.'

Similarly, the production of *Antony and Cleopatra* was built around Margaret Leighton, who had first been approached by Clements to play the part at Chichester three seasons previously, and they made what she described as 'a loose gentlemen's agreement' that she would when she could.

* See Kenneth Muir, *The Comedy of Manners*, Hutchinson, 1970.

Clements maintained that she was one of only three English actresses capable of playing Cleopatra, though she was now in her late forties. Edith Evans had been in her late fifties when she played the part opposite Godfrey Tearle, but historically Cleopatra was only about thirty-eight when she died, and the action of the play spans about ten years. Antony should be in his early forties when the action begins, and she should be fourteen years younger.

Shakespeare wrote the part to be acted by a boy and therefore contrived the action so that the lovers need never be seen embracing. Though Peter Dews, the director, and Margaret Leighton would both have preferred to avoid clinches, John Clements was in favour of them, and he had his way. This, unfortunately, highlighted the question of age. Once again critics brought out the dreaded word 'Victorian'. 'When they declare their love to each other,' wrote Milton Shulman in the *Evening Standard*, 'it is with the grandiloquent gestures of opera, the fierce clutching and clawing of passion that mocks at understatement and laughs at reticence. For my taste these early protestations of love at times achieved a Victorian dramatic splendour that bordered faintly on the risible.' Helen Dawson agreed : 'For me the physical and emotional dependence of Antony and Cleopatra does not lie in melodramatic Victorian stage clutches and whites of eyes turned to heaven.'* Clements, predictably, spoke forcefully, but was more convincing as a soldier and as a suicide than as a man who would give up half the world for a woman. Margaret Leighton was at her best in her long death scene and in the comedy, some of which was cleverly distilled out of the dialogue, some of which was imposed. Several critics singled out the moment when she strode forward to swat a fly.

The play might at first seem very suitable for the Chichester stage, but there are fifty-five scenes in it, and though Chichester, like Stratford, Ontario, is ideal for about twenty-five scenes, there is, as Michael Langham has pointed out,† a great danger of boring the audience when actors troop in, play a brief scene and then troop off as another

* Review in *Plays and Players*, September 1969.
† *Theatre Quarterly*, July-September 1973.

lot troop in to play the next. At both theatres the problem lies in the distances they have to walk between the entrances and the centre of the playing area. The dramatic points that the separate scenes are making need to follow rapidly on each other's heels, and in the Stratford production of *Antony and Cleopatra* the solution was to block very carefully, using extra lighting, so that as one scene finished, that area of the stage could be blacked out and the spectators' attention switched to another area, without having their view of it by actors making their way towards the nearest exit.

Peter Dews was invited to direct the Chichester production because he had already done the play on television – where this problem does not occur. You simply cut from one camera to another. In the theatre his solution was to use a permanent set consisting of a structure which would be used as the tomb, and he insisted that it should be possible for actors to make entrances over the top of it. But the tomb scenes are so important that it had to be brought as far downstage as sightlines would allow, and not enough space was left downstage of it. The galley scene was somewhat cramped, and, more important, there was not enough space left to use lighting and groupings as effectively as they could otherwise have been used to evoke an atmosphere of Egyptian heat, with hot bare feet on cool stone floors. As it was, the palace seemed to be rather a small one. And though it had seemed a good idea to have a cloth at the back which could sometimes suggest the sky, sometimes a sail, it turned out to have a deadening effect on the sound.

Between thirty and forty-five minutes had to be cut out of the running time, and some of the characters were cut. The dying Antony advised Cleopatra to trust none about Caesar but Dolabella, instead of recommending Proculeius, as most Antonys do. And as in the Olivier-Vivien Leigh production of 1951, the scene was cut in which Cleopatra sends Caesar a dishonest inventory of her possessions, leaving half her fortune unmentioned. To cut this is to put her hesitations about suicide in a false perspective and to make her less of a deceiver than Shakespeare wanted her to be.

If the 1970 season got off to a rather lame start, it was partly because Peter Coe, only three years after Danny Kaye's defection had aborted his production of *The Servant of Two Masters*, again had bad luck in losing his star. For over eight years – since March 1962 – when he had worked with Christopher Plummer and Sean Kenny on a production of *Macbeth* at Stratford, Ontario – the three of them had wanted to work together on *Peer Gynt*. They had discussed it in great detail, and a West End production had been planned with the Bernard Delfont management, only to fall through. Then, after the Oxford University Press had commissioned Christopher Fry to do a new verse translation of the play, a script was sent to John Clements, who was eager to première the new version at Chichester, and at last it seemed the Coe-Plummer-Kenny ideas could be put in front of a public. Plummer signed a contract to open the 1970 season in the part and they started working together again. But four weeks before rehearsals were due to begin Plummer had to go into hospital with an embolism of the lung. Although he did not want the production to go ahead without him, it had now had so much press publicity that Clements was unwilling to postpone it, and when Plummer came out of hospital he seemed fit enough to go ahead. They worked together for another week until a recrudescence of his illness made it impossible for him to continue, and there was no alternative now but to find another actor who would be willing to take over not only the role but also the ideas that he had played no part in shaping. Final arrangements were made with Roy Dotrice only two days before rehearsals started, and in the hasty revision of production plans, several unconsidered ideas somehow crept in. They had not previously intended to use either period costumes or photographic projections, for instance.

The basic idea for the production was a very clever one which was seriously underrated by the critics. It was that all the events of the play after Ase's death take place inside Peer's mind. That he imagines himself to be an attractive extrovert while actually being an introvert who has no success with women, and that instead of travelling all round the world he stays at home, imagining himself having ad-

ventures at different stages of his later life – a rich businessman who traffics in negro slaves, a phoney prophet in an
asylum, an old man confronted with the Button Moulder
who accuses him of wasting his life. The Great Boyg was
presented as a mirror image of Peer, and he had no changes
of make-up, suggesting the onset of age only with his voice
and a few props like the shawl he tossed aside at the end to
dismiss the old man that he had become inside his own
imagination.

This conception of the play is less tragic than the usual
one, for nothing irreversible happens – Peer is left at the
end with his life still in front of him. But, properly staged,
the Button Moulder sequence need be no less frightening.
Even if what we are seeing represents only what Peer is
imagining, we are still open to all the impact the two actors
can make on us. This approach could also give the play a
contemporary twist by inviting us to be conscious of the fact
that we are watching an actor acting out a fantasy – which
is what the whole play amounts to. This is not even to
violate Ibsen's intentions. Most directors have been far too
literal and naturalistic. Two years before the first performance in Christiana (1896) Ibsen was writing to Grieg asking
for a great deal of the action to be backed by music and for
the monologue in Act Two after the scene with the three
cow-girls to be accompanied by chords 'in the style of melodrama'. Most of the fourth act was to be cut for the performance and he asked for it to be replaced by 'a substantial
musical tone picture to represent Peer Gynt's wanderings
about the world'. The tableau with Solveig, now a middle-
aged woman, singing outside her house was to be presented
to the audience 'like a distant dream-picture'.

Staging *Peer Gynt* today it could be disastrous not to
treat the trolls and the Great Boyg as subjective phenomena.
They correspond to fantasies inside Peer's mind prompted
by the idea of having sex with the cow-girls. But if Peer, on
one level, represents the actor, on another he represents the
poet. Like all writers, Ibsen was fundamentally concerned
with his own predicament, and, like *The Tempest*, the play
is partly about the playwright's power of fleshing imaginary
worlds into three-dimensionality and about the relationship

between the lunatic, the dreamer and the poet. As W. H. Auden has pointed out,* one of the difficulties of translating *Peer Gynt* is that Norwegian has different words for the self which is conscious and the self of which it is conscious. The writer, like Peer, enjoys flying away from objective reality, but he refuses the operation that the Troll King wants to perform on his eyes. To identify with the self-sufficiency of animal nature is a pleasure; to be incapable of anything else would be an intolerable restriction. Peer has not only a duty but a real desire to be true to himself. But he cannot do that without the co-operation of other people, and because he feels rejected by the villagers, the death of the mother who was his playmate in acting out the stories he made up is a blow from which he may never recover.

Coe's conception, then, is an interesting one, but the physical realization it received at Chichester did not do justice to it. It is always hard to represent village life without using a regional accent, but the Yorkshire moors are very remote from the Norwegian mountains both emotionally and in folk culture, and the broad accents ruined the effect of Christopher Fry's unpretentious and workable translation by imposing alien rhythms and cadences. It was good to have the millionaire's yacht represented by the toy boat from the first scene and to have no Arabian steed but the old rocking horse. And as always, Peter Coe provided plenty of eye-catching choreography in the crowd-sequences. But there was an undeniable element of musical comedy vulgarization in both the costumes and the staging, especially in the scenes with the villagers and the trolls. Incorporating Roy Dotrice's idea of mounting one of the women from behind produced a realistic moment that stood out like a nude in a pantomime.

The big hit of the 1970 season was Robert Bolt's *Vivat! Vivat Regina!* which went a long way towards repeating the success of his earlier historical play *A Man for All Seasons.* All thirty-four Chichester performances were sold out in advance, and when it transferred to the West End it broke all box office records at the Piccadilly Theatre.

* *The Dyer's Hand,* Faber, 1963.

Robert Bolt wrote the part of Mary Queen of Scots for Sarah Miles. Before they were married she had said to him 'You may be a good playwright but you're not a great playwright because you've never written a really meaty part for a woman'.* In *Vivat! Vivat Regina!* he wrote meaty parts for both queens, but anyone who read the script before seeing the production would have thought that Mary's was the meatier, though it was Eileen Atkins, returning to Chichester to play Elizabeth, who made the stronger impression. Originally Bolt had not wanted to have Elizabeth in the play at all, and when he found she was necessary, he wrote the part so economically that Eileen Atkins found it intriguing. 'Whereas if I'd been sent the script and asked whether I'd like to play Mary, I'd have said "Yes, but slice, slice, slice, slice. It's overwritten." He wanted to put so many ideas into Mary's mouth that on the page it reads beautifully, but that isn't what anyone would actually say. But with Elizabeth you thought "Oh yes, somebody would talk like that, never wasting a second".'

Once a history master and never a historian, Bolt was not interested in exploring beyond the accepted clichés of the two queens' characters. More inclined to pathos than tragedy, he shows Mary as a victim of her passions and Elizabeth as a victim of her success in subduing hers. The narrative is neatly structured, but its fulcrum is a character-contrast which is too schematic. The plot centres almost entirely on personal relationships, which are angled to reveal the unhappiness of both queens. This derives from the inability they share – however different the reasons are – to enter into normal family relationships. Elizabeth is seen as the archetypal stateswoman, denying the female side of her own nature for political reasons; the price Mary has to pay for indulging and fulfilling herself as a woman is nothing less than the loss of her kingdom. But Elizabeth will not consent to have her killed until there is proof of her complicity in a plot against her life, and what makes Mary knowingly sign her own death warrant is the news that Elizabeth has effectively sealed her off from contact with her own son. The turning point comes immediately after

* *The Guardian*, 9 October 1970.

Walsingham's line 'It is my mistress who has exercised a mother's office towards your son'.

As Irving Wardle said, the play is 'an immensely skilful piece of cosmetic surgery: adding the common touch and the free-flowing action of epic theatre, while leaving the assumptions of heroic costume drama untouched'. The fact that the play grips the audience so powerfully makes it all the more of a pity that Bolt did not take advantage of his opportunity to penetrate more deeply into his fascinating material.

Originally the play was to have been directed in the West End by Peter Hall for the Tennent management, and contracts were signed with both Sarah Miles and Eileen Atkins before this plan was dropped. The play was then offered to Chichester because Eileen Atkins's agent, Larry Dalzell, was also Peter Dews's agent, and knew that Dews was helping Clements to look for a second play for the first half of the season. The deal was then set up in the space of thirty-six hours. Bolt's initial intention was that the play should be produced unnaturalistically, like a show at the end of a pier, rather in the style of *Oh What a Lovely War*. Dews dissuaded him by saying 'They'll call it *Oh What a Lovely Whore*'.

Dews was also instrumental in creating a new and highly effective ending which was improvized out of the necessity of bringing Elizabeth downstage after her final seated line and before the curtain calls. To show the face of the woman that Elizabeth had become to the whole audience, Eileen Atkins contrived to turn her head once to either side during her long weary move without in the least coming out of character. Like Dews, she benefited greatly from her experience of the theatre, projecting every line with firm precision, and catching the exact measure of Elizabeth's growth from pallid, demanding, unspontaneous girlhood to an exhausted and almost bored resignation to the lifeless life for which her birth had destined her and her talents equipped her. Sarah Miles was hampered by a French accent which made her vocally monotonous, but there were some fine supporting performances. Richard Pearson was memorable as a high-pitched Cecil who patiently played the role of male confidant to keep Elizabeth's ear open to his shrewd advice.

It is not often that three productions in a season of four are damaged by indispositions, but Laurence Harvey, who was to have played Sergius in *Arms and the Man* and Face in *The Alchemist* was injured less than a week before *Arms and the Man* was due to open, while rehearsing *The Alchemist*. 'Edward Atienza and I had to jump up and down with joy on an eighteen-inch board which simulated a four-poster bed . . . the board, the actor – everything – came down on top of me.' He went on rehearsing, but when his leg was afterwards X-rayed he found he had fractured his knee-cap. The production opened on 8 July with his understudy, James Warwick, who had played Darnley in *Vivat! Vivat Regina!* and had been rehearsing the small part of the Russian Officer. On 7 August Laurence Harvey returned to the cast, leaning on a stick and holding his right leg straight, but restoring some of the balance that had been missing for the first four weeks.

There had been only two major London revivals of *Arms and the Man* since the Olivier-Richardson-Margaret Leighton production at the Old Vic in 1944. It is not one of Shaw's better plays, and in a letter to Alma Murray in 1904 he dismissed it as 'flimsy, fantastic, unsafe stuff'. When it had first been produced in 1894, the Serbo-Bulgarian war had been over for only eight years, and though Shaw had wanted to puncture romantic attitudes to militarism, he had not intended to satirize Ruritanian romances like Anthony Hope's *The Prisoner of Zenda* (the novel which started the vogue for them but had not yet been published). On the contrary, the play was meant as a serious social comedy about real people. The models for Bluntschli and Sergius were Sidney Webb and Cunningham Graham, while Raina was based on Annie Besant.*

Though more straightforward than it might have been, John Clements's production was more stagey than it should have been. As Frank Marcus wrote, it 'sends up the roman-

* See Shaw *Collected Letters 1898-1910*, Ed. Dan H. Laurence, Max Reinhardt, 1972.

tic posturing more than is necessary for us to see the silliness of it', or as B. A. Young put it, 'The flapdoodle is in the words, and if it's underlined by excessively colourful playing, as it mostly is here, we're unable to take it seriously.' John Standing seemed rather suave for the doggedly middle-class Bluntschli, but Sarah Badel gave a good impression of the cool commonsensicality underneath Raina's affectation, though without making much effort not to seem Anglo-Saxon.

As a curtain-raiser Clements directed Chekhov's twenty-five-minute farce *The Proposal*, encouraging Sally-Jane Spencer, Edgar Wreford and Richard Kane to play rapidly, energetically and broadly.

Bad luck struck even more aggressively at Peter Dews's production of *The Alchemist* : James Booth, who had been engaged to replace Laurence Harvey as Face, had two weeks of rehearsal but at the end of them he was still unsteady with his lines. So Peter Dews, who as director of the Birmingham Rep had already earned himself a reputation for taking over parts at short notice, had to play Face himself for the first couple of weeks. But probably it would not have been one of his better productions even if rehearsals had gone smoothly. Although he had already directed the play on television, he did not seem to welcome the opportunity of bringing out Jonson's verse to full effect on the open stage. The play is a farce but a very serious one, a savage satire on the quacks and con men who take advantage of their victims' greedy willingness to believe in nostrums and panaceas. But Peter Dews aimed no higher than the belly laugh. He made it into yet another Chichester romp, a sort of Jacobean *Lock Up Your Doctors*.

Coleridge described the plot of *The Alchemist* as 'absolute perfection for a necessary entanglement, and an unexpected, yet natural evolution'.[*] It offers the possibility of building considerable suspense about whether the tricksters will be found out. As Subtle, Edward Atienza aimed his impersonation straight at the audience, transforming himself with

[*] S. T. Coleridge *Literary Remains*, ed. H. N. Coleridge, 4 vols., 1836-39.

virtuoso speed from a conjuring alchemist to a fidgety friar,
flagellating himself with his rope belt, and then to a
scampering dwarf in a plumed toque. But the nervous
energy was that of the performer who might fail to impress,
not the deceiver who might be caught and punished.

Nor did Dora Bryan seem happy in the role of Dol
Common. She went through the motions, manipulating her
skirts with calculated vulgarity as she stamped in and out
of the privy or up the stairs of Carl Toms's ingenious set
built on two levels, with nine entrances. But one never
believed in her as a prostitute capable of gaining power
over William Hutt's rather small-scale Sir Epicure Mammon
by flaunting her sexuality at him.

For 1971, the final year of his second three-year contract,
John Clements planned a season in which the choice
of plays was more unadventurous and the list of actors more
impressive than ever before. There were to be revivals of
The Rivals, Caesar and Cleopatra and *Reunion in Vienna*
and another English premiere of an Anouilh play, *Dear
Antoine*. But the company was to be led by John Gielgud,
Edith Evans, Margaret Leighton, Joyce Redman, Nigel
Patrick, Anna Calder-Marshall, Renee Asherson, Beatrix
Lehmann and Clements himself. Robin Phillips, who in
1970 had directed Albee's *Tiny Alice* for the RSC and
Ronald Millar's *Abelard and Heloise* in the West End and
on Broadway, was to stage the Anouilh and the Shaw, while
Clements took charge of the other two plays. But since the
last season he had spent two months in hospital and he was
obliged to relinquish *Reunion in Vienna* to Frith Banbury.

In 1970 Gielgud had agreed that in principle he would
like to come to Chichester if Clements could think of the
right play; and when Clements became involved in adapting his production of *Arms and the Man* for television with
Anna Calder-Marshall as Raina, it struck him that she
would make a good Cleopatra opposite Gielgud's Caesar.
Knowing that Margaret Leighton wanted to come back to
Chichester, he offered her the irresistible opportunity of
combining the romantic heroine of *Reunion in Vienna* with
Mrs Malaprop in *The Rivals*, a very unlikely character role

for her. The eighty-three-year-old Edith Evans had not acted in the theatre for three years, but two days after he had found himself sitting on a committee with her and told her that she ought to come to Chichester he was sent a script of *Dear Antoine* and realized he had a part he could offer her.

His production of *The Rivals* was a glaring example of what can happen when a good play is staged for no other reason than to hold out a loose posy of star performances to an uncritical public. John Clements had already played Sir Anthony Absolute in 1956 and the part suited him better than any other he had played in Chichester. He is capable of irate fulminations of stentorian sermonizing, comically punctuated with self-contradictions when warmth and paternal affection peep through the thunderclouds. But whereas the production of *The Cocktail Party* had profited from being directed by its leading actor – because of Guinness's mature appreciation of the play – *The Rivals* did not, because Clements had no clear idea of what he wanted to do with it.

Margaret Leighton could probably have been a very good Mrs Malaprop, infusing new vitality into the too-familiar lines. Occasionally she did bring them to unexpected life, but she obviously needed far more help than she got from a director. It has always been a difficult play to integrate, with the elaborate seriousness of the Faulkland-Julia sub-plot underpinning the high comedy – and sometimes poking through – and today there is the additional complication of an unusually wide stylistic gap between the older and younger generations of actors. To give himself even a chance of pulling the disparate elements together, a director would need to start off by making his mind up about what sort of play the twenty-three-year-old Sheridan had written. Is it a soft-centred and mindless romp or a hard-edged and searching satire? Does it have a deep social sub-text? How serious is it in making statements about snobbery and servants and money? Is Lydia Languish meant to seem as absurd as her name? Is Sheridan poking as much fun at the affectations of the young as at the self-importance of the old? And as much at the tottering pillars of society as at the country bumpkin and the trigger-happy Irishman who try to crash their way in? How does one prepare for the facile drift into a Mozartian reconciliation that provides a happy ending without blunting the abrasive satire on romantic attitudes to love? Not that a director needs to provide definitive answers to these questions, but unless he can give his cast some indication of having thought about them, his production will have no organic style, only a series of separate attempts at affecting or evading the stylishness that used to be thought appropriate to eighteenth-century comedy.

Clements's own inclinations were towards the traditional approach but throwing cohesion to the winds he also seemed to have made a point of being tolerant to the actors who wanted to do something different. Margaret Leighton is no Margaret Rutherford and her personality forced her to a less blustery delivery of the malapropisms than we usually get. Vocally she proved herself well capable of what the part requires, 'ranging', as Irving Wardle put it, 'between a butch rasp and an angry squawk, with a slightly tipsy middle register', but her exorbitant make-up, her Rabelaisian padding and her pantomime costume negated all the subtlety of the performance. In *The Guardian*, Catherine Stott said she was 'got up like a liquorice allsort'; and for B. A. Young she looked 'like a boxer dog in a fuzzy grey wig'. Peter Egan made a pleasant Jack Absolute, not without panache but not overdoing it. Edward Fox gave a twitchily post-Freudian interpretation of Faulkland, while his Julia (Joanna David) not knowing how to respond to it, discreetly ignored it. Clive Swift's realistic Bob Acres was handicapped by an almost surrealistic wig. As Catherine Stott said, 'This was the most refined interpretation in the least refined part', but 'he looked in the duel scene for all the world like Toad of Toad Hall in a marmalade bouffant wig'. There was a lot of facial over-reaction in Angela Scoular's attractive Lydia, and Hubert Gregg was miscast as Sir Lucius O'Trigger, lacking the quarrelsome fire he needs. There were liveried footmen to shift the furniture in the scene-changes and of course the production succeeded in looking pleasingly polished.

'In *Dear Antoine*', as Robin Phillips says, 'there isn't a character who has heard of sweat', but though the first act turns out to be an act of a play that Antoine, the playwright-hero, has not yet written when we meet him in Act Two, the fiction of the whole play is one that could have been improved enormously by the introduction of a little non-theatrical reality. *Dear Antoine* was Anouilh's first play after three years in which he wrote nothing, and seven years (1962-9) in which none of his work was staged in Paris, but it is closely in line with his earlier writing, which had often featured a play within the play, trying to focus the contrast between reality and theatrical artificiality, but usually making reality look fairly theatrical and artificial.

Had the ingenious idea behind *Dear Antoine* been fleshed out more substantially, the play would have been well suited to Chichester's open stage, for the basic intention is to let the playwright alive in his mountain retreat working with the actors and actresses who have needed him and made love to him without liking him. The first act is set in 1913 in a Bavarian castle where the dead man's friends, ex-wives, mistresses and their children gather to hear the will; the dead man's will issues from a gramophone. We then find we have been watching a company of Comédie Française actors, and the second act moves us back in time to show the playwright alive in his mountain retreat working with the actors to make a play out of their reactions to the news of his death. One of many effective moments came when John Clements, with a suavity more suggestive of Noël Coward than Jean Anouilh, lay down on a table, inviting them to imagine he was his own corpse, and to improvize what they would say. But though the play bites quite hard, its teeth are all false. The stagey aging star, the hypocritically affectionate mistress, the doctor, the lawyer, the academician, the critic are all cardboard clichés we remember from Anouilh's other plays and we even get one of his starry-eyed young girls. Perhaps the two-dimensionality of the characters would have mattered less if we had been watching them through a proscenium; J. C. Trewin found the play better after the production transferred to the West End.

Edith Evans had never played on an open stage before and did not like the idea. 'I like more illusion in the theatre . . . With the audience so close it is rather like someone holding the arm of a painter as he works.' But she had no trouble in projecting her performance into every corner of the hexagon, and Ronald Bryden found that the most moving moment of the evening was when she leaned on her fellow-actors' arms at the curtain-call. But she could play only for the first two nights. She was taken ill before the Saturday matinee and had to let her understudy, Peggy Marshall, take over for the rest of the run.

'Camp is esoteric – something of a private code, a badge of identity even, among small urban cliques . . . A sensibility that, among other things, converts the serious into the frivolous . . . To emphasize style is to slight content, or to introduce an attitude which is neutral with respect to content. It goes without saying that the Camp sensibility is disengaged, depoliticized – or at least apolitical . . . Camp is a vision of the world in terms of style – but a particular kind of style. It is the love of the exaggerated, the "off", of things-being-what-they-are-not . . . Today's Camp taste effaces nature, or else contradicts it outright. And the relation of Camp taste to the past is extremely sentimental . . . When something is just bad (rather than Camp), it's often because it is too mediocre in its ambition . . . The hallmark of Camp is the spirit of extravagance . . . The whole point of Camp is to dethrone the serious. Camp is playful, anti-serious . . . One is drawn to Camp when one realizes that "sincerity" is not enough. Sincerity can be simple philistinism, intellectual narrowness.'

I have started this section on Robin Phillips's production of *Caesar and Cleopatra*, with some extracts from Susan Sontag's 1964 'Notes on "Camp" ',* because I believe camp is the indispensible word for describing it, but one needs to be fairly careful to exclude some of its associations and to emphasize that a camp approach to some of Shaw's plays might be not only justifiable but appropriate and even

---

* From *Against Interpretation*, Secker and Warburg, 1967.

necessary. Shaw himself was playful, seriously committed to dethroning the serious, and while John Clements's 1972 production of *The Doctors' Dilemma* succeeded because of its sincere, solid and almost stolid straightforwardness, *Caesar and Cleopatra* calls for a very different treatment. If Robin Phillips's production failed, it was not because it was too extravagant.

But as in Ralph Koltai's designs for *The Tempest*, a scheme that had been worked out for another play was being applied to one it did not suit. Robin Phillips's Strat-ford-on-Avon production of *The Two Gentlemen of Verona* had been set by a swimming pool with the young people in dark glasses and swimsuits, and the old ones in transparent shirts. Silvia tore a page out of *The Tatler* to give Proteus a photograph of herself, the Duke was a cocktail-sipping university don, and Proteus's and Julia's separation was backed by the tune of 'Now is the time for us to say good-bye', rather in the way that the Eton Boating Song was to creep in as background music for the rowing in *Caesar and Cleopatra*. Not that the Shaw text deserves more reverence than the Shakespeare, but it is hard to move gracefully between larkiness and prose loquacity.

Besides, all these gas-filled balloons were tied down to a single serious point which was made with a heavy-handed insistence. On the programme we read the lyric of a song that started 'Listen hear the sound the Child awakes . . .' The performance started with voices shouting 'Hail Caesar' to a background of 'Rockabye Baby'. The nursery image was then established on the all-white set with a cut-out wooden rocking horse, and Cleopatra came on trailing a rag doll which was later to be thrown aside when, after prolonged sessions of Caesar's avuncular tutoring, the child queen matured into a queenly woman and ordered her first murder. The prologue and the Sphinx were cut, and from the high white balcony that replaced the Sphinx two play-ground slides skeltered symmetrically down to the stage. In due course Sir John Gielgud would be seen making his first descent into the palace by sliding down one of them. Appolodorus also slid down to dive through a paper hoop into the waters of the Eastern harbour, and Sir John bobbed

across the stage on a large white hopper balloon when
Caesar was meant to be swimming. If nursery games became too dominant it was partly because the basic idea of
an old politician creating a woman out of a girl had been
cultivated in an atmosphere of game-playing. On the first
day of rehearsal Robin Phillips threw a small red ball to
each member of his cast in turn, calling out their character's
name so as to identify them to each other. When the ball
was thrown to Gielgud he dropped it.

Compared with Vivien Leigh's Cleopatra, Anna Calder-
Marshall's was almost asexual, which tallied with Shaw's
writing and Robin Phillips's intentions, but probably not
with Shaw's intentions. When Gertrude Elliott (Mrs Forbes
Robertson) was playing the part at the Savoy in 1907 he
wrote to advise her to lie across the Sphinx's paws as if it
were dandling her. 'If I had such a pretty profile and such
pretty arms I would not throw them away by being propped
up against the beast like a sack of apples.' And at the copyright performance he had had the part played by Mrs
Patrick Campbell. Nor could he have wanted the Caesar-
Cleopatra relationship to be quite so one-sided as Robin
Phillips made it. As Ronald Bryden put it, 'his relationship
with Egypt becomes purely that of an imperial Mr Chips
with nothing to learn himself'.

Visually, of course, it was essential to disregard Shaw's
intentions, which were described elaborately in the stage
directions and demand an elaborate set, full of opulent
purples and golds. The designer, Carl Toms, felt that
Egyptian trimmings always look ugly on the stage and
thought that by dispensing with them completely he would
leave the audience free to concentrate on the words. But by
the end of the rehearsal period he had provided plenty of
other distractions. Hubert Gregg's Britannus wore a bowler,
a blue serge toga, a snake-clasp belt and carried a brief-case
and an umbrella. Harold Innocent's Pothinus wore a black
Afro wig and Pat Nye's Ftatateeta a white Afro wig. The
furniture consisted mainly of white cubes which were moved
about by hoola-hooping mini-skirted soldiers. And at the
end Caesar struck camp in a striking camp way, wearing a
white toga and facing the white-robed crew of his white

ship while Cleopatra wore black, and white rose-petals rained down from the roof.

Robert Sherwood's work has never reached a wider audience than when he wrote speeches for President Roosevelt during the war, but his 1931 play *Reunion in Vienna*, written as a vehicle for Alfred Lunt and Lynne Fontanne, was a great success. If Alexander Woollcott is to be believed, it brought Lunt nearer than any other play did to drying. The plot is about a Hapsburg heir currently working as a taxi-driver, who returns incognito to Vienna in 1930 to celebrate the centenary of the Emperor Franz Joseph and to see his former mistress, now the wife of a psychiatrist. He stays at a hotel he knew well. Curious to discover whether the owner, Frau Lucher, still wears the red drawers that became so well known to her visitors, he lifts her skirt to find out. One night the actress, Helen Westley, forgot to put her red drawers on and Lunt had some difficulty in coming out with his next line, which was 'Thank God there's one thing in Vienna that hasn't changed'.

After *Arms and the Man* Clements knew that Ruritanian settings appealed to the Chichester audience, but it would be difficult to strike an effective balance between satirizing the genre and indulging the audience's nostalgia. The play itself is ambivalent – not without irony but also liable to gaze, as Frank Marcus put it, 'with tourist awe at the vanished royalty of Europe'. The waltzes, the gipsy fiddlers, the dance music coming over the old-fashioned wireless sets, the elegant uniforms and ball-dresses catered for a theatrical appetite that had been starved for years, and at the box office the production was one of the two greatest successes of a very successful régime.

But the way attitudes have changed in the last forty years towards both psychiatrists and princes made the rather flat dialogue look particularly dated. Michael Aldridge needed all his charms to stay on an even keel as the understanding husband. He knows the danger of losing his wife to her ex-lover would be all the greater if he took advantage of her hesitation about whether she should go to the reunion for former members of the exiled Austrian court. In his best professional manner he advises 'Sing, dance, flirt, relax, let yourself go'. But Nigel Patrick did not quite have enough charm to sweeten the boorish brutality of Rudolf Maximilian's behaviour. He knocks valets about and slaps ladies' faces. There was one effective moment when Margaret Leighton stood with her back to the audience, taking her first long look at the man her lover had become after so many years of not seeing him. But their protracted first kiss produced a hiatus of inaction which made his ensuing line unintentionally funny. 'How long has it been since you were kissed like that?' And there were baroque reminiscences like the one of a hot summer night when he made love to her in a forest surrounded by a whole symphony orchestra, with every musician blindfolded.

11
The Clements Régime (3):
1972-73

Clements was reappointed this time only for a two-year stretch, but not surprisingly the success of the 1971 season had its effect on advance bookings for 1972. The season opened on 4 May, and by 11 April £150,000 had already been taken. If the list of stars was less impressive, it was not unimpressive: it was headed by Joan Plowright, John Neville, Millicent Martin, Richard Chamberlain, Anna Calder-Marshall, Anthony Hopkins and Robin Phillips, who was to play Dubedat in *The Doctor's Dilemma* as well as directing *The Beggar's Opera* and *The Lady's Not for Burning*. The other play was *The Taming of the Shrew*, the first Shakespeare since the 1969 *Antony and Cleopatra*.

Like *Caesar and Cleopatra*, but with far less justification, *The Beggar's Opera* was given a camp production. Even if Brecht's version of it had never been written, the indictment of bourgeois society in it would be clear enough, and the piece is disembowelled if it is reduced to a series of production numbers, revue-type jokes and picturesque theatrical effects. With a perverseness that may not have been entirely disingenuous, Robin Phillips's production began with a new ballad, sung to the tune of Bobby Shaftoe:

> *In the action of our play*
> *See the poor who slave away. . . .*

Each stanza was punctuated with a rude gesture to Robert Walpole, the originator of stage censorship, who was represented by a slumped figure in a chair. This set up a false perspective for everything that was to follow: the poor in the play do not slave away but use their wits to avoid the slavery that a flagrantly unjust society would otherwise impose on them, and the deceptions they practise are modelled on those of their social superiors.

This basic point cannot emerge clearly if the audience is repeatedly having its elbow jogged to admire clever pieces of superimposed comedy. A coach in progress was suggested by swirling umbrellas and jogging movement; the whores made a musical comedy entrance featuring a hobby-horse, a wheelbarrow and a clothes-basket; and Macheath escaped from Newgate prison by tipping a bucket of water from the balcony and pretending to swim through it, to the tune of 'Speed Bonny Boat'. Maggie Fitzgibbon's affectedly genteel Mrs Peachum broke into a vaudeville tap-dance, and after Filch had withdrawn to talk business with her, a curtain was thrown aside to reveal that he was half way up her skirt. And when Polly poured her poisoned drink over the flowers, a cloud of pantomime smoke erupted from them. There was also a swing, which was used only once. When Polly sang about swinging on the gallows she jumped up to make an obvious visual pun.

It is always a problem to find a cast that can act and sing, and there was the rest of the season to consider. John Neville was more effective in his other part – Sir Colenso Ridgeon in *The Doctor's Dilemma* – than as the highwayman Macheath, and Millicent Martin, who was engaged only for *The Beggar's Opera*, disappointingly applied her usual pertness and her usual singing style to Polly. The best singing performance came from Angela Richards as Lucy Lockit and the best acting performance from Harold Innocent, who made a greasily malevolent Peachum, but could only put over the songs in a sub-Rex-Harrison manner, emphasizing the rhythm.

The Doctor's Dilemma is a prosy and discursive piece of writing, but in one important way it was well suited to the Chichester stage. Reviewing the 1906 production at the Court Theatre, *The Times* critic, A. B. Walkley was reminded of *An Italian Straw Hat* by the way that 'our bevy of doctors career through the play, always together (one wonders what became of their patients), like the wedding guests'. The practical advantage of this, on an open stage, is that the men set the scene. Whether we are asked to imagine that we are in Sir Colenso Ridgeon's Queen Anne Street consulting rooms, in Richmond at the Star and Garter or in Louis Dubedat's studio, it is those well-fed, formally dressed bodies and those self-satisfied, argumentative voices that will create the atmosphere the plot needs, especially when we are watching well-cast heavyweight actors. Sir John Clements himself played Sir Ralph Bloomfield Bonington, with William Mervyn as Sir Patrick Cullen and Michael Aldridge as the avid surgeon Cutler Walpole.

As in Clements's previous Shaw productions, *Heartbreak House* and *Arms and the Man*, the words emerged with exemplary clarity, and this time Irving Wardle was prompted to salute the Chichester Theatre: 'It preserves the tradition of eloquently literate speech. It is Britain's main stronghold of the spoken word'. Critics greeted the production with superlatives. Frank Marcus called it 'by far the best production of the play I have seen', and in *The Sunday Times* J. W. Lambert wrote 'the play seems to have here more substance than I have ever found in it before'. He applauded the nuances in the central characterization. 'At first Mr Neville draws a man pleased with his achievements but suspicious of his wordly success, tired and infected with a loss of purpose. Then he subtly lets us see determination creeping back under the spur of belated sexual arousal.' He saw Joan Plowright's level gaze as evidence that Jennifer Dubedat was an accomplice in her husband's dishonesty, while other critics noticed other subtleties in other performances. While urging Jennifer to remarry, the dying Dubedat clasped the hands of Ridgeon, the man who could have saved his life but wanted to marry his wife. The death scene was staged exactly as Shaw intended it – as a performance.*
'He is quite conscious of the fact that he is dying splendidly as an artistic spectacle (note how thoroughly he understands Ridgeon's allusion to "the dying actor and his audience"),

---

* Letter to Siegfried Trebitsch, 17 May 1910.

and he wants the world to hear about it. The newspaper man is the world : it is the presence of that spectator which has nerved him to the scene.' Even the apparent age-gap between husband and wife was turned to advantage. Joan Plowright made no attempt to look younger, and her age added irony to her dry-eyed acceptance of his death. One was reminded of her stoicism as Sonya at the end of *Uncle Vanya* on this stage when she was ten years younger. As Bloomfield Bonington Clements showed, as he had shown in *The Rivals*, that he could play a booming part with delicate self-irony, and the excellent Michael Aldridge gave us a clear impression of his technique with the scalpel every time he lengthened his wrists in greedy anticipation of another opportunity to cut out a nuciform sac.

The disadvantage of a book like this is that it can never convey the full feeling and flavour of a theatrical experience ; it can only describe what happened on stage, analysing the ideas in the play, production and performance, and the way they were realized. The disadvantage of most productions by our most erudite director, Jonathan Miller, is that while the ideas behind them are almost invariably fascinating, their relationship to what actually happens in performance is often unstructured and haphazard. The productions often get better reviews than they deserve because it is so easy for a critic to write interestingly about the ideas, passing briefly over any inconsistencies in the way they are applied and any patchiness in the resultant performance. Critics also tend to be intimidated by the cultural references Miller throws out in his statements to the press. He says that his main inspiration is often visual and that for *The Taming of the Shrew* he considered and rejected Hogarth's work before settling on a Veronese fresco and Brueghel's *Peasant Wedding* as containing the quality he most wanted to recreate. If everything in his production had had the same vitality and earthy solidity, it would have been very good, but in practice a more important influence seems to have been Germaine Greer's remarks about the play in her book *The Female Eunuch* : 'Kate has the uncommon good fortune to find Petruchio, who is man enough to know what he wants and how to get it. He wants her spirit and her energy because he wants a wife worth keeping. He tames her like he might a hawk or a high-spirited horse and she rewards him with a high-spirited love and fierce loyalty'.

According to Miller, Shakespeare's main interest was in the power-structure within the family. Who has the right to rule and what are the duties and obligations attached to ruling? But whereas Shakespeare obviously felt that women have as clear a duty to be submissive as men have to be responsible, Miller confused the basic issue by exaggerating the contrast between Baptista's household and Petruchio's in terms of luxurious comfort and Puritan austerity. Kate is shown as the spoilt product of soft living and fine clothes; Petruchio has close-cropped hair, practical leather clothes and says grace piously before eating. As Irving Wardle pointed out, Anthony Hopkins's performance in the part was rather like a continuation of his Frankford in John Dexter's production of Heywood's *A Woman Killed with Kindness* at the National. But to characterize Petruchio like this is to drain a great deal of the humour out of the aggressiveness he affects to subdue his shrewish bride. Instead of putting on a performance to get his own way, he seems to be motivated by a sincere, semi-religious disapproval of her way of life. Joan Plowright's shrew was correspondingly lacking in shrewishness. Of course it's unfortunate when a character is labelled with a one-word temperamental summary, and a performance centred solely on shrewishness would be as bad as one of Molière's Alceste aimed exclusively at misanthropy. However, Shakespeare was writing about a tough but likable and humorous soldier subduing a virago into an obedient wife, and Miller showed us instead a spoilt but likable girl deciding to humour a difficult husband. Shakespeare's Kate is defeated; Miller's yielded voluntarily, and the change in her was less marked than the change that came over Petruchio once he had reduced her to tears.

Any serious approach to the play would have to make sense of everything that Shakespeare wrote, including the induction that presents the story as a performance given in front of a drunken tinker. As in *The Caucasian Chalk Circle* the prologue was cut, and Miller, though excessively serious in most areas, was frivolous in others. Petruchio enters with his servant Grumio on his back and when they ring at the entrance of Baptista's house we hear a modern door-chime. The puzzling business of the piggy-back ride was never justified and never explained until an interview revealed that it had been Anthony Hopkins's idea. Grumio, he said, 'is an army-type batman, but because the two have soldiered together there is no longer the gulf between servant and master. They are good friends and this fact leads to what some people have said is a rather quirky reaction from Grumio when he sees his master is happily married . . . the fun and scrapes they enjoyed together and the in-jokes that have developed between them are finished.' The interview also revealed that so far as Hopkins was concerned, Kate's shrewishness was only superficial. 'The woman he chooses has a personality problem . . . she perpetuates an image because she believes a certain kind of behaviour is expected of her. Her real personality is discovered at the end, and she and Petruchio developed a great deal of love and respect for each other.' This is to apply modern psychology to a character conceived in terms of Elizabethan psychology, to weaken the play's central conflict and undermine its basic point. If the shrew is only a shrew because she thinks she's expected to be, very little taming is necessary. The big moments – like the first confrontation between shrew and tamer and his insolent arrival at the wedding in grotesque clothes – lost most of their comedy and their tension.

The starting point for the production of *The Lady's Not for Burning* – the only contemporary verse play apart from *The Cocktail Party* to have been staged at Chichester – occurred when John Clements took Richard Chamberlain out to lunch. Clements asked him whether there was any play he particularly fancied, and when he asked for *The Lady* Clements said he had already been thinking about it. As a proposition for the Chichester stage it could hardly be more different from *The Cocktail Party*. The setting is medieval, the action is comic-heroic and the verse could not possibly be made to sound like prose. The original production had been at the Arts Theatre in 1948 with Alec Clunes as Thomas Mendip, but it was the Gielgud revival of 1949 which made the play famous. Both Gielgud's performance and his production were influenced by a misleading remark of Harcourt Williams's: 'If you do not play it with artlessness, the simplicity of children, you will be lost'. Oliver Messel's sets helped to create an atmosphere of golden enchantment, and Fry's intentions were submerged. Wanting to capture the opposite mood of post-war disenchantment, he had centred the play on the bitterness of a suicidal soldier returning from the war. A less romantic production in 1949 would probably have been less successful, but an open-stage production in 1970 should have provided an opportunity to see whether the play could stand up to a rougher, more realistic treatment. The basic question is whether the chirpiness of the language and the easy brightness of the rhythms would in any case dilute the bitter into a lemonade shandy.

Apart from one musical pun, when he brought in the tune of 'Keep the Home Fires Burning', Robin Phillips checked any inclination to camp the play up, but his production did not answer the question. Richard Chamberlain may, as he said, have been thinking of the soldiers who were fighting in Vietnam, but his performance as Thomas Mendip was more sweet than sour or bitter. He was engagingly modest in holding himself back from striking romantic poses, but fairly perfunctory in the disgust he professed at the carnage he had witnessed. A professional soldier is paid to kill, and on this level he was no more convincing than Gielgud had been. Anna Calder-Marshall was energetically sincere in her protestations about not wanting to be burned, but she found the part too slippery and undefined to get a firm grip on it, and it was the character actors who provided the main pleasure of the evening – Michael Aldridge as a fidgety major with wispy hair sticking out from a balding crown, Harold Innocent as a petulant, dyspeptic Justice of the Peace, and Leslie French as a meek, emaciated chaplain. But again, as in the Gielgud production, the villains were far too charming to be frightening and far too amiable for all the uses of this world to seem anything like as weary, stale, flat and unprofitable as Thomas Mendip would have us believe.

Ever since the Canadian company's guest season in 1964 there had been discussion about a winter season. Heating had been installed and it was very wasteful to leave the theatre empty for over thirty weeks each year, but, with no assistant, Clements was unable to cope with more work than he had already, and it was not until the Christmas of 1972 that an extra-curricular production was mounted – a two-and-a-half week season of *Toad of Toad Hall* starring Harold Innocent and Christopher Guinee and directed by David Conville, who had been presenting the play regularly for a Christmas season in London ever since 1960 and latterly been directing it himself. About £20,000 was taken at the box office.

After *Dear Antoine* Anouilh had promised Clements 'My next play will be for you'; apart from that the only conceivable reason for starting his final season with *The Director of the Opera* was that it provided him with a long leading part that commented aptly on his situation as retiring director. Antonio di San Floura, an aging hero with a strong resemblance to the General in *The Fighting Cock* and the playwright in *Dear Antoine*, is reaching the end of his career as director of an Italian opera house – though Anouilh hardly troubles to sustain the pretence that he is not thinking of a French theatre. Sometimes he even refers to the operas as plays.

The Times review ended with an inspired misprint referring to the play's 'maudling development'. This is the *mot juste*, neatly combining references to sentimentality, muddliness and conservatism. There is no spine of developing plot, no moral centre, no clarity of statement, and when John Clements and the director, Peter Dews, went over to see the Paris production, they thought it so bad they were in two minds about whether they ought to go ahead with their own. It is a solipsistic play, an interview the playwright conducts with himself, illustrating it with scenes that dramatize his persecution complex. Bathing his feet in a tub of

hot water in the opening scene, Antonio tells us that he has
no other way of disposing himself to feel kindly towards his
fellow-creatures. Without making any ambivalent suggestion
that the man may be a scatterbrain, the play which follows
acrimoniously attempts to vindicate his misanthropy. His
family exists in the play only to plague him. One daughter,
unhappy in a love affair with a married man, tries to kill
herself, and after her father has saved her life his concern is
rewarded by an accusation of indifference. Another daughter nags him to buy her a new coat, which prompts his
extravagant and predatory wife to make the same demand.
'My mink is worn to the back binding'. His loutish, fur-
coated son refuses to work, fathers an illegitimate child,
expects his father to buy the mother off and, like Mendigales
in *The Fighting Cock*, knocks the old man down. His
equally self-indulgent youngest daughter takes advantage of
her pregnancy to throw a series of tantrums. 'You're selfish,
the lot of you. You're thinking of yourselves, not me'.

None of this is subtle enough to need commentary nor solid
enough to warrant discursive interpolations, but Antonio's
attitudes are explicated further by providing him with a
stooge, a subservient business manager who has to ask the
right questions, and listen to the long answers. The character
is called Impossible. What is the root of all Antonio's tribulations? It must be 'the impossibility of getting out of one's
skin and really giving'. Accordingly the second half of the
play puts that proposition to the test. Trying to act generously to a total stranger, Antonio offers to divorce his wife
and marry his son's discarded mistress. He is rebuffed. He
tries to offer sympathy and understanding to three of the
chorus who turn up in *Boris Godunov* costumes and settle
down on the floor of his office, occupying it as part of a
strike. He gets nowhere. He tries to make friends with the
business manager he has always taken for granted. He discovers that Impossible has cordially disliked him for seven-
teen years.

A scene with a dancer from the *corps de ballet* who offers
herself to him is intended to establish the admirable will-
power of a man who decides not to go on taking advantage
of his power over these young things, and at the same time

to strike a note of poignancy – aging hero bids farewell to pleasures of promiscuity. But the worst scene of all was the proposal of marriage to his son's girl-friend – another recurrence of the evergreen Anouilh innocent. Impossible tells Antonio he is cheating 'I rather thought you had a fancy for the girl, sir : it would make a good theme in the opera in the old tearjerker style'. This is as near as Anouilh can get to telling himself that he is cheating.

It is very much a proscenium play. Neither Alan Tagg's set nor Peter Dews's production took advantage of the Chichester theatre's shape, and scenically the best moment came in a sequence they had thought up together to replace the awkward ending Anouilh wrote, in which Antonio presides over an opera rehearsal from an armchair in the centre of the stage while the other characters sing to him. At Chichester a miniature opera house auditorium, complete with chandelier, was built into the inner stage, and as Clements walked up finally towards it in full evening dress with silk hat, cloak and cane, it lit up.

There were plenty of flaws in Jonathan Miller's production of *The Seagull* but it cannot be faulted for being either romantic or old-fashioned, and Clements's willingness to employ directors whose approach is totally different from his own could not have been brought more sharply into focus. This was a production that recoiled vigorously against the tradition of centring the play on Nina and extracting a maximum of pathos from the way she is casually destroyed. She became almost peripheral : the emphasis was shifted to the conflict between Trigorin and Kostya, not as males fighting for both women but as writers. Trigorin represented complacent conventionality; Kostya the apostle and the victim of Darwinian truth. His play that is performed in Act One is a frightened celebration of evolution; the suicide in Act Four is a defeated recognition of the survival of the fittest while the weakest go to the wall. As Eric Rhode pointed out* this Kostya did not seem to shoot himself

* In a discussion with the author on *Arts Commentary*, BBC Radio 3, 25 May 1973.

because of his failure to win back either his mother or Nina from the pusillanimous writer who has exploited both of them without loving either. He was a victim of his own philosophy. The main turning point in his progress towards self-destruction came when Nina repeated what he had written about the death of the world in the speech she had delivered in Act One.

Whether this interpretation of the play could ever be embodied successfully in an actual production we do not yet know. Miller did not have the technical savoir-faire to bring it off at Chichester. He failed to create an impression of space or place. He failed to eliminate distracting mixed metaphors from the translation. 'Like a deer badgered by the hounds'. He used the vomitories in a distractingly random way. In Act One, for instance, Nina enters out of breath and leaves in an equal hurry. He brought her on through a vomitory and gave her an upstage exit in the opposite direction. Had he perpetrated the opposite inconsistency we would at least have seen more of her face, but he confused us about relative positions and showed us her back both times. Nor did his casting of Nina and Kostya allow them to lose their hopefulness as they lose their youth during the years that elapse between the beginning and end of the play. Kostya should be twenty-five when the play begins and Nina a young girl, perhaps about nineteen. But Peter Eyre, though he is an excellent actor with all the requisite intelligence, intensity and capacity for ascetic dedication, never looked less than thirty-five, while Maureen O'Brien did not look much less than thirty.

Irene Worth and Robert Stephens, as Arkadina and Trigorin, were splendid in the physicality of the tussle on the chaise-longue. He was excellent in his bouts of self-loathing and his apprehensive reaction to the shot in Act Four could not have been better. Penelope Wilton was a good Masha who got the production off to a very good start with her abrasively ironic delivery of the second line, 'I am in mourning for my life'. But the component elements neither came sufficiently together nor created a satisfactory starkness by staying sufficiently apart.

Compared with most of the plays that Clements had put on, *The Director of the Opera* and *The Seagull* both did poor business at the box office, but the last pair of productions in his final season, *R Loves J* and *Dandy Dick* compensated with near-capacity business, despite the drubbing that *R Loves J* received from the critics. In 1956, while the Cold War was still on, Peter Ustinov's play *Romanoff and Juliet* had seemed amusingly up to date; in 1973 the book that he derived from it, Alexander Faris's eclectic music and Julian More's lyrics all gave the impression of having been written a long time ago, and the references to Spiro Agnew and Jane Fonda seemed to have been added at the last minute in a desperate effort to restore the vanished effervescence, as did a topical reference to an Investigating Committee checking on the American Senate.

Altogether this was a lump-fish caviar and cream musical, bursting with clichés, many of which would have already been clichés in 1956, and since then we have had enough jokes about the Russians and Americans to take the edge off any appetite for them, especially now that the two sets of values and the two ways of life no longer seem as different as they did then. Nevertheless we get Hooper Moulsworth, American Ambassador to this rather improbable Central European country called Concordia, threatening its President: 'I'll have you bombed by mistake even if we have to apologize afterwards'. We get his wife enthusing: 'I love history; it's so old.' And on the Russian side we get a renegade spy and a nubile Party-liner who strides about the stage in pillar-box red, fulminating about decadence and perpetrating mispronunciations like 'disgriceful' and 'tchaotic'.

As in *The Unknown Soldier and His Wife* Ustinov makes perfunctory gestures in the direction of political satire, using them to camouflage the sentimentality of the underlying attitudes. Concordia is presented as a happy country whose citizens could have gone on enjoying a quiet life of eating, drinking and making love if only they had not been constantly invaded and occupied. The action of the musical depends on the rivalry of the Russians and Americans who are both over-eager to befriend Concordia: the Americans feel 'committed to come to your assistance, even against your better judgment. That's how generous we are'. But there is only a very far-fetched analogy between the two world powers and the two warring households in *Romeo and Juliet*. A love affair between the Russian Ambassador's son and the American Ambassador's daughter would create neither a diplomatic disaster nor a situation that the President could easily exploit, though in the musical version he does not seem even to be trying to exploit it for his own ends, or for any reasons other than to contrive a happy ending.

The character Ustinov wrote for himself, the General who is the President, has a great many lecture-type speeches full of jokes on his usual level, and altogether the part is more a vehicle for a heavyweight comedian than a character for an actor. Topol found there was very little he could do with it. He speaks English with a pleasing accent and a thick axle-grease charm oozes upwards under steady pressure through the baritone relaxation, but the cheerfulness which had seemed so admirable when emerging from under Tevye the Milkman's tribulations in *Fiddler on the Roof* rapidly became monotonous when all he had to do was stand on the two hexagonal steps at the centre of the stage like a human fountain of friendly rapport with the audience. His best scene gave him a series of alternate visits to the two embassies on either side of the stage and a series of conversations about code. This was effective vaudeville, mainly because of his progressive drunkenness, but the plot failed to supply him with any motive for telling the Americans that the Russians had broken their code or the Russians that the Americans knew or the Americans that the Russians knew they knew.

In the West End production of *Romanoff and Juliet*, two structures like doll's houses on either side of the stage represented the two embassies, with a picture of Lenin in one and of George Washington in the other. Tim Goodchild's Chichester set replaced Washington with an astronaut, and made very clever use of restricted space with interiors that pushed forward and manually operated flaps that folded over them, painted to suggest exteriors that might belong to a European market square. The upper rooms had to be replaced by balconies, but the set was a miracle of compression, accommodating an eight-piece band, almost invisible on the upper level between the two balconies, as well as the outline of an unfinished Hilton, stage right and a town clock, with a death figure making an unpunctual appearance when it was nowhere near striking the hour. But it would have taken more than this to disturb the waves of euphoria that were pouring forwards out of the auditorium strongly enough to keep the fuzzily sentimental philosophizing afloat. Wendy Toye's bland production contributed a good deal to the atmosphere of mindless merriment, with its lively deployment of a colourful crowd of supporting characters. Though they were all much more shabbily dressed than the aristocrats in musical comedies by Franz Léhar or Rudolf Friml, they were no less unreal. Ustinov's musicalized Concordia was Clements's final Ruritania.

After the success and the West End transfer of John Clements's production of Pinero's farce *The Magistrate* in 1969 with Alistair Sim and Patricia Routledge, it was very unlikely that the 1973 revival of his farce *Dandy Dick*, (directed by Clements with Alistair Sim and Patricia Routledge) would be less successful or would fail to transfer to the West End. *The Magistrate* had been produced in 1885 at the Royal Court Theatre, which was then under the management of John Clayton and Arthur Cecil. Another farce, *The Schoolmistress*, followed in 1886 and *Dandy Dick* in 1887 with Clayton as the Dean and Cecil as his villainous butler Blore.

The basic subject is once again Victorian respectability and the comedy formula is very much the same. A pillar of society, irreproachable in his morals but vulnerable in his naïvety, allows himself to become involved in disreputable goings-on, which lead to his spending an uncomfortable night in a police station. The final act, which takes place on the following day, clears up most of the misunderstandings and reinstates most of his dignity.

Dandy Dick is very much a proscenium play, and this time Alan Tagg resorted to building a false proscenium at the back of his set to contain a castellated wall representing the outside of the deanery, which had two arches in it, with elaborately painted backcloths behind them. The second act is set indoors in the morning-room, and after the interval we move from the police station to the morning-room, but the scene-changes were contrived very cleverly. The central section of the wall was built on a turntable, flaps could conceal the archways and to the rousing sound of circus music a very large crew of scene-shifters pony-trotted onto the stage to clear away one set of furniture and replace it with another while the audience laughed and applauded.

Alistair Sim occupied the central role quite delightfully. He made his first entrance into the deanery garden chanting absent-mindedly and then the benign smile prompted by the presence of his two decorative daughters froze into horror when he caught sight of the two young officers who had been plotting to smuggle them out of the deanery to a fancy dress ball. Alistair Sim is a highly idiosyncratic actor, but no one can dither better, and gaiter parts enable him to exploit his technique of half crumpling at the knees. When he is under comic stress, long fingers clutch feverishly at twitching wrists, while the hollow eyes stare balefully out of an uneasy silence. The lines are all spoken with a misleading semblance of speed and carelessness. Every word is clearly enunciated but the syllables seem to tumble over each other, whether he is lamenting ('Oh what a dreadful wave threatens to engulf my deanery'), apostrophizing his dignity ('that priceless possession of a man's advancing years') or self-righteously dismissing his horse-owning sister for the night ('In the meantime you are my parents' child, and I trust that your bed is well aired').

He is at his best in moments of being pulled in two directions and his playing of the temptation scene was superb. Driven, for the sake of his spire, to overcome his scruples about gambling and put money on his sister's horse, he hands over his fifty pounds to the butler and immediately checks himself so violently that there's no avoiding a spindly collapse on to the chaise longue. Then he calls the butler back, but so faintly there is not the slightest chance of being heard.

Some of Pinero's best effects are scored by applying the machinery of melodrama to the subject-matter of farce. A thunderstorm is already making itself heard as the Dean wrestles with his conscience about whether he would be justified in administering a bolus to the horse which is being lodged against his will in the Deanery stables. It has been moved because of a fire and is in danger of catching cold, so would he be trying to improve his chances of winning tomorrow or merely fulfilling the courtesies a host to his guest? Then as the butler, who has placed not only his own bet but also the Dean's own on a rival horse, Bonnie Betsy, puts strychnine in the bolus, the lights are lowered and the thunder is providing the same background as might accompany the poisoning of an innocent damsel.

Just as the actor in farce needs to exude an air of very serious belief in what he is doing, the solidity and straightforwardness of Clements's Pinero productions has provided an admirable base for their lunacy. The Dean, preaching a sermon from behind the birdbath to his miscreant daughters about the size of their dressmakers' bills, is solemn and ridiculous at the same time, and Patricia Routledge made Georgiana Tidman endearing and appalling at the same time by treating the absurdly horsey dialogue with brisk matter-of-factness. 'I'll tootle off upstairs and have a rubdown' she remarks with the utmost casualness. 'I shan't be sorry to get my nosebag on'. Even exclamations like 'Ye gods, old cock, steady on!' are made to sound almost plausible.

Of course it is a very slight play and sometimes, even during the performance, it was difficult to shake off the feeling that too much effort had been put into it, but it was keeping the audience very happy and it was undeniably an appropriate choice for Clements's final production, giving him a chance to do everything he can do best, combining heavy solidity with a dexterous lightness of touch, affectionately reviving both the body of Victorianism and its amiable capacity for laughing at itself. Though Clements had to rewrite the end of *Dandy Dick*, introducing a very funny final speech for the Dean, with liquor going quickly to his teetotal head, the productions have proved that Pinero is worthy of a place in the English comic repertory. If they have not proved that he is worthy of three Chichester productions in the space of eight years, it is mainly because so many other plays were being elbowed out.

12
The New Régime

The announcement that Keith Michell was to take over from John Clements caused a good deal of surprise. Both Laurence Olivier and John Clements had been primarily actors and secondly directors; they were to be succeeded by another actor, and one who had neither directed a play nor run a theatre, although it was known that several experienced directors, including at least two who had worked successfully at Chichester, had applied for the job and been interviewed. Why had it been offered to an actor who hadn't even applied? And, more important, how well would he do it?

What the Chichester theatre needs, above all, is an Artistic Director who knows how to use an open stage, who can choose the right plays, the right directors and the right designers, encouraging them to explore and exploit the theatre's possibilities, taking enough risks to revive the feeling of adventure that had disappeared during the Clements régime, but without losing too much of the audience that he had built up. One point in Keith Michell's favour was that his training had been visual. Before deciding to become an actor, he'd been an art student and later an art teacher in his native Australia. As an actor in Olivier's first season at Chichester, he'd been sufficiently excited by the new theatre to make several sketches of it, and after his appointment, his choice of plays for his first season seemed to promise that he was genuinely interested in how the space could be exploited theatrically – Pirandello's *Tonight We Improvize*, Vanbrugh's *The Confederacy*, Sophocles's *Oedipus Tyrannus* and Turgenev's *A Month in the Country*. The Vanbrugh and the Turgenev plays might have been selected for a Clements season, but the other two represented a brave departure from Chichester tradition. It was high time that a Greek tragedy was attempted on the open stage there, and it was good to open with a late Pirandello which had never been seen in England. It ought to be possible to make the play and the theatre show each other up in the best possible light.

Though Pirandello had to write for theatres designed for illusionistic drama, his own inclinations were anti-illusionist, and he came to react more and more violently against the restrictions of the proscenium. *Six Characters in Search of an Author* (1921) still relies on the pretence that the audience isn't really there, but by 1925 he had come to dislike the rigid separation between acting area and auditorium : the new edition of the script made the six characters enter through the stalls, preceded by a commissionaire. With *Each in His Own Way* (1924), the second play in Pirandello's *teatro nel teatro* trilogy, the action starts outside the theatre with newspaper sellers shouting about a scandal involving a Baron and an actress. In the foyer we find both of them, arguing with friends who are trying to dissuade them from going inside to see a show based on their affair.

The final play in the trilogy, *Tonight We Improvize* is the only one to be written after Pirandello had actually had the experience of running a theatrical company, as he did from 1925 to 1928. It is also the only one to establish a clear distinction between setting and substance. Rejected in Italy, the play was premiered in Konigsberg early in 1930, and produced in Berlin later on in the year, when the audience became involved enough to riot, exchanging insults with the actors. It was revived in 1959 by the Living Theatre, with the text reworked by Julian Beck. It needs to be updated and adapted for each new production, and Chichester's open stage naturally had its effect on the new adaptation by Peter Coe, the director, and Keith Michell.

Pirandello's ambivalence about the domination of the director is fundamental to the play. He dedicated it to the autocratic Max Reinhardt 'whose unequalled creative power had given magical life to *Six Characters in Search of an*

Author on the German stage'. But he also attacked Reinhardt viciously in the characterization of Dr Hinkfuss, a
self-possessed, irritable Tom Thumb with tiny hands and
fingers as white and fuzzy as caterpillars. Yet Pirandello
puts a great many of his own ideas into Dr Hinkfuss's
theorizing, and at the same time a good deal of the action
is formed by fleshing out ideas propounded by other theore-
ticians and directors, especially Meyerhold, who paralleled
Reinhardt in his methods of liberating the play from the
dramatist. There are episodes in *Tonight We Improvize*
which dramatize his ideas about actors freeing themselves
from the director's authority as he has freed himself from
the writer's, about the use of lighting to produce self-
sufficient theatrical effects, about the role of the spectators
as co-creators of the play and about incorporating opera
into drama.

Tonight We Improvize is a play about theatre and reality;
the danger is that it can seem to be about actors and a
director. The play-within-the-play is more fragmented even
than in *Six Characters in Search of an Author*, and, as in
Each in His Own Way, the story does not arrive at a conclusion. It is a truly experimental play – not only ahead of
its own time but still ahead of ours, as reviewers showed in
their objections to a script designed to give the impression
that the actors were improvizing. Like the play, the production had a lot of flaws, but in approaching *Tonight We
Improvize* it is important to differentiate between failure to
achieve consistency and refusal to attempt it. Pirandello had
the courage to let his own uncertainty surface in the play's
movement. In the arguments between the characters and
the director in *Six Characters in Search of an Author* we
always know who is in the right; in *Tonight We Improvize*
Pirandello is more ambivalent, and the structure is not only
dialectical but contrived so that the conflicting elements can
almost topple it. Who are we to believe when Hinkfuss tells
us that the actors' protests were pre-arranged and the actors
deny this? The argument about whether they can manage
without him seems to be settled when they throw him out
of the theatre, but when he reappears later, he claims to
have been in control all the time.

On another level the play is about the relationship between the moment of living experience and its crystallization into a work of art. In his introductory remarks to the audience, Dr Hinkfuss says:

> The poet is under an illusion when he fancies that he has found perfect peace and achieved liberation by crystallizing forever, in an immutable form, his work of art. He has merely stopped living his work. Liberation and peace are not to be had except by ceasing to live. If a work of art survives, it is only because we are still able to take it out of its crystallized state, to dissolve its form within us in a vital motion; and it is we then who give it life, varying from occasion to occasion and from one to another of us; what we have being not one life but any number of lives, as may be inferred from the incessant discussions to which the subject gives rise, and which spring from an unwillingness to believe just this: that it is, indeed we who give it life, and that it is in no wise possible that the life which I bring to it should be the same as that bestowed upon it by another.

This tallies with Pirandello's beliefs, but he also maintained that there was no possibility of translating into art the chaos of actuality. Real life would always be a disruptive force on a stage, and if he allowed the structure of *Tonight We Improvize* to be fragmented, this was partly a failure but partly the successful result of generating tensions that no play could contain.

Keith Michell is not a Tom Thumb with fingers as fuzzy as a caterpillar, and the name Hinkfuss wasn't used in the Chichester production, but there was a resonant irony in having the part of the director played by the newly appointed Artistic Director, who would seem to be having trouble with his actors and would later be thrown out of his own theatre. When the houselights dimmed at the beginning there was a sufficiently prolonged black-out for the audience to think something might have gone wrong, and then an anxious female voice was heard over the loudspeakers. 'Would Mr Keith Michell please contact me in the control box?' Music was brought in immediately, but above it we heard a hubbub of backstage voices raised in altercation.

Instead of making the irate entrance Pirandello prescribed for Dr Hinkfuss, Keith Michell came forward in a dinner jacket and patent leather shoes, to be greeted by applause. The opening speech is too long and too much like a lecture – it was a mistake not to cut it substantially, but he did seem to be referring to this particular theatre when he wandered through the auditorium to make the point that each theatre's shape brings a different version of the play into existence. The audience's uneasiness seemed to be contributing creatively to the play – and in a way Meyerhold would have approved – when the actors were called forward under their own names and there was a quiet, intent argument between Keith Michell and Keith Baxter, who was objecting to the use of his name while in costume. As if to be farther away from the audience, they retreated under the umbrella formed by the upper platform of the permanent set.

As Signora Ignazia Palmiro, Miriam Karlin had to introduce her four attractive daughters, Mommina, Dorina, Tottina and Nenè. Her aside to Keith Michell afterwards – 'It's going well, isn't it?' – seemed spontaneous, as did Keith Baxter's dudgeon as he stalked off the stage.

This was followed by the first of the genuine-seeming arguments about whether it was all a pretence, all going according to a preconceived plan. Keith Michell wandered round the front of the stage and interrupted Miriam Karlin: 'Don't anticipate the story, Miriam, please.'

The value of wordless theatrical effects was another point on which Pirandello was ambivalent. During the interval and at the beginning of Act Two Dr Hinkfuss uses lighting and sound effects to create the impression of an airfield, creating a scene which he then decides is superfluous. In the first act there is a religious procession which some of the reviewers dismissed as irrelevant, not realizing it was in the script, but Pirandello was deliberately testing the theatricality of effects like this against other kinds of theatricality, refusing even to umpire the tug-of-war between them. At Chichester, Peter Coe displayed an appropriate virtuosity in building theatrical effects gradually and dissolving them abruptly, as when the stage was transformed into a nightclub at the end of the religious sequence. Before it started,

the stage was suddenly empty, so, materializing out of
nothing, there came a Fellini-like procession with music
reminiscent of Nino Rota's. The revolve was used to bring
on an altar laid out with electric candles. The procession
itself corresponded fairly closely with Pirandello's description. At the head came the band. The first of the choristers
was swinging a censer, white-clad girls followed with flowers
and then a chorister with a tall cross, another with a censer,
a life-sized holy statue on a platform supported by masked
carriers, a priest walking under a canopy, a group of girls
in black. The smell of incense was growing stronger. The
characters were now in the auditorium as if we were all part
of the congregation for the Mass which followed, with bells
rung at the right moments and the Host administered to the
kneeling characters. The cut to the nightclub was effectively
brutal – as the music changed we saw semi-nude girls performing a slow, sexy, casual dance. Under a massive mane
of frizzy red hair, Annie Ross was singing ultra-emotionally
in a follow-spot, while men in caps chatted, ignoring her.
Between phrases she sipped wine, and at the climax she was
prostrate on the stage, as if she couldn't go on.

Suddenly we were outside in the electric moonlight,
with projections representing the exterior of the building.
Habitués of the nightclub were mocking Signor Palmiro,
who did not see the paper horns they'd put on his head
until his family arrived in the street, with young officers
escorting the girls. Again the level of the action changed
when Alfred Marks appeared to be getting fed up with
having so little to do.

Following Meyerhold, who towards the end of his career
wanted both to 'cinefy' the theatre and to achieve a
Wagnerian synthesis of all the arts, Pirandello introduced a
sequence of filmed opera into his play, but at Chichester
this was replaced by an operatic dumbshow to music from
a gramophone on an old-fashioned stage created by placing
working footlights on the actual stage, while the Palmiro
family and the officers noisily took their places in the Dress
Circle. The trio from the first act of *Il Trovatore* was mimed
rather too balletically, by three masked singers in cothurni,
but there was some good comedy in the parody. The volume

of the singing was turned down when the family dialogue had to be audible above it, until Keith Michell appeared with a loud-hailer. 'That's enough, Miriam. Don't go too far.'

For the interval the audience had the choice of staying to watch his lighting effects or going out to watch the drama between the four girls and their young men which would continue in the foyer and on the lawn. Keith Baxter seemed to be getting angry with the spectators who overheard his conversation with Mommina. 'Why do you have to listen to everything we say? We've got as much right to be here as you have.' The end of the interval was signalled by an air-raid warning accompanied by an announcement over the tannoy. 'Please take cover in the auditorium.' Pirandello's airfield had been developed into an air-raid, and searchlight beams were coming out of a trap-door in the stage. We heard the whistle and crash of bombs dropping. As the searchlight beams whirled round the darkened auditorium, there were flashes, smoke and flame effects on the steel doors at the rear. The All Clear was followed anti-climacterically by Keith Michell's apparently spontaneous decision, 'Yes I think we can do without this air-raid scene. It was my idea.' The more authentic the spontaneity sounded, the more chaotic the play seemed. At the risk of enraging his audience Pirandello had been illustrating his theory about the relationship of art and life.

The confusion was compounded when, apparently at random, Keith Michell invited members of the audience to describe what had been going on outside for the benefit of those who'd stayed in their seats. Planted actors, masquerading as spectators, described what they'd seen in unflattering terms – 'It was a bit of a mess.' Could Pirandello have written that too?

The living-room was created out of nothing with commendable speed. A swinging shaded light. Draped furniture. On the upper level Totina was being undressed by a young officer, but only to exchange clothes with him. Signora Ignazia was suffering from toothache, but it didn't stop the singing and dancing which culminated in a spirited rendering of the Anvil Chorus from *Il Trovatore*, with the rhythm marked by the clinking of silver cups. The fun was interrupted by the entrance of Keith Baxter as the jealous lieutenant who accused Mommina of being 'tarted up' and refused to believe she had really wanted to join in. The level of the action changed again when, after his knocking at the door had been ignored, Alfred Marks burst in with blood on his stomach and sleeve. 'Nobody let me in.' They tried out his death scene in various ways, but he insisted that it couldn't be done without the entrance – 'Death enters with me.' After repeating the entrance, he proceeded to die melodramatically, and the audience, which had responded well to the change of level, clapped when he abruptly revived.

The scene of throwing the director out of the theatre harks back to *Six Characters in Search of an Author*. If the roles are taking possession of the actors as they should be, why should a director be necessary? Alfred Marks volunteered to work the lights and Miriam Karlin asked for the stage to be cleared. Scenery is unnecessary. She made up June Ritchie's face in front of us, applying greasepaint, rubbing it in, adding whitened bags under the eyes, and then powdering her and untidying her hair. With the three other girls, she backed away. The scene had begun. Mommina was now arguing against the accusing voices of her mother and her sisters.

In the ensuing scene Pirandello tries to show the role taking possession of the actress. The dominant idea is of imprisonment – for the actress, inside the role; for Mommina, inside the room to which the lieutenant's jealousy confines her. The sequence begins with her line 'Is this a wall?' In Pirandello's script the walls have been erected in the darkness by stagehands; in the Chichester production, the walls were imaginary, suggested only by the lighting. The real objective of her husband's jealousy is to destroy her past. He loves only his own idealized image of her, not the woman she has been throughout her life, so when she says 'You want to kill me', it refers both to the damage he is inflicting on her by keeping her shut up and to his wish to destroy the woman she really is.

The final sequence would probably be too operatic to

work on a modern audience, even if Pirandello had not introduced an operatic aria. Peter Coe removed some of the sentimentality by letting June Ritchie indicate the presence of Mommina's two daughters through mime, using four follow-spots, two on her and two on the children's empty seats. Like Dr Hinkfuss's speech at the beginning, Mommina's final monologue is too long, and the revival of the actress after her stage death is too much like a repetition of the point already made in more comic terms with the actor playing her father. All the same, the play has proved its importance by making unusual and interesting connections between apparently unrelated areas of theatrical and non-theatrical experience, and the Chichester production used the theatre as it had never been used before.

This could not be said about Wendy Toye's production of Vanbrugh's *The Confederacy*, which used the stage in an unimaginative and all too familiar way. An adaptation of Dancourt's 1692 play *Les Bourgeoises à la mode*, it was first produced in 1705, eight years after Vanbrugh's two best comedies, *The Relapse* and *Virtue in Danger*, and a year before Farquhar's *The Recruiting Officer*. Popular in its day, *The Confederacy* has been neglected recently, but it was impossible to gauge how stageworthy it still is from this production, which gave the impression of having been put together without any genuine interest in what the play could communicate to a modern audience.

Ignoring the new tradition of staging early eighteenth-century comedy in terms of social realism – a tradition inaugurated by the Berliner Ensemble version of *The Recruiting Officer* (seen in London in 1956) and introduced into the mainstream of English theatrical style by William Gaskill's National Theatre production of the play in 1963 – this *Confederacy* was more in line with the cheerful, colourful, comfortable, musicalized version of Fielding's *Rape upon Rape* which opened the Mermaid Theatre under the title *Lock Up Your Daughters*. *The Confederacy* was not turned into a musical, but it was produced as though it had been, with no finesse and a lot of coarse-grained comedy.

It looked as though the prime concern was to please the

audience with a bevy of television stars – Dora Bryan,
Peggy Mount, Peter Gilmore and Richard Wattis. As
Moneytrap, a sad scrivener with straggly hair and wilting
Puritan clothes, Richard Wattis gave the only performance
which was both funny and truthful : he was alone in giving
an impression of genuine feeling trapped inside a personality
that had become ridiculous because of a pointless social pose.
'Perhaps I'm not so young as I was,' he conceded ruefully,
gesturing towards his genitals. Dora Bryan looked considerably too old to play Clarissa, the witty, intriguing, beautiful
wife of another scrivener called Gripe. In her ribboned
blonde wig and her orange dress with black rosettes and
black gloves, she produced a phoney petulance that made
her seem like a suburban aunt of Fenella Fielding's. Peter
Gilmore overacted energetically, while Peggy Mount,
dressed like an Eskimo on a package tour of the Soviet
Union, let a lot of the dialogue go for very little, especially
at the beginning.

In Mrs Bracegirdle's old part of Flippanta, Clarissa's
conspiratorial maid, Patsy Byrne was solidly persuasive but
the role required the quick, slick charm of a female Figaro.
Frank Middlemass is a good actor, but as Gripe he was
handicapped by balloon trousers and a long frizzy spaniel
wig, which he kept clutching. Generally the delivery of the
lines was far too unvarying, but Gemma Craven had one
delightful sequence, cooing, chortling, warbling over a love
letter, and making the most of dialogue which looks dis-
concerting on the page :

> Let me read it, let me read it, let me read it, let me read it,
> I say. Um, um, um, Cupid's, um, um, um, Darts, um, um,
> um, Beauty, um, Charms, um, um, um, Angel, um, God-
> dess, um – (*kissing the letter*) – um, um, um, truest Lover,
> hum, um, Eternal Constancy, um, um, um, cruel, um, um,
> um, Racks, um, um, Tortures, um, um, Fifty Daggers, um,
> um, bleeding Heart, um, um, dead Man. Very well, a
> mighty civil letter, I promise you; not one smutty Word in
> it : I'll go lock it up in my Comb-box.

This is Vanbrugh's invention; in the French original there
is only one conventional sentence about the love letter.

Joe Griffiths's breezy music, Anthony Powell's toytown rooftops and Wendy Toye's trite stage business of carpet-beating and market bustle had nothing to do with either the social or the personal realities that could have been evoked in moving the action between Covent Garden, Clarissa's house and the much humbler home of Mrs Amlet, a woman 'that sells paint and patches, Iron-bodice, false Teeth and all sorts of Things to Ladies'. The market set was designed so that it could be transformed briskly into an interior setting by placing a cloth over the table and closing the shutter of the stall to reveal a hat-rack on the other side of it. The play does not demand realistic visual treatment but it does pose problems for the Chichester stage. Wendy Toye evaded them with a jokeyness that verged on the twee. After two of the ladies went out through the vomitories we heard the clatter of horses' hooves, and during an indoor scene there was birdsong over the loudspeakers in the auditorium.

In short, the production wasted its opportunity of testing whether Vanbrugh's social criticism measures up to Farquhar's. Satire in lines like 'Women of rank buy things because they don't have occasion for them' could be given a resonance that would extend to the institution of bourgeois marriage. Clarissa's attitude to the bed she has made for herself is summed up in her line 'The want of a thing is perplexing enough, but the possession of it is intolerable.' As unhappy with their wives as their wives are with them, the two scriveners would like to do a swap, and each showers expensive presents on his friend's wife, while grudging his own her extravagances. Meanwhile the working-class boy in the sub-plot, Dick Amlet, masquerades as a colonel to woo Clarissa's step-daughter. Just after promising his mother a daughter-in-law with a coach and six horses, he has to put on a patronizing act of not knowing her. 'I was making aquaintance with this good gentlewoman.' The servants are accomplices in the affectations of their employers. 'Not one word in prose,' promises Brass (Peter Gilmore) as he delivers a love-letter for Clarissa to Flippanta, who as a servant, is not entitled to expect verse in the letter he gives her for herself. In his energetic over-projection as Dick Amlet,

Nicholas Clay failed to differentiate between the affected gallantry of the Colonel he was impersonating and his behaviour in private with his mother. But when it is performed without any real interest in its subject-matter, a comedy of manners is full of traps for actors who can be tempted into making immediate effects without contributing to the over-all design.

Hovhannes I. Pilikian, the thirty-two-year-old Armenian graduate of a directors' course at RADA, whom Keith Michell entrusted with the production of *Oedipus Tyrannus*, had written several articles on Greek tragedy for the quarterly magazine *Drama*. In a piece called 'Comedy in Greek Tragedy' (Autumn 1970) he claims that Aristotle 'almost certainly had never seen any of the unique master-pieces of that time [the classical age] performed in the context of their original meaning.' Pilikian attacked modern Greek productions of them as being founded either on Renaissance misinterpretations of Aristotelian concepts or on 'concepts crystallized by eighteenth-century French classicism based on Seneca'. He went on to call Oedipus's scene with the messenger from Corinth 'the most powerful comic scene'. While Jocasta is silent, understanding she is his mother, Oedipus 'indulges in a torrent of sex-humour, enjoying it to the full with child-like joy and exuberance' and 'the Corinthian shepherd overflows with folk-wisdom and practical humour, jollity and cleverness.'

There is a dangerous mixture of sense and nonsense in Pilikian's ideas about *Oedipus Tyrannus*. The feature titled 'The Swollen-footed Tyrant', written for the Summer 1974 issue of *Drama* and excerpted in the Chichester programme, presents Oedipus as a madman and a villain. His murder of an innocent old man at the cross-roads was not only un-necessary but blasphemous. Laius was a pilgrim on his way to the Delphic oracle, while both Hermes, the god of travel-lers, and Hecate, a goddess of the underworld, had roadside images posted at the cross-roads, which implies the presence of improvized altars. To the original audience Oedipus must have epitomized the same blind passion that possessed Xerxes, who had just led the Persians against the Greeks, a madman who ordered his slaves to whip the sea that had destroyed his pontoon bridges. Thebes had been pro-Persian throughout the wars, so the nationalistic Sophocles must have wanted to represent Oedipus in a negative light. Tiresias is a nasty, vengeful old man who publicly calls for Oedipus's impeachment because he'd hoped to solve the Sphinx's riddle himself, winning Jocasta and the throne. 'Oidipous' (Οἰδίπους) means 'swollen-footed' or 'swollen-legged', and the deformity, resulting from the vicious injury done to the child by its father when he was trying to get rid of it, must be intended to highlight spiritual deformity. Oedipus is not a hero but 'a murderer, a rogue, a grotesque-looking thief-of-the-(cross)-roads, who rises to political power (just like Brecht's Arturo Ui) and whose successful cover-up at last cracks down and destroys him (like Spiro Agnew)...' Oedipus was also dark-skinned (like Othello), being semitic, a descendant of Cadmus, son of a Phoenician king. He is very proud of being a foreigner, and not one of the people he rules as a dictator. Jocasta is 'whorish, perverted, de-generate', and Creon 'being Oedipus's father-substitute (and homosexual power-companion) perversely fathers Oedipus with his sister.'

The self-contradictions in this reading of the play are so blatant, it is inconceivable that a group of intelligent actors could work through the rehearsal process without stumbling up against them. By the time they did, it may have been too late to correct most of the mistakes they were committed to, but at least the fallacy of the dark-skinned foreigner could have been avoided. This idea would be tenable only if the Messenger proved that Oedipus was not the son of Laius, who was presumably as white-skinned as Jocasta, so why should their son's pigmentation be darker?

Nor does the original Greek meaning of 'tyrannos' seem to have the same connotations Pilikian ascribes to it, but only to mean 'self-made ruler' or 'dictator', but not in a derogatory sense. The main movement of Sophocles's play is fairly straightforward. Oedipus's reign is founded on Laius's defiance of the oracle that had warned him he would die by the hand of his own child. (He had once violated the laws of hospitality by seducing the son of his host, and far from presenting him as an innocent old man, the play shows that Nemesis worked by letting Oedipus inherit his father's explosive temper.) The main theme of the Priest's first speech is that the city is being punished by the gods, afflicted with pestilence. An evil has to be expiated. The unhappy people need their ruler's help, and in using his capacity for riddle-solving, Oedipus destroys his own happiness. The chorus's closing words are that no one can be called happy until he has carried his happiness down to the grave. If you make Oedipus into a Nixon-like villain who is trying to deceive his people by concealing the evil facts, you destroy the central irony. The detective must exert all his powers to arrive at the solution that reveals him as the murderer.

In trying to confute the scholars, Pilikian made a lot of elementary theatrical mistakes. Making all the leading characters into villains, he alienated our sympathy from them, and we were not even allowed to feel pity for the Thebans, because he used the chorus to illustrate his idea that tragedy preserved vestiges of the obscene satyr plays. In fact there was nothing at all revolutionary in his insistence on the presence of comic elements in the tragedies, but the comedy he actually introduced into his production seemed curiously imposed. The chorus of bald-pated dotards did a funny little jig as they chanted 'Never again I'll make my journey to Delphi', beating rhythmically on the ground with their sticks, and as the messenger from what he called 'Horinth', Willoughby Goddard was made to talk like a comic Dutchman and roll his large body about the stage, cackling. There was also some unintended comedy in Diana Dors's monotonous hand gestures and in her tantrums, which suggested a spoilt wife in the stockbroker belt. 'I'm sick of it all,' she grumbled, and the exit that was meant to lead up to her suicide would have been more appropriate if she'd been refusing to cook dinner. Over-literary in some places and over-conversational in others, Gail Rademacher's translation gave Jocasta the line 'And the same to you' as a retort to a long speech of the Messenger's.

Ralph Koltai's set suggested a vaginal entrance to a cave in the back wall and there was a breast-like mound, stage left, which Diana Dors sat on. There was also a pile of stones downstage, forming a platform that could be used for speech-making. Keith Michell's Oedipus was bare-chested, with a huge cod-piece. In one rehearsal which was written up in *The Guardian* (17 July), Pilikian told him that 'Oedipus' meant not only 'swollen foot' but 'big prick'.

A few of the images had impact – the six old men prostrate between stones and mound before the action started; the four soldiers with knives sitting at the top of the Stage Right vomitory until Tiresias made his exit and Oedipus signalled that they should go after him and finish him off; the entrance of the old shepherd, bare-bottomed and clinging to a pole carried by four soldiers. But the infallible sign of bad direction is that good actors are pushed into giving bad performances. Alfred Marks tried to remain neutral as Creon, but he was given an impossible task in the final scene because Pilikian insisted there was no proof that Oedipus's children were on stage. Why shouldn't this be the fantasy of a blind madman? And why shouldn't Creon encourage it? As Oedipus Keith Michell gave no sign of physical deformity and he suffered the fate that often over-takes an actor playing a ruler in a production where a director has imposed a fashionably anti-authoritarian reading on a play written from the premise that people need a good ruler. In the first part of the play Michell had to be a hypocritical politician putting on an unconvincing act of paternalistic benevolence; in the final scene, with his blood-daubed body naked but for an antique jock-strap and the cloak he held in front of him, he had to emote, scream and writhe in an agony of self-pity against background music provided by the group called Tangerine Dream. After driving him offstage with their sticks, the bald old men began to caress their new ruler.

Toby Robertson's production of *A Month in the Country* was the undisputed success of the season. Unfavourable comparisons were made, as they always are, with Chekhov, though the play was written in 1850, ten years before he was born; but the reviewers who had been almost unanimous in giving all three productions the thumbs down, were almost unanimous in their enthusiasm for the only nineteenth century play of the season, the play which would intrinsically have seemed least likely to succeed on the Chichester stage, even if it had the most appeal for the Chichester audience.

Had the actors found their way to their places in a blackout, each scene could have begun as Turgenev wanted it to, but Toby Robertson resorted to the device of bringing them on in a stylized parade to polka-like music by Carl Davis. This meant that our first impression of them came from the way they moved to the music. As Natalya, Dorothy Tutin had to arrange her skirts visibly for the position she should have started in. As Rakitin, Derek Jacobi needed all the help a director could give him to make his presence felt more in the first half of the play. Natalya's neglect of him is put into the wrong focus if he is made to seem negligible, but at the end of the parade he was required to sink onto a footstool at her feet.

Later, when background music was brought in under soliloquies, they stood out more than they needed to – especially his at the end of the second scene. There was an awkward moment when an imaginary window was opened in an imaginary downstage wall and birdsong floated in from outside. Nor was the problem of suggesting a garden solved by putting potted plants against the wooden slats of the back wall. But the main failure of the production was in holding the balance between the four men around Natalya. Rakitin represents Turgenev himself, the unsuccessful would-be lover, who has stayed on hopefully for four years as a friend of the family, well-liked by the husband, Arkady, whose only real passion is for his estate. 'Rakitin is myself', said Turgenev to Savina, the young actress who was Vera in the Petersburg production of the play in 1879. 'I'm always the unsuccessful lover in my novels.' He was himself still living in the household of Pauline Viardot, a singer who kept him on leading strings for forty years. Belyayev, the tutor of Natalya's son, is young, gauche, inarticulate and lacking in self-confidence, partly because he is so acutely conscious of his social inferiority. This was the element that was missing from Nicholas Clay's elegantly dressed young man, who had no need to apologize for his old frock coat. John Turner was very good as the un-imaginative, unsuspicious Arkady, but it is essential that the honesty of these three honourable men should be weighed against the dishonesty of the family doctor, Schpigelsky. This is a very well written part but the actor playing it should not be able to run away with as much of the show as Timothy West did.

If Toby Robertson was given more credit than he deserved for his production, the main reason was that it contained two such richly enjoyable performances as Timothy West's and Dorothy Tutin's. She was courageously honest in throwing so much of herself open to the character, exposing layer after layer of private-seeming ambivalence as Natalya careered her hesitating way between *grande dame* dignity and an immature embarrassment, the destructive pride of the *femme fatale* and the desperation of the frightened quarry. Her timing was perfectly controlled as she gave every indication of being out of control, agonized at being unable to go on in both directions at the same time, to be generously open and meanly secretive, nobly self-sacrificing and greedily jealous. There was something helpless in her scheming and calculated in her helplessness. Moments of the most vicious emotional in-fighting were followed by moments of languid resignation to boredom. Charmingly, tantalizingly, she dealt out reproaches like endearments, endearments like complaints. She seemed innocent, even when she was inflicting unnecessary pain on everyone around her, so she never forfeited our sympathy. She seemed to feel so much for her victims that, like a man-eating Miranda, she could have said 'I have suffered with those that I made suffer.'

Having said all that, I have still not said enough, and it is worth quoting Benedict Nightingale's description in the *New Statesman* of the way her performance developed :

At first she looks merely uncomfortable and a bit shifty as she seeks to keep her embarrassing love hidden; but, as the secret becomes increasingly intolerable, she begins to fret and fidget and laugh nervously, jumping up and prowling about the room, snapping out in exasperation and promptly apologizing. It's a memorable picture of a woman caught between passion and self-respect at a time of her life when the future seems to hold nothing but more games of cards and more decorous little conversations about land prices. The performance makes no play for our pity – indeed, Miss Tutin implies that Natalya is enjoying the drama of it all – but it ends by winning it. Renouncing her male Lolita, she crumples up and weeps; and it is as much a complaint against the common enemy, time, as a threnody for a lost love.

If she gave the impression of having started from the inside and characterized by going outwards, Timothy West seemed to have started from the outside and worked inwards. Which is not to say that he didn't succeed in penetrating to a very considerable depth. We learnt a great deal from his characteristic stance, knees slightly bent, burly body poking inquisitively forward, from his characteristic mannerism, tapping the money in his pocket, and from his characteristic expression, the skin beneath the eyes puckering in quizzical calculation. The most realistic man in the play, the doctor is the least romantic, the least sexually ambitious, aspiring only to a convenient marriage with Liza, the unglamorous companion of Arkady's mother, and wooing her in the manner of a farmer buying a cart-horse that happens to have a dowry attached. It was an extremely funny performance, vibrantly alive with a comedy that was felicitously complementary to Dorothy Tutin's. When she got laughs, as she often did, it was when a neatly gauche modulation revealed Natalya's stumbling lack of self-awareness. Timothy West's Schpigelsky knew exactly what sort of man he was, and didn't in the least approve, but still went on sucking greedily at each tasty gobbet of gratification that came his way. Free meals were an occupational perquisite he valued, and he was not above mediating for a rich, fat, landowner, Bolshintsov, who had promised him three horses if he was instrumental in making Natalya marry her foster-daughter to him.

Leonid Grossman's book *Turgenev*, (Moscow, 1928), which is excerpted in Andrew Field's *The Complection of Russian Literature* (Penguin Press 1971) produces compelling evidence to suggest that in writing *A Month in the*

Country, Turgenev plagiarized Balzac's *La Marâtre*, which had been produced in May 1848. 'I am dreaming about a salon comedy where everything is peaceful and calm and proper,' said Balzac.

> The gentlemen calmly play whist by green-shaded candle-light, while the women laugh and converse over their embroidery. They drink tea. In a word, everything bespeaks order and harmony. But underneath passions seethe, a drama ripens and stirs until it finally bursts forth like a sudden conflagration.

The plot centres on a rivalry between a married woman and her step-daughter for the love of a young man employed in the household as a tutor. In both plays the older woman has the opportunity to get rid of the girl by marrying her off to a provincial, middle-aged man who would obviously make her unhappy, and in both plays the family doctor has an important role as a droll observer on the edge of events. Grossman's quotations of dialogue indicate that Balzac's play was the source of Bolshintsov's talk about his timidity, of his ineptness with girls, and his recourse to the weather as a topic when confronted with Vera, while Arkady's remark on surprising his wife with Rakitin echoes the remark that Balzac's General makes in the same situation. Natalya's sequence with Vera, luring her with promises of sisterly friendship into confessing her secret love, is suspiciously similar to a sequence in *La Marâtre*, where the step-mother also manoeuvres the girl into losing more and more of her freedom of choice until she agrees to marry the middle-aged man. Unlike Balzac's previous plays, *La Marâtre* was a success, but a modern audience would find it highly melodramatic, whereas Turgenev's play comes across very freshly not least because of it subtlety in fulfilling the programme that Balzac set for himself, passion seething under the calm surface of polite boredom in a country house.

For the two main characters, Natalya and Rakitin, the passion is calibrated by their idleness: they have nothing to do except cultivate their own sensitivity, inflame their own emotions by playing with them, torture themselves and each other, indulge themselves romantically, ignoring not only the reality of the outside world but the reality of their own situation. The outcome is inevitably unhappy for them, as it is for all the romantics in the play. While Natalya loses both the young man she has briefly loved and the older man who has loyally befriended her, the materialistic doctor and the fat landowner both win the women they had unromantically been bidding for.

Keith Michell's first season had at least proved that he was willing to take risks and, in spite of the mistakes he made over choosing directors, there is more hope than there used to be that the possibilities of the space will be explored.

Plays and Players 1962-74

PLAY	AUTHOR	DIRECTOR	DESIGNER	LEADING PLAYERS	PAGE
1962					
The Chances	John Fletcher	Laurence Olivier	Malcolm Pride	Rosemary Harris Kathleen Harrison Keith Michell John Neville Joan Plowright	65
The Broken Heart	John Ford	Laurence Olivier	Roger Furse	Fay Compton Joan Greenwood Keith Michell Andre Morell John Neville Laurence Olivier	69
Uncle Vanya	Chekhov	Laurence Olivier	Sean Kenny	Joan Greenwood Laurence Olivier Joan Plowright Michael Redgrave	39, 72

PLAY	AUTHOR	DIRECTOR	DESIGNER	LEADING PLAYERS	PAGE
1963					
Saint Joan	Shaw	John Dexter	Michael Annals	Max Adrian Jeremy Brett Joan Plowright Robert Stephens	36, 75
Uncle Vanya (as above but with Rosemary Harris replacing Joan Greenwood)					77
The Workhouse Donkey	John Arden	Stuart Burge	Roger Furse	Frank Finlay Robert Lang Mary Miller Norman Rossington Robert Stephens	79
1964					
The Royal Hunt of the Sun	Peter Shaffer	John Dexter and Desmond O'Donovan	Michael Annals	Colin Blakely Robert Lang Robert Stephens	39, 58, 88
The Dutch Courtesan	John Marston	William Gaskill and Piers Haggard	Annena Stubbs	Frank Finlay Joyce Redman John Stride Billie Whitelaw	92

PLAY	AUTHOR	DIRECTOR	DESIGNER	LEADING PLAYERS	PAGE
Othello	Shakespeare	John Dexter	Jocelyn Herbert	Frank Finlay Laurence Olivier Joyce Redman Maggie Smith	88, 93
1965					
Armstrong's Last Goodnight	John Arden	John Dexter and William Gaskill	René Allio	Albert Finney Geraldine McEwan Ian McKellen Robert Stephens	55, 96
Trelawny of the 'Wells'	Arthur W. Pinero	Desmond O'Donovan	Alan Tagg	Graham Crowden Doris Hare Louise Purnell Billie Whitelaw	50, 103
Miss Julie	Strindberg	Michael Elliott	Richard Negri	Albert Finney Maggie Smith	105
Black Comedy	Peter Shaffer	John Dexter	Alan Tagg	Albert Finney Derek Jacobi Louise Purnell Maggie Smith	57, 106

PLAY	AUTHOR	DIRECTOR	DESIGNER	LEADING PLAYERS	PAGE
1966					
The Clandestine Marriage	George Colman and David Garrick	Desmond O'Donovan	Alan Tagg	Bill Fraser Margaret Rutherford Alastair Sim John Standing	112
The Fighting Cock	Anouilh	Norman Marshall	Alan Tagg	Michael Aldridge Sarah Badel John Clements John Standing	113
The Cherry Orchard	Chekhov	Lindsay Anderson	Alan Tagg	Tom Courtenay Bill Fraser Celia Johnson Ray McAnally Hugh Williams	14, 115
Macbeth	Shakespeare	Michael Benthall	Alan Tagg	Michael Aldridge John Clements Tom Courtenay Margaret Johnston	118

PLAY	AUTHOR	DIRECTOR	DESIGNER	LEADING PLAYERS	PAGE
1967					
The Farmer's Wife	Eden Phillpotts	John Clements	Peter Rice	Michael Aldridge Diana Churchill Bill Fraser Irene Handl	121
The Beaux' Stratagem	George Farquhar	William Chappell	Peter Rice	Fenella Fielding Maureen O'Brien Anton Rodgers John Standing	123
Heartbreak House	Shaw	John Clements	Peter Rice	Michael Aldridge Sarah Badel Diana Churchill John Clements Bill Fraser Irene Worth	41, 125
The Italian Straw Hat	Eugène Labiche and Marc-Michel	Peter Coe	Peter Rice	Sarah Badel Fenella Fielding Anton Rodgers	127

PLAY	AUTHOR	DIRECTOR	DESIGNER	LEADING PLAYERS	PAGE
1968					
The Unknown Soldier and His Wife	Peter Ustinov	Peter Ustinov	Michael Warre	Clive Revill Prunella Scales Peter Ustinov Simon Ward	131
The Cocktail Party	T. S. Eliot	Alec Guinness	Michael Warre	Eileen Atkins Hubert Gregg Alec Guinness Pauline Jameson	133
The Tempest	Shakespeare	David Jones	Ralph Koltai	John Clements Richard Kane Clive Revill Simon Ward	137
The Skin of our Teeth	Thornton Wilder	Peter Coe	Michael Warre	Hubert Gregg Pauline Jameson Millicent Martin	139
1969					
The Caucasian Chalk Circle	Brecht	Peter Coe	Michael Knight	Heather Sears Topol	143

PLAY	AUTHOR	DIRECTOR	DESIGNER	LEADING PLAYERS	PAGE
The Magistrate	Arthur W. Pinero	John Clements	Carl Toms	Michael Aldridge Renee Asherson John Clements Christopher Guinee Patricia Routledge Alastair Sim	145
The Country Wife	Wycherley	Robert Chetwyn	Hutchinson Scott	Keith Baxter Hugh Paddick Patricia Routledge Maggie Smith	148
Antony and Cleopatra	Shakespeare	Peter Dews	Carl Toms	Keith Baxter John Clements Gordon Gostelow Margaret Leighton	60, 149
1970 Peer Gynt	Ibsen	Peter Coe	Sean Kenny	Sarah Badel Roy Dotrice William Hutt Beatrix Lehmann	152

PLAY	AUTHOR	DIRECTOR	DESIGNER	LEADING PLAYERS	PAGE
Vivat! Vivat Regina!	Robert Bolt	Peter Dews	Carl Toms	Eileen Atkins Sarah Miles Richard Pearson	60, 61, 154
Arms and the Man	Shaw	John Clements	Peter Rice	Sarah Badel Laurence Harvey John Standing	157
The Alchemist	Ben Jonson	Peter Dews	Carl Toms	Edward Atienza James Booth Dora Bryan William Hutt	158
1971 *The Rivals*	Sheridan	John Clements	Carl Toms	John Clements Peter Egan Margaret Leighton Angela Scoular	160
Dear Antoine	Anouilh	Robin Phillips	Alan Tagg	John Clements Edith Evans Peggy Marshall	160

PLAY	AUTHOR	DIRECTOR	DESIGNER	LEADING PLAYERS	PAGE
Caesar and Cleopatra	Shaw	Robin Phillips	Carl Toms	Anna Calder-Marshall John Gielgud	163
Reunion in Vienna	Robert Sherwood	Frith Banbury	Carl Toms	Michael Aldridge 62, 166 Margaret Leighton Nigel Patrick	
1972 *The Beggar's Opera*	John Gay	Robin Phillips	Daphne Dare	Harold Innocent Millicent Martin John Neville	168
The Doctor's Dilemma	Shaw	John Clements	Michael Warre	John Clements John Neville Robin Phillips Joan Plowright	169
The Taming of the Shrew	Shakespeare	Jonathan Miller	Patrick Robertson	Anthony Hopkins Joan Plowright	171

213

PLAY	AUTHOR	DIRECTOR	DESIGNER	LEADING PLAYERS	PAGE
1974					
Tonight We Improvize	Luigi Pirandello	Peter Coe	Anthony Powell	Keith Michell Keith Baxter Alfred Marks Miriam Karlin June Ritchie	186
The Confederacy	John Vanbrugh	Wendy Toye	Anthony Powell	Dora Bryan Peggy Mount Peter Gilmore Richard Wattis Nicholas Clay	193
Oedipus Tyrannus	Sophocles	Hovhannes I. Pilikian	Ralph Koltai	Keith Michell Diana Dors Alfred Marks Willoughby Goddard	196
A Month in the Country	Turgenev	Toby Robertson	Robin Archer	Dorothy Tutin Derek Jacobi Timothy West Nicholas Clay	199